Deadly Luck: A St. Patrick's Day Romantic Suspense

Love, Lies and Alibis

Judith A. Barrett

Wobbly Creek, LLC

DEADLY LUCK: A ST. PATRICK'S DAY ROMANTIC SUSPENSE

A LOVE, LIES AND ALIBIS NOVEL

Published in the United States of America by Wobbly Creek, LLC

2026 Georgia

wobblycreek.com

Copyright ©2026 by Judith A. Barrett

All Rights Reserved. No parts of this book may be reproduced, stored, or transmitted in any form or by any means, electronic, mechanical, photocopying, recording, or otherwise, without the prior written permission of the copyright owner, except for brief excerpts for reviews.

DEADLY LUCK: A ST. PATRICK'S DAY ROMANTIC SUSPENSE is a work of fiction. Names, characters, businesses, places, events, locales, and incidents either are the products of the author's imagination or used in a fictitious manner. Any resemblance to actual persons, living or dead, or actual events is purely coincidental.

Cover by Wobbly Creek, LLC

ISBN 978-1-967288-57-1 eBook

ISBN 978-1-967288-58-8 Paperback

Dedication

Deadly Luck is dedicated to the color green and to big dogs, little dogs, and cats of all sizes.

Chapter One

Grace clutched the rafter with both hands as she leaned over the wide opening to the main floor of her grandmother's old house. "Granny, if you want this attic completely cleared out, we'll need help to bring these larger boxes down."

Nora shouted from the bottom of the attic ladder. "Come on down. I just got a phone call from the mayor, and we have to talk." A faint rustle in the far reaches of the attic had caught Grace's attention, and she glanced at the boxes in the dark corners she hadn't even touched. *I swear Granny's fairies sneak more boxes in when I'm not looking.*

When a tiny light flickered, she picked up a medium-sized box hidden behind larger boxes.

If the light hadn't blinked, I wouldn't have seen the box.

"We need to get an electrician here before this old house burns down," she muttered.

"I heard that, and I already had it checked last fall. There's nothing wrong with the electrical system in this house. The electrician said any dimming was likely a rolling brownout, and there's nothing we can do about that. Now, quit fiddling around and get down here," Nora said.

Grace carefully backed down the pull down ladder with the box clutched in her left arm while her right hand gripped the rung above her.

On the way down, her breath caught as the scent of baking apples, cinnamon, and sugar wrapped around her. *Takes me back to when I was three and the first time I helped Granny make shamrock cookies.*

"This box was really light." Grace set the box on the kitchen table and peered inside. Her heart leaped at the sight of the puppy, its brown corduroy body showing signs of wear from childish hugs and its ear missing.

Her voice cracked. "I found Rosie, Granny."

She pulled the toy out and held it against her chest while she buried her face. "She smells just the same and hasn't changed a bit. I'll be right back. I'm taking the box to my room so I can go through it later."

When Grace returned, Nora said, "The mayor said he has a big problem and asked if you could take over the parade. I told him he'd have to talk to you himself."

"Take over the St. Patrick's parade? Isn't that in five days? Did you tell him I already have a job in Atlanta and I'm on vacation? Besides, I wouldn't know where to start."

"I don't know about that; I know you could handle it, but he'll be here in just a few minutes. He didn't want to just bring it up the second he walked in the door."

"So he let you spring it on me ten minutes before he pops in."

Nora put her hand on Grace's arm. "He wouldn't ask if his back wasn't against the wall. Hear him out and help him."

"I'll listen."

"I know, and I'll help you if you need me. I've finished going through my box; it can join the rest of them in the dining room that we're taking to the thrift shop. I have to check my apple cakes."

Grace carried the box into the formal dining room and scanned the room as she lovingly rubbed her hand along the back of the chair next to Granny's chair. *My chair when I graduated from kids' table.*

When she set the box on the dining table along with the other boxes she'd brought down earlier, her gaze drifted to the head of the table, Poppy's place. A small ache tightened in her chest.

"We miss you, Poppy."

As Grace strolled down the hallway, she subconsciously sang along with Granny who was belting out one of her favorite country songs. The spice blend of oregano, rosemary and thyme tickled Grace's nose. *Granny is roasting a chicken for dinner. Mama called Granny's roasted chicken a mantrap recipe.*

Granny stood at her old kitchen table with its ancient vinyl tablecloth while she gave a raw whole chicken a rubdown of butter and spices. Granny had always complained that the kitchen table was too small, but Poppy pointed out it seated eight, and even that was too many for a man before he finished his second cup of coffee.

"Grace, come check my apple cakes that are in the oven."

When Granny wasn't in the kitchen, the monstrous old style gas stove was the dominant fixture in the kitchen. Grace smiled, remembering the first time Granny trusted her to open the oven door and check a cake with a toothpick by herself. She was six. *The toothpick is clean, Granny.*

Grace grabbed a toothpick, and when she opened the heavy oven door, she turned her head to protect her face from the heat, just like Granny had taught her long ago.

"The cakes are done, Granny." Grace pulled the pans out and set them on cooling racks. *I'm just as proud now as I was then to help Granny.*

"Put the last two in the oven for me."

While Grace positioned the last two cakes in the oven, Granny said, "The new teacher at Briar Glen High School offered to help with the boxes in the attic after school. I invited him to stay for dinner to compensate for his time."

"That's great because there are boxes up there I can't budge."

Grace glanced at her spreadsheet on the kitchen table she had created to track the progress on their decluttering project, and frowned. "I grossly underestimated how much going up and down the attic ladder would affect the time it would take to empty the attic. I'm already half a day behind, and I brought down the lighter weight boxes first. I feel like such a rookie."

"It's your first attic project. Adjust your schedule."

Grace tapped her fingers on the paper. "I've never had to adjust a schedule on the first day. There has to be a way to finish on time. How's your baking?"

"I have five Irish apple cakes in the freezer, four cakes cooling, the two you just put in the oven, and one in the refrigerator for us. I'm freezing them after they cool so I can take them to church for the church's St. Patrick's Day bake sale and luncheon." Nora brushed back the stray strands of her silver-gray hair and put them behind her ear, then adjusted her tortoise frame glasses.

"I'm looking forward to the parade. I even found green jeans to wear with my shamrock T-shirt. I need to find a green scarf to tie up my hair." Grace pulled her long black hair back and pulled it into a ponytail using the hair band she kept on her wrist.

"Don't you go dyeing your hair green or you'll look like you soaked your head in muddy creek water just like the high school girls," Nora said.

A knock was followed by the front door creaking open. "You here, Nora?" a man called out.

"In the kitchen, come on back, Daniel."

Mayor Daniel Reeves sauntered into the kitchen, fully embracing the upcoming holiday, from his bright red hair down to his shamrock tie tack.

"Ahhh. Your Irish apple cakes are always a big hit, Nora."

"You look like you're ready for St. Patrick's Day with your lucky shamrock."

Nora asked as she sliced a piece of still warm cake and put it on a plate on the table in front of him. She handed him a fork, and he dug in.

"Coffee?"

His mouth was full. He nodded as she poured a cup.

"How is everything going with the parade?" Nora asked.

After he swallowed, Daniel said, "I actually need my luck to change. Grace, I could use your help. The parade is falling apart because the float owners are dropping out."

Daniel cleared his throat. "Somebody told them they had to have proof of insurance, or the state would wade in with hefty fines."

"That's nonsense," Grace said.

"Tell me about it. I can't say too much, but I'm worried the point was to shut down the parade so all the merchants would lose their biggest day of sales for the year."

"Who would do that?" Nora asked.

"I have my suspicions, but I need proof. I'm scrambling to do damage control because word got around before I knew about it, and floats are pulling out."

"That's terrible," Grace said.

"I agree." Daniel put his fork on his empty plate. "I was hoping you'd jump in and contact all the float owners and settle everyone down while I work on a much larger project."

Nora patted Grace's hand and gave a slight nod.

"We have a lot to do, Granny, and I hate to get even farther behind. What do you think?"

"We'll be fine. It won't take much time for you to get the parade back on track."

Grace asked, "Can I get a list of all the approved floats?"

"We have all the applications at the office, but have never needed a list."

"Are there any other problems?" Grace opened a box and peered inside.

Daniel used the napkin Nora handed him and dabbed at his mouth, then wiped his damp forehead. "I didn't want to mention it, but the party at the distillery was canceled."

Grace's eyes widened, and she closed the box. "Why? That has always been my favorite part of the festivities. What's going on?"

"Sounds like sabotage to me." Nora peered into the oven, then gently closed the oven door.

Daniel shot a look at her, then frowned. "I don't know about that, but it's definitely a mess."

"I'll be at your office first thing in the morning," Grace said.

"I was kind of hoping you'd go back to the office with me now."

Grace raised an eyebrow. "This isn't a quick, one day assignment, is it?"

Daniel shrugged. "No, but I have an open full time position for a Deputy Mayor."

"If you're going to be throwing your weight around, Grace, you'll need the title to get things done." Nora turned to Daniel. "A paid position with a professional salary, I assume."

"You're right."

Grace stared at them, then rubbed her forehead. *I haven't had a vacation in three years. I expected to recover from burnout while I was here, not to step into another challenging role.*

"But I'm not looking for work. I'm here to help Granny and relax."

Daniel jutted out his chin. "It's not work; it's community service, and the community needs professional leadership with experience in delivering and meeting deadlines. We might be able to cut back a bit on scope, but we can't change the deadline. Step one is to put the parade back together."

Grace raised an eyebrow. "I can see why you're mayor. That was definitely a polished speech, but at least it came straight from the heart."

Daniel raised his eyebrows at Nora. "Did she just say I went too far?"

"Maybe, or maybe it was a compliment."

Grace studied her grandmother's face. *The parade is important to Granny.*

"Nobody else could pull it off," Nora whispered.

I've never turned my back on a challenge. Grace hugged her. "Okay, Granny. I couldn't live with myself if we didn't have the parade."

The mayor patted his shamrock tie tack. "I don't ordinarily believe in luck, but I sure appreciate you being in Brier Glen when I needed a talented project manager, Grace. Thank you. Are you ready to go? I hope you don't mind walking. I've always considered it a bonus for living in a small town."

She glanced down at her clothes. "I've been crawling around the attic in my jeans and T-shirt. I need to clean up before I go into an office to work."

"We're small town casual; most of our contact with the public is by phone or through email. But you'll want to grab a long-sleeved shirt because we keep the office cold."

After Grace went into her room for her warmest long-sleeved flannel shirt and her backpack, she slipped her holster into her waistband and then joined the mayor who had waited in the kitchen for her.

On their way past the town park, the mayor glanced at the sky. "We're all weather watchers in Briar Glen. I certainly am the closer it gets to parade day. I heard some in town won't commit to a decision if the signs are wrong, especially in the clouds."

"Sounds like that's not so much weather watching as superstition," Grace said.

"That's exactly what I think too, but there's something about it that makes me nervous."

Grace widened her stride to keep up with the mayor's pace, and she was breathing hard when they were only halfway to the office. *Five years as a corporate desk jockey has made me soft.*

Daniel said, "I'm turning the parade completely over to you. Ask me questions, but I won't be sticking my nose into your business. I have a political issue I can't hand off as easily. It's tricky."

He's over his head. "As long as I can ask questions, I'll be fine," Grace said.

"That is why I asked you to step in. I have to have somebody take over who will make the parade successful. I don't know if you remember Bella. She's the licensing clerk and has been pretty entrenched in her version of how things should be every time I suggest any changes. We seem to have a conflict in our styles."

Grace side-glanced at Daniel. "What are my other obstacles?"

Daniel ticked off the items like he was reading a list. "You'll need to issue a permit for the parade. That's something else that got shoved under the rug. Hire an assistant of your own. I suggest checking at the technical college. If you get some resumes, I'll give them a quick review to be sure you aren't getting anyone who will sabotage you. Unfortunately, that's where we are right now because of my political issue."

"So if I can issue myself a permit, can't I just issue a blanket permit for all the floats?"

"Since we don't have any written procedures, you can do whatever you want. You'll have signing authority so you can fast-track whatever needs to be done."

When they stopped at the door to the mayor's office, Daniel said, "I've only been in office for a month; I'd still be selling cars if Mayor Dorsey hadn't suddenly taken off for parts unknown, so I understand how difficult it is to jump into a messy situation."

"Do you miss selling cars?"

Daniel smiled. "I would except remember my community service speech? I've got the bug."

Grace returned his smile. "I can tell that."

When they went inside, Grace shivered and pulled her flannel shirt closed against the sudden drop in temperature. *It's not just the temperature; the entire office is cold with no personality.* She was chilled even further by a gaze locked on her. Grace glanced to her right.

A woman with thinning hair dyed black scowled, and her chair squeaked as she shifted her weight to lean away from Grace. She sat behind a large, gray metal desk like the captain of a battleship. The office-style nameplate was engraved with Receptionist.

Grace smiled at the woman. The woman didn't return the smile.

"Bella, this is Grace Callahan."

Bella narrowed her eyes. "Nora's granddaughter."

Grace smiled and put out her hand. "Nice to meet you."

Bella straightened her back but left her hands on her desk.

Grace raised her eyebrows. With a slight nod, extended her hand closer to Bella.

Bella pinched her lips tight and briefly shook Grace's hand with a gruff, "You too."

Daniel cleared his throat as he motioned to the rest of the office. "We're not fancy, as you can see." The three-foot high wooden railing cut the room in half, separating the hum of machines from the rest of the space.

Grace ran her fingers lightly along the wood railing that served as a line no one was meant to cross and had been smoothed by countless fingers touching the wood over the years just like she was now. "How long has this been here?" she asked.

"I don't know," Daniel said.

"Thirty-seven years." Bella's voice was soft and reverent.

Grace turned. "Thank you; it's beautiful."

Bella ducked her head behind her computer screen and typed on her keyboard, with the keys clicking a staccato rhythm that echoed in the room.

Daniel stepped closer to Bella's desk. "Grace needs signing authority. How do I do that?"

Bella continued typing. "Just write out a statement and sign it."

Grace turned her attention to the area beyond the railing. The room had a sterile look of a mocked up office highlighting equipment and furniture for sale, with the smooth metal surfaces reflecting the harsh fluorescent overhead lights.

The machines, a copy machine and a printer stood ready, their plastic trays empty, against the far wall near the corner storage room.

The three desks were crammed together in the middle of the room, with no regard for personal space. Two of the desks were bare except for desktop computers, screens dark and impersonal. The third desk had papers sprawled across its surface, as if someone had left in a hurry or simply stopped caring.

Along the back wall, three closed doors offered no clues about what was behind the doors.

Daniel said, "We have two offices and a conference room. Both of the offices have back doors that exit to the back parking lot. I'll give you your key."

"The only back doors are from the two offices? That seems odd."

"They must have been required by the building code when the building was constructed, but I only use my back door after hours when I work late. It's convenient for everyone when Bella knows whether I'm in or out of the office."

Bella beamed. "You're right about that, Mayor."

"Bella, Grace is our Deputy Mayor. Call our bookkeeper so we can get her lined up on the payroll."

Grace's eyes flicked when Bella pursed her lips, then reached for the office phone on her desk.

Daniel opened the gate to the rest of the office.

"I'll show you my office first, and then the conference room and your office."

As they strolled into his office, the door automatically closed behind them with the latch clicking a little louder than she expected.

Grace took her time in the room. The desk dominated the space; solid wood, positioned squarely in the center like a command post. Two large computer monitors were on the desk, their black screens reflecting more authority than warmth. Across from the desk, a pair of visitor chairs were neatly aligned. *Set up for listening, not lingering.*

On one side, a table with its six chairs tucked in tight, as if meetings here were efficient and strictly controlled.

Grace peered at the shredder tucked almost invisibly under the meeting table.

Daniel cleared his throat. "I bought the shredder because there wasn't one in the office. I use it occasionally, but I always empty it after I use it."

He motioned toward the opposite wall, where three gray metal file cabinets stood shoulder to shoulder, functional and unadorned. Nothing was out of place. Nothing was personal.

Daniel scanned the room as if for the first time. "I haven't had time to do much to the office since the previous mayor left. I don't spend a lot of time in here anyway what with trying to stop..."

Grace examined his face as the mayor gazed over her head in deep thought. She remained still and resisted the powerful urge to look behind her.

"Well, we'll talk later." He picked up a file folder from his desk and handed it to Grace. "I pulled this together for you. It's a copy of our budget and our expenses for the year so far. I thought you might like to review it."

He pointed toward the file cabinets. "There's nothing in here. There are a few files in your office that I should probably move somewhere else more secure, but I was in a rush when that car...anyway, they'll be safer with you for now."

Grace remained quiet, hoping the mayor would explain what was in the files that needed to be in a safer place.

"I should take some notes," he mumbled.

"Have you noticed Bella has her own style?" he asked. "I live to close the deal, but she focuses on trivial details and slows everything down."

"We'll work it out. Who has the other desk?"

"Zoey. The only actual management decision I've made is to rewrite her job description to include flexible hours. She'll be here in a few minutes after she drops her two children off at school. She leaves at three to pick them up. Zoey maintains our office calendar...one second."

Daniel opened the door. "Bella, we need Grace added to the office calendar."

"I'll tell Zoey, Mayor."

The door automatically closed behind him. "I've kept Zoey on because I can trust her, and she fills in for Bella. Give her assignments, but make sure...what am I saying? Managing a staff is not an area where I could give you any advice at all."

When they went into the office next to his, Grace was immediately struck by a sense of isolation after the door closed.

The once-prized wooden desk seemed to have shrunk in the room, and its chipped legs and scratched top told of years of neglect. The computer, screen, and keyboard sat on the desk with their cords in a tangle, and a black generic desk chair with a mesh back had been shoved into a corner with its back to the door.

Grace ran her fingers lightly over the top of the desk and noticed the large drawers with locks on both sides of the desk.

"Ask Zoey to order what you need in your office. I'd suggest a personal printer and a second monitor for starters. If you tell Zoey to order the basics, your office will have what you need."

After they left her office, Grace asked, "Bella, what else will I need besides a login to the office system?"

Bella stared at her. "Keys to the building, security code, and a list of the staff with phone numbers."

"Can you take care of all that today?"

"Yes, ma'am; I can. I'll need your number so you'll be on the list."

"Thank you." Grace picked up her backpack and handed Bella her business card, which had her cell phone number on it.

After she put the folder into her backpack, Grace followed Daniel into the conference room. She raised her eyebrows at the scent of stale cigars and bad whiskey as she surveyed the room, absorbing its atmosphere of secrets and under the table deals.

Daniel said, "I was impressed. It's been difficult for me to get any information out of Bella. We are a total mismatch of personalities."

He motioned with a wide sweep of one arm. "The city council meets here once a month and has since the first city council was formed in the early 1900s."

"It looks like it's been painted recently."

"I think it was repainted three years ago. I'm not sure anything can erase the room's history."

"The door didn't automatically close," she said.

"The city manager, a paid position here in Briar Glen, closes the door to signal the meeting has begun, and no one arrives late. None of them have keys to the building because I'm required to attend their meetings. This room's schedule is on the calendar, so you and I will never clash for the resource. I know I've thrown a firehose worth of information at you, but I think you'll be okay from here. Do you have any questions for me?"

"Who is on the city council?"

"Dr. Valerie Higgins, the vet for the animal shelter; Piper Franklin, the new banker who replaced Henry Donaldson when he retired after the old bank was bought out; Sam Macklin, a farmer; and Walt Lassiter, the owner of the gas station. Anything else?"

He could use a sounding board. "No, except to tell you I will help you anytime you need me."

Daniel stared at her. "I've been careful to keep it quiet and close to my chest, which makes me the center of bad luck for someone who is more superstitious than I am."

Chapter Two

Before the mayor reached the conference room door, he paused.

When he turned, his face was grim. "On second thought, Grace, maybe we should go over a few things that have been weighing heavily on my mind. Thanks for the offer. It's easy to lose sight of what's right without any feedback."

Grace strolled to Bella's desk. "What do you think about the parade being canceled?"

Bella's eyes widened. "Canceled? Nobody's canceling the parade."

"What about the float permits?"

Bella jutted out her jaw. "People should follow rules."

"I agree completely. We have to call every single float that has applied. How many entries do we have?"

"Seventy-eight."

"Wow. Wouldn't that be a parade?"

Bella's back straightened, and a hint of pride crept into her voice. "It's the most we've ever had apply."

"Too bad so many float owners backed out. We have confirmed with the state that no insurance is required, so I wonder if there is anyone who needs help with their float. I'll ask my grandmother. She knows everybody."

"No insurance is required by the state? That changes everything. I know somebody, and I'll bet Nora does too," Bella said. "I have a neighbor who had to quit entering his float because he couldn't manage it anymore by himself."

"We should know if we'll need more floats by the end of the day. Do you know how to manage a parade?"

Bella glanced up at the ceiling, then shook her head.

"I don't, but I could learn." A woman who had just come into the office stuck out her hand. "Hi, I'm Zoey. Are you taking over the parade?"

"Appears so. I'm Grace." Shaking hands, Grace returned Zoey's smile.

Bella sniffed. "Grace is our new deputy mayor."

"It's about time," Zoey said.

"Getting the parade back on track is not a solo activity; we'll need to divide and conquer to get every float we can committed to the parade," Grace said.

"But the permits..." Bella said.

"Who can write a permit to cover the entire parade for me?"

"I can," Zoey said.

Bella growled, "That's my job."

Bella's willing to take part. "How about going through all the parade applications?" Grace asked.

Gritting her teeth, Bella said, "That's my job too."

"I'm happy to help," Zoey said.

"Divide and conquer. Which one do you want to do, Bella? Write the permit for the parade or go through the applications?"

"I'll write the permit." Pulling up a form on her computer, Bella began typing.

"Zoey, if we write a script to follow when we call the parade applicants, could you pull together a spreadsheet to track them?"

"That would be easy."

"What should our script say? First, we want them to know they have an approved permit, so all they need to do is to be at the gathering site at...I need details. Where should they gather and at what time?"

"The high school parking lot is the usual place. The parade starts at ten, so we always have them in place before nine," Bella said.

"We need to talk about the details, so we'll have a written plan. Bella, join us as soon as...oh, wait. Does the parade have a marshal or an official St. Patrick who rides in the parade?"

"Mayor Dorsey was always the parade marshal," Bella said.

"I think the mayor would be perfect, but we'll have to ask him if he has time."

Scanning the office, Grace said, "I need to make a sign for the front door."

Zoey pulled out a pink sheet of construction paper from her desk drawer and then picked up a black marker. "How's this?"

"Perfect." After printing "Closed until three o'clock", Grace taped the sign on the outside of the front door and locked it.

"Now we can focus. Bring a notepad and a drink and snack if you like, and let's go into the conference room. You can finish the permit after our brainstorming session, Bella."

Scanning the conference room, Grace asked, "Where's the whiteboard?"

Bella sniffed, then went to a wall with draperies and pulled a cord, exposing a large whiteboard.

"That's what I'm talking about." Grace picked up a dry erase marker and strode to the board.

After an hour of brainstorming, Grace asked, "What do you think? See any holes?"

Zoey compared the board with her notes. "No holes."

Bella squinted at the whiteboard, then rose from her seat and studied the board.

Grace leaned back in her chair to give Bella time to analyze the board.

Returning to her desk, Bella said, "I don't see any holes. After I call my neighbor, I'll write up the permit for you to sign it, and then I'll post it on the door."

Zoey hurried to her desk. "I'll start calling."

Grace examined the notes and arrows on the whiteboard then sat at the conference table with a yellow legal-sized pad and jotted down more thoughts.

Bella tapped on the conference room door. Grace tilted her head. "Wow, you're finished already?"

Bella's cheeks reddened as she continued into the conference room with three sheets of paper in her hand, two white and one green.

Tentatively handing the papers to Grace, Bella said, "I think this works for the overall permit you wanted. Sign all three copies, and we'll post the green one on our public board, and I'll file the other ones."

She stared at the floor. "So it will be handy in case anyone wants a copy."

"This is absolutely perfect. I have a couple of thoughts and need to know what you think," Grace said.

Hurrying to the front door, Bella beamed while Grace waited for her at Zoey's desk.

Running her hand through her hair, Grace said, "Y'all are doing great, but we're only three people. We need an army here. If we buy lunch, how many people do you think we could get here to help? I think there are five people in Granny's Bible study class."

"My neighbor belongs to a quilting club," Bella said.

"I belong to a book club, but are we okay with babies and toddlers as part of our army?" Zoey asked.

"We could take over an office for napping," Bella said.

Grace side-glanced at Bella. *I expected her to complain; shame on me.*

"We'll use my office for the littles," Grace said. "As soon as we have an idea of how many people we have, we can order lunch."

"How long will we need them?" Zoey asked.

"If we have lunch at eleven thirty, then we can get started by noon and work until two. If they could stay longer, that's wonderful."

Bella's face grew dark. "What about chairs? We don't have enough for everyone to sit."

"I'm grateful you thought of it, Bella. Let's ask everyone to bring a camping chair."

"I'm sending a group text to the book club members." Zoey said. "Want me to keep a tally of how many will be here for lunch?"

"Yes, please." Grace picked up her phone and called her grandmother.

"You haven't been fired, have you?"

"No, but we need help. We have to call all the float owners who applied for a spot in the parade and tell them they have a spot because the permit issue is covered."

"My Bible study group will help. When do you need us?"

"Come at eleven thirty for lunch, and we'll have a brief training session while everyone eats so we can start calling at noon. They'll have to bring their own chairs, and we'd like them to commit to staying until two. Let me know how many will come from your group."

"Seven, counting me."

"I thought there were only five in the study group."

"There are but two members will bring their sisters who are visiting, but what about husbands?"

"If they come to lunch, they have to make calls."

Nora said, "We can count on six."

After she hung up, Grace announced, "Husbands are welcome, but they have to make calls unless they want to pay for everyone's lunch."

Bella chuckled. "Good plan, boss."

Grace said, “Six for Granny’s Bible study group, Zoey.”

Grace grabbed a small stack of the float applications and called a float owner.

After tallying the number of people who could help, Zoey said, “We have a count of seventeen, but should I pad it and call it twenty? What do you want me to order?”

Grace sighed as her call finally ended. “I’d say ham and cheese sandwiches with a side of chips and a cookie, but what about...”

Bella broke in. “I know who won’t eat a ham and cheese sandwich in the groups we’ve invited, so I’ll take care of ordering them something they’ll enjoy for lunch. Quite a few of our callers will want only half a sandwich for lunch, so fifteen sandwiches will work for us, but I’ll order extra chips and cookies. I’ll call the café right now so they can plan their morning.”

“And we’ll want to put a sequence number on the applications with our initials and the same number and initials on the form,” Zoey said.

“I created a tracking form for the callers to use.” Bella went to the printer and picked up a printout, then handed it to Grace who skimmed it.

“This is exactly what we want.” Grace handed the sheet to Zoey. “Do you see anything missing?”

Zoey squinted as she slowly read the form. “Not a thing; I’ll make copies.”

Zoey stood at the copy machine, watching as the printer spit out copies of their form, one at a time. “This copy machine is too slow. Are we trying to do too much in such a short amount of time?”

Grace raised her eyebrows. "Of course, we are, but that's the nature of an important project. What do you think, Bella?"

Her face flushing, Bella glanced at Grace. "It will make planning the parade and managing the lineup much easier."

"We can judge our progress by taking a count of how many have been called after thirty minutes, then decide at one o'clock if we need to trim back or ask people to stay another half hour."

"I like it." Bella rushed to her desk with her tally sheets and began making calls.

Completing her second call, Grace said, "I can't make any more calls. People want to talk to me about why Daniel hired me and not a local person, or tell me all about the previous mayor."

"I was afraid of that," Bella said after she finished her current call. A coin slipped from her hand and clinked when it landed on her desk. Bella's cheeks reddened, and she quickly picked the coin up and dropped it into her pocket.

Grace glanced toward her office. "My time would be better spent creating our database." When Grace went inside her office, the door closed automatically.

She frowned at the door.

She stepped out of her office. "Does anybody have a screwdriver or a hammer?"

"What kind?" Zoey asked. "I have both."

"I have a hammer," Bella said. "What are you going to do?"

"Relieve the automatic door closer of its duties."

Bella's eyes widened. "But what about fire safety?"

"That's an excellent point, Bella. I'll have to be very conscientious about closing my door before I go home."

"Thank you."

Grace pulled a visitor's chair from Daniel's office to hers. "I'll need somebody to hold the door open while I take it apart."

Zoey joined her at the office door and handed her the screwdriver. "Can I add experienced doorstop to my resume?"

Grace laughed. "If we pull this off, you can add project facilitator to your resume."

After Grace climbed up on the chair with the screwdriver, she examined the pieces of the automated door closer unit. *Now what?*

Bella breathlessly rushed into the office, waving a sheet of paper. "I did a quick search and found instructions on how to remove an automatic door closing system."

She handed the printed instructions to Grace. "Don't detach the spring mechanism."

After Grace had read the instructions, she handed the printed sheet back to Bella. "Thank you, Bella. You are definitely the safety officer on this team. Read the instructions to me step by step."

After Grace detached the unit from its mounting points, she handed it to Bella. "This is our team trophy for our first project."

Zoey giggled as Grace handed her the screwdriver.

"As tempting as it is to display our trophy, I'll find a box for it and put it in the storage room," Bella said.

Grace's eyes widened, then she laughed as she climbed down off the chair. "Now I can work in my office with the door open, so y'all can see I'm not slacking."

While Grace created the simple parade participants database using the collection form as her template, Bella and Zoey made phone calls.

Grace's alarm on her phone went off at ten thirty, and Zoey and Bella glanced up.

Grace asked, "Do we need to verify our order?"

"We can, but I did that fifteen minutes ago," Bella said. "The café assured me our order would be ready at eleven. I'll pick up the order."

Grace said, "You don't have to..."

"Yes, I do because I would enjoy the fresh air."

"I can't argue with that," Grace said.

"I'll leave at ten minutes before eleven; they won't pack up the order until I'm there."

"That's great; the database is almost finished. Zoey and I can test it while you're picking up lunch."

After Bella left, Grace pulled up a chair and sat next to Zoey as she guided her to the database.

Zoey raised her eyebrows. "It looks exactly like the form."

"Thanks." Grace rose. "I wanted to make entering the data from the form as easy as possible."

As Zoey entered the first form, Grace stood behind her.

"You have a typo," Grace said.

"Of course, I have a typo." Zoey sighed. "Do you want to enter the data into the forms, and I'll stand behind you?"

Grace stepped back. "It's been ages since I've done any coding. I just wanted to make sure..."

"Grab a form and enter it yourself." Zoey resumed entering the information from the form.

Grace picked up a form and went into her office. When she was in the middle of entering her third form, Zoey came into her office.

"We need an indicator of some type that we can check. I'd forgotten about this guy." Zoey handed a completed form to Grace.

"Why did you write 'do not approve' on the form?"

Zoey crossed her arms. "He told me he'd be in the parade, but only if Bella wasn't involved. I didn't want to write that down, but we don't need anybody with a negative attitude in the parade."

"You're right. I'll put checkboxes in the database we can use to show we had an application that needed more review. Will that work?"

Zoey relaxed her arms. "Perfect."

"I haven't had any firm commitments. What about you? I wrote call back tomorrow on the form, but what about a checkbox for call backs?"

"I have one firm commitment for the parade. Are we going to have too many checkboxes?" Zoey asked.

"We'll be okay. I can sort on any of the checkboxes after we enter them into the system."

Bella burst into the office. "I have the lunches, and I picked up water on the way to the café."

Grace slowly surveyed the room. "Do we have a break room? Where's our coffee pot?"

Bella and Zoey exchanged a glance.

"There's no break room," Bella said.

"We'll fix that; let's set up our food and drinks in the conference room like a buffet so people can help themselves."

While Bella and Zoey set up the food, Grace updated the database with the checkboxes and explained the checkboxes to Bella.

"I was worried some people might bully our callers," Bella said.

Grace picked up her notepad and then said, "I added this to my speaking notes: if you become uncomfortable on the call, interrupt and say, 'Thank you for your time.' And hang up."

"And write that on their sheet," Bella said.

Grace hurried to the door as people began coming into the office carrying either camping chairs or toddlers.

"Hi, I'm Grace, and lunch is in the conference room. After everyone eats, we'll go over our plan of action for this afternoon."

"Grace is our new deputy mayor," Bella added, "and a professional project director, so the parade is in excellent hands."

Grace smiled when Zoey stared at Bella, then rushed to help a woman who was struggling with an errant toddler, a large diaper bag, a backpack, and a folding canvas chair.

"Hi, Grace. Thanks for the help."

"How do you do all this?" Grace asked.

The mom dropped the diaper bag and scooped up her toddler as he made a beeline for the open door when someone else came in. "Poorly."

The nearby women chuckled.

"We're laughing, but we've all been there, honey," a woman said. As she walked back with the toddler, he said, "Hi Grace."

When Nora came in, she hugged Grace, then beamed as she introduced her to her Bible study group.

While everyone was eating, Grace grabbed a sandwich and bolted it down.

She picked up her notepad and stood in front of their whiteboard. Bella stood at the door and held up copies of the forms.

When Grace cleared her throat, Zoey whistled between her fingers, and even the little ones became silent at the piercing sound.

"What an amazing talent. Thank you, Zoey," Grace said. Zoey smiled and shrugged, then joined Bella in handing out the forms.

Grace quickly explained the purpose of their task and the process. "If you have any questions or run into any difficulties, flag down Bella, Zoey, or me. We plan to call all of our float owners by two, but I think we can beat that goal."

"Beat that goal!" Zoey shouted, then led the chant, "Beat that goal! Beat that goal!"

After the rowdy group cheered, they scrambled to claim a work spot and soon were making calls.

Grace motioned for Bella to join her near the front door. "I just heard the party at the distillery was canceled. Is that true?"

"I heard the same thing. Mr. Pearce, Senior is not happy, but his grandson claims there's nothing he can do."

"Grandson? I knew Mr. Pearce, Senior, had retired, but I thought his son took over."

"His son had a fatal heart attack year before last," Bella said. "Mr. Pearce Senior's grandson left his job in Atlanta and stepped in."

"I'm sorry to hear that. So, Trey Pearce runs the distillery now?"

Bella chuckled. "You must have gone to school with him. He goes by Ryan now."

"Yes, I did until eighth grade when Mama and I moved to Atlanta." *Trey Pearce was an obnoxious jerk.*

Grace shook her head and headed toward the working group.

Bella caught up with her. "I'll bet you could help Ryan fix whatever the problem is."

She shook her head. "I have to focus on the parade."

Bella's eyes narrowed. "You built a team in one morning. I think you can trust us to beat that goal."

Grace shook her head. "I'd have to walk to Granny's and get my car."

Nora lifted her head when Grace mentioned her, then joined them. "Did you call me?"

Grace glared at Bella. "I just said my car is at your place."

"If there's somewhere you need to go, take my car." Nora handed Grace her car keys, then returned to her work.

Grace stared at the keys in her hand. "I guess it would be common courtesy to let him know the parade won't be canceled."

"You're right," Bella said. "Bad news gets around fast. You might want to stop at the gas station on the way back and tell Walt the parade is still on schedule. He'll get the news out faster than anyone else." She pulled a coin out of her pocket and rubbed it with her thumb.

Grace glanced at Nora who was gesturing while she talked on the phone.

Grace shrugged. "It will be a good excuse to fill up her gas tank for Granny."

After Grace picked up her backpack, she headed toward the distillery at the edge of town in Nora's compact sedan.

As she approached the driveway to the distillery, the old wooden sign appeared, waiting.

It still hung from the same black iron bracket, the metal now more rust than paint, swaying gently in the breeze like it had been waiting for her to come back. The wood had darkened with age; the edges rounded and softened by years of weather. Time hadn't ruined it. Time had settled into it.

Carved into the face was the same hearth, its little flames painted in worn shades of amber and brick red. Beside it rested the round-bellied barrel with its iron bands faded to charcoal. On either side, sheaves of wheat stood tied with twine, their once-bright gold now the color of warm honey.

Nothing about it was precise. The carving wavered slightly. The lines weren't straight. The letters arched just a little crooked. HEARTH & BARREL. Cut deep into the wood, not painted on. She remembered that.

She remembered thinking years ago that whoever made it had done so by hand. It didn't feel like a business sign. It felt a promise.

It still did.

And for a moment, turning at the driveway with fifteen years pressing at her back, Grace had the strange, steady feeling that the sign hadn't aged at all.

It had simply been here. Waiting.

Grace continued up the driveway, and there it was. Just as she remembered.

The building looked exactly like what it had been built to be, a distillery that had never pretended to be anything else.

A long stretch of painted cinder block ran beneath a weathered metal roof, practical and unadorned. But across the front, the gift shop softened it. Wide windows caught the light, and the simple door beneath a narrow metal awning felt more welcoming than the rest of the structure had any right to be. Someone had wanted to invite people to come inside.

Behind the shop, the roofline stepped back into the original living quarters. The windows were smaller, set in a tidy row, hinting at a home built into the bones of a working place. Not fancy. Just steady. The space that promised shelter at the end of a long day.

A narrow drive ran along the side of the building toward the larger structure attached at the rear, the distillery proper. It was plainer, broader, and marked by a roll-up door and vent pipes that rose past the roofline like silent sentries. That part of the building didn't invite anyone in. It existed to do a job.

Together, the whole place carried a quiet contradiction.

Warmth in the front. Shelter in the middle. Work in the back. A family place wrapped around a working one. And every bit built to last.

When Grace opened the door of the distillery shop, an electronic tone announced her arrival, and her first impression was the sense of calm in the shop.

All the items on display were aligned with such quiet precision she imagined the shop was patiently waiting to be noticed. Shelves ran true; each product was spaced just enough to look intentional but not fussy. Colors flowed in a gentle gradient, guiding her gaze naturally.

Her shoulders loosened, the way they did when she walked into a well-loved home rather than a business.

She drifted forward, fingertips hovering just above the nearest display. The owner had arranged the items to curate a moment of tranquility when customers stepped into the shop.

While she admired the barware and glassware with the distillery logo and the table in the corner with the banner "Local Artisans" draped on the wall above the table, she inhaled the aroma of a sweet, malty cloud with hints of fruity and spicy notes from fermentation.

When a lanky man with blond hair and a cowlick strode out of the rear of the shop removing a white bib apron, she peered at the golden retriever at his side, and then him. "Trey?"

Chapter Three

He tilted his head as he gazed at her. "Welcome to the distillery. I'm Ryan; are you looking for anything special?"

"I was admiring your Local Artisans corner, but I actually came to tell you the parade is still on. Who's your companion?"

Ryan scratched his dog's ears and smiled as he glanced down. "This is Willow."

"Can I pet her?"

"She'd love it."

Grace slowly approached Willow with her hand out. Willow cocked her head, then whined as she stepped toward Grace.

"What a good girl," Grace cooed as she stroked the side of Willow's neck. Grace smiled at the tufts of blonde dog hair that popped up, then floated to the floor as she ran her fingers through Willow's coat.

"So, the parade is still on? I'd heard it had been canceled; that's fantastic news." He examined her face. "You must be the new deputy mayor. Are you new here?"

"Not really; I just haven't been around in a while. I'm Grace Callahan."

"Crazy Gracie?" Ryan stared at her, his nose twitching as he inhaled sharply, and his head tipping a fraction to the side, like he was listening for something she couldn't hear.

"Yes, Tacky Trey, the one and the same."

Grace turned to leave.

Ryan went still for a beat. "I am so sorry, Grace. Please don't go. It was just such a shock to see you grown up."

Grace turned back and faced him with her eyes flashing. "You haven't grown up a bit, and you still do that weird thing."

Ryan stared at her, then burst out laughing. "You're imagining things, but I suppose I deserved that. Would you like a cup of coffee as a peace offering?"

Grace glanced over her shoulder at Granny's car, then lifted her chin. *I won't run away crying this time, Tacky Trey.*

"Sure."

Maybe he'll tell me why he canceled the party.

Their footsteps clicked on the worn brick floor as Willow walked alongside Grace who followed Ryan down a short hallway to a room behind the distillery showroom.

When he opened the door, the scent of used books and leather reminded Grace of an old library as it wrapped around her before she even stepped inside. Her gaze went immediately to the floor-to-ceiling bookcase, with neatly shelved books that looked read, reread, and valued.

“What do you read?” she asked.

Ryan poured two cups of coffee and set them on a table. “I spend most of my spare time studying my grandfather’s chemistry and science books. I still have a lot to learn.”

Grace forced herself to look away from the shelves. Only then did she take in the coffee station tucked away in a corner and the modest living space stretching between her and the books she already wanted to explore.

“What brought you to Briar Glen after all these years?” Ryan motioned to the table with its two chairs, and Grace sat.

As she leaned over her cup, the smoky aroma of her coffee reminded Grace of sitting around a campfire. “I still occasionally visit my grandmother on weekends, but I’m here on vacation to help her clean out her attic.”

“So how did you go from attic worker to deputy mayor?”

Willow flopped down next to Ryan as Grace leaned back and raised her eyebrows. When he took a sip of coffee, she shrugged. “Demotion.”

When Ryan sputtered and then spewed out his coffee, she smiled. Ryan covered his mouth as he coughed and glared at her.

“Dang it, Grace. You haven’t changed a bit. I should have known you were up to something when you leaned back.”

“Actually, the mayor asked me to get the parade back on track.”

Ryan grabbed a kitchen towel to dry the table. "I heard about that. What exactly happened?"

"Officially, a misunderstanding."

"Got it. So, unofficially..." Ryan finished drying the table and tossed the towel into the sink.

"Somebody started a rumor that the existing permits were invalid."

"How do you fix something like that?"

"I issued a new permit that covers everyone, and this afternoon, an army of volunteers is calling all the parade applicants to tell them all is well. We'll know how many floats we have confirmed this afternoon."

"I know you, Grace. What's your plan if that number is too small?"

"We're going to find retired float owners and offer to help them decorate their floats."

"Just like when we were kids; I always knew you'd have something up your sleeve if someone needed help."

Grace wrinkled her nose. "You certainly didn't act it."

He shrugged. "Didn't seem right for you to be so much smarter than me."

"I thought you hated me."

"This may be a first, but you were wrong."

Grace narrowed her eyes. "Was I that insufferable?"

Ryan's eyes twinkled as he picked up his cup. "I'm not falling into that trap."

They relaxed as they sipped coffee; when Ryan smiled, Grace returned his smile, then self-consciously peered into her coffee.

Grace asked, "What did you do before you came here to run the distillery?"

"I was a research chemist for a pharmaceutical company. What about you? What was your career before attic cleaner?"

Grace smiled. "I'm a project director at a tech company." *Wait for it.*

Ryan peered at her. "Project director?"

Now. "You need a project director?"

"I don't know. I thought I was stuck; maybe I do need some help."

Ryan rose and picked up the coffee pot. When he hovered near her cup, Grace shook her head; he refilled his own and then joined her at the table.

Grace finished her coffee. "I have to go see how the army is doing. They're on a quest to beat my deadline of calling all the applicants by two o'clock."

When Grace leaned forward to rise, Ryan casually rose to pull back her chair.

Grace's eyes widened. *He developed manners.* "Thank you."

Ryan cleared his throat as they headed toward the front door. "How do I get in touch with you if I need a project director?"

Grace pulled a business card out of her backpack. "Call or text me."

"I'll text you so you'll have my number."

Before Grace reached her car, her phone buzzed with a text. She glanced at it, then replied, "Got it."

On the way to the gas station, Grace suddenly remembered when she was six and someone at school stole her lunch. *I was crying while I was sitting on the swing, and Trey gave me his chocolate bar. The entire thing.*

Grace pulled into the gas station and parked next to a pump. After she filled the tank, she went inside for a receipt.

The young clerk grinned as she handed Grace the receipt right away.

Grace smiled. "Is Walt around?"

"He's in the back working on the books." She shouted, "Papa! Someone is here to see you."

Walt stepped out of his office and then strode to the front when he saw Grace. "Gracie, I didn't know you were going to be here. Are you going to be around for a few days?"

"Two weeks."

"That's wonderful, but it's too bad you'll miss the St. Patrick's Day parade." He snorted. "It's been canceled."

"Actually, it hasn't been canceled. That was an unfortunate rumor."

His eyes widened, then he guffawed. "So, you are the new deputy mayor. I should have put it together quicker. Chalk it up to old age. Well, isn't that something? Congratulations, and I can't tell you how happy I am that the parade isn't canceled. The town's economy relies on the boost from the annual parade. I'll make sure everybody knows."

"If you hear somebody complaining about not being in the parade, tell them to call the mayor's office. We think we got everyone, but just in case..."

"You got it, girl. Did you let the high school know?"

Grace's cheeks burned. "I didn't think about that."

"The band director is my cousin; I'll call him for you."

"Excuse me, Miss Grace," the young clerk said. "Are you really having dinner with Mr. Sharpe?"

"He's helping my grandmother with a project, so I'm sure he'll stay for dinner."

Her shoulders slumped. "Oh, so it's not a date."

"Not at all unless he's having a date with my grandmother."

The girl giggled. "That's funny, but I'm sad it's not a date."

After she left the gas station, a small herd of cows in a field was headed toward the barn with two calves scampering ahead and then returning to their mothers' sides. *Bella was right in more ways than one when she told me to stop at the gas station.*

As she neared the office, she smiled. *I wonder if Mr. Sharpe knows he has a classroom of matchmakers rooting for him.*

Zoey met her at the office front door and whispered, "This is our last call. I can't believe how many people showed up, can you?"

A woman with a toddler on her lap put down her phone. "Done!"

Loud clapping and whistles filled the room.

"When's our next army day?" A young woman asked as everyone shuffled to gather their things.

Grace chuckled. "We'll let you know."

Nora hugged Grace on her way out. “I called in a few favors, but today was definitely worth the few cookies this cost me. Absolutely impressive, Grace. Dinner’s at six.”

After the helpers left, Grace asked, “How many floats do we have?”

“Four confirmed and nineteen maybes out of our seventy-eight applications,” Bella said.

“We’ve got a bunch of forms for you to review,” Zoey said. “They are on your desk. A few applicants didn’t list a working phone number.”

“What’s that all about?” Grace asked.

Bella and Zoey exchanged a glance.

“Last year we had eighteen floats,” Bella said.

“We think someone was trying to overwhelm us so we’d get behind, making the mayor look bad,” Zoey added.

Grace snorted. “They didn’t count on an army.”

“I know. They didn’t know how many moms would be tickled to have an impromptu mom playdate that included a free lunch,” Zoey said.

“They didn’t count on a deputy mayor,” Bella said.

Grace headed toward her office. “I’ll start going through the applications on my desk.”

“While you’re doing that, we’ll work on the lineup. Zoey has a spreadsheet we’re going to use.”

While Grace reviewed the applications, Zoey called out, “Next year we want a photo of their floats.”

“Start a list,” Grace said.

“We did,” Bella replied, and Zoey giggled.

At three o'clock, Grace rose from her desk and stretched before she joined Zoey and Bella.

"What's next?" Zoey asked.

"Isn't it time for you to leave?"

"Oh, gosh, it is. Don't do anything fun without me."

"We need to send a confirmation letter to everyone who has been accepted. We'll draft one today and then review and revise tomorrow."

"Thank you. Bye!" Zoey dashed out the door.

After Zoey left, Bella said, "I'd like to clean up the office before the end of the day."

Grace scanned the room. "You're right. We have some trash to pick up, and I'll bet the conference table is sticky."

"I'll wipe down the tables and desks," Bella said.

"I'll pick up trash."

When she was picking up the conference room, Grace found a yellow sticky note.

After she had read it, Grace carried the note to Bella. "I found a folded sticky note. It says, How many for you? I fixed four. Then the reply says two. Was there an error on the form that we should fix?"

Bella looked at it and shook her head. "No one asked me a question about fixing something, and they would have."

"I don't know if I'm suspicious or paranoid. I'll ask Zoey about this in the morning; she may just explain it right away, but meanwhile, would you review the applications on my desk to see if I missed anything like locals or usual participants that you recognize? I took the comments at face value; maybe I should have asked you or Zoey to scan them too."

"You think someone who was here was sabotaging us?"

"I don't want to jump to any conclusions, but I don't ignore anything either. I'll finish cleaning the conference room so I don't mess up your system."

After Grace had cleaned the conference room, she went into her office. "How are you doing?"

"Just finished. I found eight applicants who are local. Six of them say the phone number is not valid and the initials are MM. We didn't have anyone here with the initials MM. The other two were marked no answer, but with the initials of someone who was here."

"Let's call our eight then."

Bella peered at Grace. "I'll call them because I can call all of them in less time than it would take for you to call one."

Grace chuckled. "True."

"I'll call them from my desk."

Sitting at her desk, Grace drafted the notification email to the float owners.

Bella returned and dropped into the visitor's chair. "We've picked up four more from our list of eight. They were marked as having invalid phone numbers, but the numbers were fine." She sighed. "What's going on?"

"I don't know, but can you imagine what those four would say when they learn almost everyone they know will be in the parade? And here we'd be all proud that we took care of everyone. I think we should call all the invalid numbers tomorrow. It shouldn't take too long. Go home, Bella. I'll lock up and turn on the security alarm."

Bella unlocked her desk drawer and removed her purse then headed to the front door and paused at the door. "Thank you for coming to work with us, Grace. Good night."

"Good night." Grace locked the front door after Bella had left.

Grace was on her way to her desk when she wheeled around at the sound of a loud click at the front door. The mayor came in, and she relaxed.

"Oh, Grace. How did today go?"

"We've made some progress toward getting the parade back on track; what about you?"

"My cousin was relieved the parade was back on schedule. He told me we'll enjoy the high school band's new routine. They've been practicing since they came back from the holiday break. That's my only good news, though. Today has been an uphill battle. Our electrical system has been a little flakey, and I think it's being caused by the drain of power by our water system, but I'm not an expert."

"Water system? How are the electrical and water systems connected?"

"You have to have power for the pumps to work, and they've been running in an emergency mode for I don't know how long. I have a meeting with Sully, the town's water system manager on Wednesday. He said if I could give him a list of what to look for, he'd get right on it."

Grace went into her office and picked up her backpack, and then closed the door behind her when she came out. “I’m still not clear how the brownouts are being caused by the pumps at the water station, but getting the water system manager involved sounds promising.”

“That’s what I thought, but I don’t have a list or even a hint of what should be on the list. I thought I’d drop in on Ryan tomorrow to see if he has any ideas of what could help. Say, maybe you could go with me. I never understand what Ryan is telling me when he talks about hydraulics and all that. Maybe you could interpret for me.”

“I don’t know anything about hydraulics, but maybe I can ask questions so we’ll both understand. What time were you planning to go?”

“About ten. Do you mind driving? I could ride with you.”

“That’s fine.”

“Good.” Daniel glanced around the office. “Where is everyone?”

“We worked through lunch. I was just getting ready to go home myself as soon as I do a few more things.”

“Go ahead; I’ll lock up.” Daniel glanced down and fiddled with his shamrock tie tack.

He doesn’t know the security system. “That’s okay. I want to have a draft ready for review in the morning.”

Daniel remained motionless, seemingly lost in thought, until he pulled a thick envelope out of his back pocket. “If we’re going to see Ryan in the morning, there’s no reason for me to carry it around. It will be safer with you. I’m afraid I’ve become a target. Ryan knows hydraulics, and I know budgets and how to spot a phony.”

He examined her face. "And so you do. I'll see you in the morning. Be careful." Daniel dropped the envelope on Bella's desk, then rushed out the door.

Grace stared at the envelope. *This is the second time he has said something was safer with me.*

She slipped the envelope into her backpack and then went into her office. She pulled on her large desk drawer, but it was locked. *Isn't there a way to unlock a drawer with two paperclips?*

She turned on the security lights and alarms, turned off the overhead lights, and then locked the front door as she left.

"Brr. It is definitely nippier than it was this morning." Grace jogged to her grandmother's house at a pace faster than her normal jog.

When the colors on the horizon shifted from a blaze of orange to a deep gray blue, and the shadows along the deserted street deepened around her, she shuddered and broke into a run when she was half a block away from Nora's house.

When she dashed into the house, the warmth embraced her like a long-lost friend, and she was surrounded by the aroma of roasting chicken with its tantalizing spices.

Nora called out, "Is that you, Grace? Tristan is working in the attic."

Grace joined Nora in the kitchen. "Granny, would it be rude if I took a shower?"

"Not at all; in fact I suggest it. You smell like that conference room."

Grace gathered clean clothes from her bedroom. When she was shampooing her hair with the hot water streaming down her back, the tension in her shoulders from the day dissipated. *I could stand here all night, except Granny has chicken roasting in the oven.* After she reluctantly turned off the water, she quickly dried and dressed.

When she sauntered into the kitchen, Nora said, "Oo-la-la, you smell good."

Grace smiled. "Thanks, Granny."

The pull down ladder creaked and groaned as a man came down from the attic. "Miz Nora, I've moved all the boxes from the back of the attic to the front. I have an idea..."

He stopped on the last rung of the ladder when he saw Grace then cleared his throat. "I'm sorry; I didn't realize you had company."

"This is my granddaughter."

Grace stepped toward him and put out her hand. "I'm Grace Callahan."

They shook hands. "The deputy mayor. I'm Mister, I mean, Tristan Sharpe." He chuckled. "I've obviously spent too much time with eighth graders."

Grace smiled. When Nora gave her the side-eye, she shrugged.

"What's your idea?" Nora asked.

"It would be much quicker and safer if we had a relay line to move the boxes from the attic. I think I could find two or three sturdy boys that would help if you'd be willing to wait until tomorrow afternoon."

Nora checked the potatoes on the stove. "That's an excellent suggestion. I can promise them cookies and lemonade for a job well done. Give me about thirty minutes, and I'll have our dinner on the table. Would either of you like a small glass of wine before dinner? We have appetizers." Nora pointed to a plate of crackers and cheese on the counter.

"Looks good to me, but I'll need to wash my hands," Tristan said.

Nora pointed toward the hall. "Turn the corner after the dining room, and it's the first door on your right."

After Tristan was out of sight, Grace whispered, "Wine? We never have wine."

Nora peered at her. "Did you become a teetotaler in Atlanta?"

"Not at all, but this isn't a special occasion. It's not your birthday or mine."

"It wouldn't hurt us to be more social."

"I don't know about that. After a long day at work, the last thing I'd want to do is spend more time with the people I saw all day. Mama told me Dad said he'd rather socialize with her and me than with the people he worked with all day."

Nora sighed. "His father was the same way. My mother asked me one time how your grandfather and I ever got together because he was such a homebody."

"Who was a homebody?" Tristan asked.

"My father," Grace said.

Tristan chuckled. "The teachers at school keep telling me I won't get acquainted with anyone my age if I don't go out once in a while and see people."

While Nora drained the potatoes and tossed in half a stick of butter before mashing them, Grace reached into the silverware drawer. "I'll set the table, Granny."

Tristen followed Grace into the dining room. "So what brings you to our sleepy town of Briar Glen, Grace?"

"Granny asked me if I'd help her clear out the attic, and I was long overdue for a vacation. What about you?"

"I thought it would be a great opportunity to branch out and make new friends. When I asked the teachers in the lounge for suggestions on where I could go mingle, they couldn't come up with anything besides the gas station," Tristan said.

"That's kind of sad," Grace said.

"Not really. Have you met Walt? He's better than the local radio station for news and the latest dirt, although he does seem to embellish the details to make the story more interesting. Not that I mind. I stop by the gas station every day after school to get the latest updates on what's going on in town."

"So, that's how you knew I was the deputy mayor. What's the local thought about that?"

Tristan side-glanced at her. "I have to be careful about how I say things at school, and it's difficult for me because my natural inclination is to be direct."

"I'm not delicate," Grace said.

"I don't think Walt would argue with you about that. You're getting things done, and everyone is excited you're here. Walt told me Daniel was over his head, but I got the impression he was talking about more than just a few administrative tasks."

"He didn't explain?" Grace asked as they left the dining room.

"No, which is why it struck me as odd. Walt is usually a tell-all kind of guy. Like who is slipping out at night for a meetup with someone they shouldn't, but he didn't explain at all."

Chapter Four

While they were still in the hallway, the scent of the roast chicken, mashed potatoes, and Nora's chicken gravy beckoned to them from the kitchen.

Tristan followed Grace into the kitchen. "Smells good in here."

"What can I do to help, Granny?" Grace asked.

"I've set up our food in here buffet style. I still have the bottle of wine if we'd like to have it with dinner," Nora said.

"Go right ahead," Tristan said. "I'll toast you with a glass of water. I drove here, and I never drive after even one sip. A teacher's curse. I can't walk home because it would be worse to leave my car here overnight."

Nora chuckled. "If I were the only one here, it would be worth it to see who got their garters in a knot, but Grace doesn't need that kind of grief. Thank you for being so thoughtful. What does everybody want to drink?"

"Hot tea for me," Grace said.

"Coffee or water will be fine for me," Tristan said.

"I made hot tea for you and me, Grace." Nora poured a cup of coffee for Tristan. "Grab a plate and serve yourself, and we can go to the dining room to eat."

While Grace and Tristan took their plates of food and drinks to the dining room, Nora followed them with her dinner plate and a plate of hot rolls.

As she passed the rolls, Nora said, "I was thrilled to see how quickly everyone jumped in to help with the parade." She told Tristan about the phone calls and how many floats there would be after all.

Tristan reached for the butter and knocked over the salt shaker. He dashed a bit of salt into his palm and tossed it over his left shoulder.

Nora raised her eyebrows.

Tristan didn't miss a beat. "Why was the parade canceled in the first place?"

"It wasn't really canceled," Grace said. "There was a misunderstanding about the permits, but we cleared that up right away."

"I know for a fact that couldn't have been a simple task," Tristan said. "It happens in the classroom more often than it should. Somebody says something, then someone else repeats it but misses a critical point or slightly revises it." He raised an eyebrow. "I don't suppose you could bring the army in for damage control at the school, could you?"

Grace laughed. "I can just imagine our twenty moms and grandmas swarming into a classroom, handing out cookies and telling kids to sit up straight and pay attention while the toddlers run wild around the room."

"So, what time can you be there tomorrow?" Tristan asked.

When Nora and Grace laughed even harder, Tristan beamed.

"Y'all are good for my soul. I crack the funniest jokes in school, and all I get are blank stares."

Nora cut a bite-sized piece of chicken and smiled. "Kids these days have no sense of humor, do they?"

Tristan buttered a hot roll. "This dinner reminds of meals at my grandmother's house."

"Where are your folks from?" Nora asked.

"Atlanta, and they're still there. I'm one of the rare true Atlanta natives."

"Do you miss the city?" Grace asked.

"When I do, I just think of the traffic," Tristan said.

"As soon as I reach our county line, I feel like I can loosen my steel grip on the steering wheel," Grace said.

"Speaking of the county, a teacher mentioned a county-wide water shortage that could affect the town's water system. Have you heard anything along those lines?" Tristan asked.

"A friend of mine who has a well complained last week that her water pressure was low. She was afraid the pump was going, but I haven't heard anything about a water shortage in our area," Nora said.

"Maybe that's what she was saying, and I wouldn't have understood it because I've never had a well."

"That makes sense," Nora said.

"I should have asked her to explain because I just realized I don't know much about city water systems either. We do tend to jump from one topic to another in the breakroom, but most of the time I can keep up. For example, yesterday a teacher announced she had adopted a new dog from the animal shelter, and that certainly sparked a huge debate about the best way to care for a dog. It's amazing how many experts there are on certain topics, isn't it?" Tristan asked.

Grace rolled her eyes as she swirled a small bite of mashed potatoes through the overflow of gravy from her chicken, then ate the warm, blended bite.

"Your gravy is always delicious, Granny."

"Thank you. Did you want more?" Nora put the gravy boat in front of Grace.

"I have plenty for now."

"We were talking about the animal shelter being overcrowded today," Nora said. "I miss having a dog around. I may visit the animal shelter tomorrow."

"Petey was a wonderful dog," Grace said.

"I'll send you photos from the shelter. Maybe you can take a quick lunch break to help me decide if we need a dog right away."

Grace chuckled. "I should probably plan on taking my lunch break at the animal shelter."

"My lease doesn't allow dogs," Tristan said, "but the neighbor across the street from me has a Pomeranian, and I take Mitzi for a walk almost every day."

"That sounds ideal," Grace said.

"It is. If it weren't for Mitzi, I wouldn't have the motivation to be outside every day."

After they finished dinner, Grace and Tristan cleared the dining room table, and Grace loaded the dishwasher while Nora put away the leftovers.

"We have apple cake for dessert," Nora said. "It's still warm. Anyone care for ice cream?"

"Just apple cake for me, Granny."

"Same; except with ice cream," Tristan said.

Nora chuckled. "I'm with you, Tristan."

While Granny dished up dessert, Grace refilled Tristin's coffee cup from a fresh pot, the fragrant steam rising and the rich coffee aroma filling the air. "Do you want more hot tea, Granny?"

"I think I'll switch to coffee." She set the desserts on the table and then sat down while Grace poured her a cup.

Grace and Tristan joined her at the table, and everyone dug in.

"What time do you plan to be here tomorrow with your helpers?" Nora asked.

"Is five too late? That will give the guys to finish up any homework. I don't think it will take us over twenty or thirty minutes if you can tell us where you want them."

"Why don't you plan on staying for dinner?" Nora asked.

"Believe me, I'd love to, but I already have an obligation. I'm having dinner with one of my colleagues and her husband."

"That sounds pleasant," Nora said.

"Normally I'd agree with you because her husband and I enjoy talking about fishing, but she casually mentioned her younger sister would be there."

Nora chuckled. "Sounds like a bit of matchmaking."

"My thought exactly," he said. "We'll see how bored she gets with fishing tales."

After dessert, Tristin rose. "Dinner was delicious, and I enjoyed the conversation. I apologize, but Mitzi is watching for me."

While Nora walked with him to the front door, Grace cleared the table of the dessert dishes.

After Nora joined Grace in the kitchen, she put the leftover dessert away and side-glanced at Grace. "I like him. What did you think?"

"He was nice and actually refreshing." Grace loaded the dishwasher.

Nora ran a sink of hot soapy water and slipped in the pots and pans. "Refreshing? What does that mean?"

"Good conversationalist, and I loved how much he cares for Mitzi."

""I'll wash, and you can dry." Nora sighed. "No fireworks, then."

"No fireworks, but I was surprised to see he was superstitious."

"I was too, but then, most folks are to a degree," Nora said. "Or at least most of the people I know are, even though they'd deny it."

"Do you have a spare coffee maker? I'd like to have a coffee station in the office."

"I have two, and I know where they are." She pulled a box out of the pantry. "This is the newest one. I bought it and then decided there were too many buttons and settings for me. It's still in the box."

After she set it on the kitchen table, Nora pulled an empty tote bag out of the pantry and then added an unopened container of coffee, a coffee scoop, and four coffee cups to the tote bag.

She squinted as she read the side of the new coffee maker box. "You'll need a few other things." After she jotted down a few things, she handed the list to Grace. "None of this is urgent."

"Thank you so much."

After the dishes were dry and put away, Grace headed toward the living room with Nora not too far behind her.

When Grace went into the living room, she beelined to her longtime friend, the broken-down sofa, with its faded green upholstery and its sagging seats that were perfect for lounging but not sitting.

Grace pulled out a book and read the first few pages, which included a note to the reader from the author. *I'm not sure I understand what the author's point was.*

Her mind wandered from the note in the book to the note she had found in the conference room. *Another note I don't understand. Was it even related to the form?*

"Granny, was there something on the applications or the form that had to be fixed? Did you notice anything unusual?"

"The forms were fine. I was surprised to see Melba there, and she brought a friend I didn't recognize, which doesn't mean much anymore because kids grow up so fast."

"Who's Melba?"

"She got into a little trouble a few years ago and was away. About a year ago she returned to take care of her aunt, whose health is poor."

"When you said away, did you mean like jail?"

"Not many people know it, so I don't mention it. She's served her time, and she's devoted to her aunt."

"That is admirable. Very few people would do that, especially someone so young."

"I agree with you, but not everyone in town would. She has rough edges, but she picks up all the shifts she can at the restaurant for the extra money."

"Why were you surprised to see her?"

"She never goes anywhere except to take her aunt to the doctor, or go to the grocery store or work. I was surprised she would take two hours off like that."

Unless someone was paying her.

"Did someone say something about the forms?" Nora asked.

"Not really. I found a note and obviously read too much into it. I don't want any more rumors spun up."

"No kidding." Nora glanced at the book Grace was holding.

"Where are you going to read?"

"I thought I'd put my feet up and read in the living room."

"I'll grab my crochet and join you."

After Grace turned on the table lamp next to the sofa and kicked her shoes off, she began reading.

Her phone buzzed with a text from the mayor. "Meet me at the office about seven?"

She replied, "Will do."

Nora entered the living room, settling into her upholstered rocking chair adorned with huge blue blossoms on a cream background. "Who was that?"

"The mayor. He wants to meet me at the office at seven tomorrow morning."

"I get up at five thirty, so I'll have coffee and a breakfast taco ready for you."

"You don't have to do that, Granny."

"I'd have to turn in my granny card if anyone left my house hungry."

Nora picked up her project and crocheted while she listened to a podcast, and Grace read.

"Granny, the mayor said something about bad luck. Do people think that?"

Nora waved a hand toward the window, where the street banners flapped in the breeze. "People will tell you the parade's cursed."

Grace snorted. "Of course they will."

"It's not a curse," Nora said mildly. "Just timing."

She set her crochet project down. "Years back, there was a drought bad enough to make folks desperate. The mayor insisted the parade go on anyway because he claimed canceling it would invite worse luck."

"And?" Grace asked.

"And that night, the river jumped its banks." Nora shrugged. "Turned out a gate upstream had been neglected for years. The parade didn't cause it. It just happened right before everything failed."

Grace frowned. "So, people blame the parade."

"People blame whatever's easiest," Nora said. "Ever since, they say when the parade goes on despite warning signs, something breaks."

Grace smiled faintly. "Sounds like a coincidence."

"It was," Nora said. "But stories don't need to be true to stick."

Nora picked up her crochet needle, and Grace resumed reading.

Two hours later, Grace yawned.

Nora rose from her chair. "I'm ready for bed. What about you?"

"I'm ready." Grace carried her book to her room while Nora checked the locks and then turned off the living room and hallway lights.

After Grace changed into her pajamas and set her alarm for five thirty, she pulled back her covers, including her faded green and white patchwork quilt, and fluffed her pillow before she climbed into bed. She switched off her bedside lamp and rolled from side to side. *I'm too hot.* She stuck her foot out from under the covers and groaned. *Now I'm too uncomfortable.*

Grace turned the lamp on and repositioned the quilt. She sat up and put the pillows behind her so she could read.

She stared at her book. *I'm too restless to read.*

Grace quietly slipped into the kitchen where she had left her laptop. She searched for how a city's water system and electricity were related, and one article led to another.

After her head jerked, she opened her eyes and yawned as she ran her hand through her hair. *Water. There's something about water I have to remember.* She closed her laptop and went to bed.

Chapter Five

When her alarm went off at five, she sat up in her bed. *Water. What am I supposed to remember about water?*

She shivered as she gathered up her clean clothes, then went to the bathroom for a hot shower. *If I don't try so hard, it will come to me.*

After Grace dressed and made her bed, she went down the hallway, lured to the kitchen by the pops of hot grease and the gurgle of a steaming pot of coffee. As she got closer, her mouth watered at the aroma of the blend of smoky-sweet bacon and freshly brewed coffee.

"I poured you a cup of coffee, Grace, and I'm planning to make breakfast tacos this morning," Nora said. "It's going to be windy today, but no rain."

"No breakfast for me this morning. I'd like to go by the café and see if I can catch Melba. What time do they open?"

"The café opens at six and closes at three."

"What does Melba look like?"

"She's tall, and what they call big-boned. She has short brown hair. She's around thirty years old but looks older."

"Thanks. If she's there, I'll see if she's willing to talk to me."

"Ask her about Mittens who is Melba's aunt's cat. Melba adores Mittens."

"That helps a lot."

"The mayor told me everybody is town is a weather watcher, especially around St. Patrick's day."

"He's right. Some people like to plan, a few like to fret, and some are downright superstitious, but nobody ignores the weather."

"In the city, nobody pays attention to the weather unless the forecast includes snow, then everybody panics."

Nora chuckled. "We'd go into deep hibernation around here if the weather folks even breathed the word snow."

Grace's phone rang. She peered at the number. *Bella?*

"Good morning, Bella."

"I'm sorry to be calling so early. Did I wake you up?"

"Not at all. I'm almost ready for my second cup of coffee. What's up?"

"I couldn't sleep. I want to go into the office so I can review the rejected applications. I'm worried I might have missed something yesterday because I was trying to go as fast as I could."

"How long do you think that would take?"

"I think I can be thorough and still easily finish by noon."

"Starting when?"

"I'd like to be at the office this morning by seven, except that means I would have to leave at three so you wouldn't have to pay me overtime."

"You're welcome to the overtime if you want to stay until five, but that's up to you."

"Really? I'd like to stay and finish the rest of my work so I won't get behind."

"I'm going to be there at seven for a meeting with the mayor, so you won't be alone. If you want to work in my office or the conference room so you'll have privacy, be my guest."

"A meeting with the mayor at seven? I'll work in the conference room so I won't interrupt your meeting."

"I don't expect him to stay long. He probably just wants a status from me. I'll see you soon."

Nora put a napkin and a plate with three slices of bacon on it in front of Grace. "Let it cool a minute. Is Bella okay?"

"She wanted to go into the office at seven and review the applications again. She said she couldn't sleep..."

"Do you think she's feeling guilty?"

"She might. The mayor was overloaded and probably not available for her to talk to him. I hope she realizes the parade is my responsibility now. What are your plans?"

"I want to be at the animal shelter at eight when they open."

. "What an exciting way to start your day. Do you know what type of dog you'll be looking for?"

"A laid back dog that likes to go for walks, not runs."

While Grace gathered all her things to leave, Nora asked, "Who should I invite to dinner tonight? My friends are vetting a list of single men for me."

"Granny! You'd better be kidding me."

"I told them you wouldn't take it well, but turns out there are very few young men in our county or any of the surrounding counties who can meet my friends' standards. It's actually a short list of one, but..."

"What about Tristan? Was he vetted?"

Nora peered at her coffee cup, then poured a splash more coffee into it. "Would you look at the time? Shouldn't you be leaving for your meeting?"

Grace chuckled. "He didn't pass the vetting process, did he?"

"Do you want me to pack a lunch for you?"

"Thanks, but I don't think so. If I don't see Melba there this morning, I'd like to go to the café for lunch."

"They're awfully busy at lunchtime."

"I didn't think about that. I'll stick my book into my backpack." Grace kissed Nora on the cheek. "Don't forget to send me photos from the animal shelter."

When Grace pulled into the gas station, there were already trucks at all the pumps and only a few parking spots in front of the store. She parked, entered the noisy store, and slipped past the line of people jostling at the register. She hefted two gallons of water, feeling the strain in her muscles, and joined the quickly moving line as more people bustled into the store.

When she put the water on the counter, Walt frowned as he glanced at the sky. "Did Nora send you for emergency water? I hadn't noticed any signs of a storm coming."

Grace cocked her head as she examined his face. *He's not kidding.* "No. This is for the office so we can have coffee when we feel like it."

"Now that makes sense. Bad weather might get people thinking it's a sign the parade is supposed to be canceled after all." He handed her the receipt. "Take care now."

Grace shook her head as she left the gas station. *I've never paid much attention to the weather. Now, it's probably number one on my list of looming threats for the parade.*

The café parking lot was packed. After cruising the aisles, Grace found a spot near the road. When she went inside, the cashier said, "We have a seat at the counter, or if you want to wait, we should have a table open soon."

Grace glanced at the counter and the tall server with brown hair. "I'll grab a seat at the counter so I don't take up a table."

The cashier smiled. "Thank you."

When Grace sat at the counter, Melba sat a cup down in front of her and poured a cup of coffee. "What can I get you, Miz Grace?"

"I feel like something sweet."

"The blueberry Danishes just came out of the oven."

"That's sounds great."

While Grace sipped her coffee and nibbled on the Danish, the counter cleared.

When Melba returned to refill her coffee, Grace asked, "Granny told me Mittens was a sweetheart. How old is she?"

Melba's smile softened her face. "She's ten years old. Not quite a senior, but she still acts like a kitten."

"She sounds like a sweet girl. I wanted you to know how much I appreciated your help. Did you get your money okay?"

"Sure did. Fifty dollars for me and the same for my friend, Marcia. Did that come from you?"

"No, it was an anonymous donor who couldn't get away from work." *MM was Melba and Marcia.*

"I really needed it for medicine for Mittens. I hope I did it right." Melba felt in her pocket, then handed Grace a scrap of paper. "I followed the instructions the best I could."

Grace read the instructions. "Mark any phone number you don't know as Phone Not Valid."

Grace handed the paper back to Melba. "You followed the instructions perfectly. Remember this was confidential because we don't want to embarrass any of our float owners."

"Yes, ma'am, and I know how to keep my mouth shut, especially if it might hurt somebody's feelings."

"Thank you so much. We knew we could count on you."

Grace finished her coffee and Danish. When the man at the end of the counter left five dollars under his plate, Grace did the same.

"How was everything?" the cashier asked.

"Delicious." Grace smiled.

As Grace headed toward the office, she glanced at the passing landscape of dry brown fields dotted with cows gathered under the trees. *Why would someone pay a hundred dollars to sabotage the parade?*

Grace parked behind the building and went inside through her office's back door. After setting her backpack on the desk, she carried the coffee maker and tote into the conference room before going back to her car for the water jugs.

She set up the coffee maker, and with a familiar click, the pot of coffee began its brewing cycle with a gentle gurgle. While it brewed, she hurried to her office and sat down at her desk, examining the drawers.

Maybe this will work. She opened the wide middle drawer in front of her and then tried to open the drawer on the side, but it remained locked.

Grace inspected the empty middle drawer. *No pens or paperclips.* She pulled out the drawer and put it upside down on the desk. *I knew it!*

She removed the key taped to the bottom of the drawer and inserted it into the lock on the side drawer.

She opened the drawer and pulled out the thick file folder, and set it next to her backpack.

While she was sliding the middle drawer back into place, the front door was unlocked with a distinct, clear click. Grace quickly swept the thick folder into her backpack and closed the side drawer.

By the time she reached the front door, Bella had come inside.

"Good morning, Bella."

Bella jerked her head up, startled, when Grace spoke. "Morning. I saw the lights on and thought the mayor must have been here. He never remembers to turn off the lights. Did you walk?"

"No, I parked in the back. Come see our new breakroom."

Bella followed Grace into the conference room. "You said we needed a breakroom. I never thought..." Bella bit her lip as she stared at the coffee maker. "This is really nice," she muttered.

Grace cleared her throat. "I thought we could move one of those spare desks back here for our coffee station. What do you think?"

Bella lifted her chin. "We've never had any use for them. I think it's a great idea."

"We don't have any sweetener or creamer yet. I thought I'd run to the grocery store later and grab some."

"I have some at my desk. I'll bring more from home tomorrow," Bella said.

"That's great. Fix yourself a cup of coffee before you review the applications."

Grace went into her office and pulled out the file folder Daniel had given her of the annual budget and expenses for the past two years. She glanced through it. *Nothing has been spent on the upgrades listed as planned in the budget.*

Grace turned on her computer. *It's almost seven thirty. I lost track of time.*

She sent a text to Daniel. "Are you running late?"

While she waited for him to respond, Grace took notes as she reviewed the budget and expenses, carefully comparing line item by line item. *How old is that copy machine? I'll make a list of suggested upgrades for Daniel.*

While she dug further into the expenses and the budget on the online system, Bella tapped on the open door. "I'm sorry to interrupt, Grace, but you've been heads down and it's eight o'clock. Didn't you say you had a meeting with the mayor at seven?"

Grace frowned at her phone. *No response from Daniel.*

Grace rose from her chair, then stretched. "I did. I'm surprised he wasn't on time."

"I was going to tell him, but since he's late...our banner on the front of the building has slipped."

I didn't know we had a banner. "I'll take a peek."

Grace went outside and crossed the street to see the banner. The colorful banner announcing the St. Patrick's Day parade spanned across the front of the building, attached at its four corners. One corner had become loose and danced wildly with each gust of wind as the fabric flapped and strained in its battle to hold on to the building.

Grace raced back into the office building. "Is there a way to get up to the roof? Do we have anything I could use to secure the loose side?"

"I have some long cable ties that the technician left when the server was installed," Bella said. "There's a ladder on the side of the building outside, and a ladder built into the storage room that goes up to a hatch in the roof."

"Show me. Let's look at the outside one first."

Bella followed Grace out the back door, then pointed at the iron ladder that looked like it was built into the side of the brick building. Grace strained upward to stretch her arms as high as she could, but her fingertips didn't quite reach the bottom rung.

Grace stood back and peered up at the ladder. "Inside the storage room, you said."

Bella handed her stash of cable ties to Grace, and then the two of them went inside and into the storage room.

After turning on the light, Bella opened what looked like a tall cupboard door. Grace craned her neck. "That's really narrow."

"It looks really tight, but it's wider than it looks," Bella said.

Grace climbed up the ladder, then pushed up, but the hatch didn't move. "This is heavy. I can't budge it."

"Let me see if I can lift it for you. I can't go on the roof though..."

"That's okay. I'll take care of that part."

Bella had pulled her coin out of her pocket and rubbed it with her thumb. After she dropped it back into her pocket, she squeezed up the ladder with her eyes tightly closed. She examined the hatch, then slid it to the side. She slowly descended, with her eyes squinched.

When her feet touched the floor, Bella exhaled.

"Thanks, Bella. How did you know to slide it?"

"I don't know. Just lucky, I guess. When it didn't push up, I pushed it to the side."

Grace climbed up the ladder with the cable ties stuck in one of her jeans belt loops. After she stepped out onto the roof, she gasped.

The mayor was lying motionless on his back near the corner where the banner was loose. She stared at his chest, willing for it to move, but it was still. When the wind howled, and she was rocked by a gust, she clutched for something to steady herself, but there was nothing. Gazing over the roof's edge, her breath hitched, and she dropped to her knees, crawling towards him. Each stone felt like a tiny dagger as the sharp gravel dug into her knees and jabbed her hands.

He was pale, almost white. She touched his throat to feel for a pulse, but there was no pulse. His skin was cold and unyielding, and his lifeless eyes stared at the sky.

Grace pulled her phone out of her back pocket with tears streaming down her face.

When the dispatcher answered, her voice caught as she said, “This is Grace Callahan. Daniel Reeves is on the roof of the mayor’s office building. He isn’t breathing, and I can’t find a pulse.”

“Are you still on the roof?”

“Yes, but I’m getting down.”

“Be careful. It’s very windy.”

Before she shifted to return to the ladder, Grace brushed back her tears with her arm and caught sight of a shimmering golden speck dancing over Daniel's left arm. His partially curled hand hid a sparkle of green on the roof. *His tie tack.*

Grace picked up the tie tack and stuck it into the small pocket of her jeans, keeping Daniel's shamrock safe for him.

Her stomach was in knots as she crawled painfully back across the graveled roof, with the wind whipping her hair across her face, adding to her tears in further blurring her vision. Before she reached the hatch, a chorus of mournful sirens wailed, their piercing cries accompanied by the sorrowful blasts of air horns.

She climbed down the ladder, protecting her wounded palms by holding onto the rungs with her fingertips. When she reached the bottom of the ladder and stepped down onto the floor, Grace leaned her head against the ladder. After she wiped her face with her forearm as she faced Bella.

"What is it?" Bella asked. "Are you okay? What's wrong?"

"Daniel was on the roof, and he wasn't breathing, and I couldn't find a pulse."

"All the sirens are coming here? What happened to him?"

"I don't know."

"He was always tired, but he's too young to have had a heart attack, isn't he?" Bella swayed slightly and grabbed onto a nearby shelf.

"Let's go into the conference room and sit down. I'm feeling a little wobbly myself." Grace followed Bella to the conference room.

Tears slipped down Bella's face. "I was mean to him because the mayor left, and I blamed him. But even after

I knew I was wrong, I was too proud to tell him I was sorry."

"I'll be right back." Grace rushed to the restroom.

She winced as she ran water over her hands to rinse away the grit and blood. She lightly lathered them, then rinsed off the soap. She lightly blotted her palms to dry them before she returned to the conference room and joined Bella.

The two of them sat in silence. Grace's hands shook as she rubbed her temples, attempting to erase the image of Daniel's chest, forever as still as a sculpted statue.

When the sheriff came in the front door, Grace rose and met him. "Where can we talk, Grace?"

"We can go into my office."

"Will Bella be okay alone?" he asked.

"Yes, I think she could use some time to pull herself together."

After they were in her office, Grace sat in her desk chair, and the sheriff sat in the visitor's chair facing her. She told him about the meeting Daniel missed, the banner, climbing the ladder in the storage room, and finding Daniel.

"He was supposed to be here at seven? What time was it when you texted him?"

Grace pulled her phone out of her back pocket. "About seven thirty."

After a few more questions, the sheriff asked, "Do you want my office to announce the parade is canceled?"

Grace's eyes flashed. "That is the last thing Daniel would want. The parade was very important to him."

"I'm going to have a press conference around ten o'clock. You should be there so you can announce the parade is not canceled because that is what the mayor would want. I can't speculate about the cause of his death. That's the coroner's business, but you can tell people he passed away trying to fix the banner. You'll have to get the word out as fast as you can. I understand you had an army in here yesterday. I'm not telling you your business, but I'd advise you to get them back in here today."

"I'll get as many as I can."

"If you think of anything else, let me know. Be at the sheriff's office fifteen minutes before ten." The sheriff handed her his business card and left.

Grace stared at her palms, which were still weeping blood from the shallow cuts, and then angrily brushed away a tear that escaped down her cheek. *I have to do this.*

She blotted her hands with a tissue and shoved the stained tissue into her jeans pocket, then strolled into the conference room and sat at the table with Bella. "How are you doing?"

Bella gazed at her. "I'm okay; it was such a shock."

"Yes, it was. Would you like to take the rest of the day off?"

Bella narrowed her eyes. "No, I wouldn't. What are we going to do now?"

"I told the sheriff the parade was not canceled. He suggested we gather the army to make phone calls and line up the floats for the parade. We need everyone here as soon as possible. Tell them we are rallying the group because the mayor unfortunately suffered a heart attack while rehanging the parade banner and did not survive. We're continuing with the parade in his memory and need their help."

"Thank you. That's exactly what we're doing."

"I'll call Zoey and Granny. The sheriff wants me to speak at a press conference at ten. Are you okay with encouraging the group while I'm gone?"

Bella rolled her eyes. "That's a Zoey skill. I'll try if she can't be here."

Grace sent Zoey a text. "Call when you can."

Her phone immediately rang. "We were just getting ready to leave the house. What's up?"

"This is sad news." Grace told her about Daniel and the plan to continue the parade in his memory.

"If you don't feel like coming in, I understand."

"I'll send some quick texts and then be there in five minutes."

After Zoey hung up, Grace called Nora.

"Something's wrong, isn't it?" Nora asked.

Grace repeated what she had told Zoey.

"I'll make a few quick calls, then be right there."

Bella came out of the conference room. "Grace, I've made two calls, and both of them asked if you were going to be the new mayor. I told them it was too early to be thinking like that, but I thought you should know."

Grace groaned. "I didn't expect that, but your answer was perfect because that's not a discussion we want to encourage at all. We want people to talk about the parade."

“Thank you.” Bella’s cheeks turned splotchy pink, and she rushed back into the conference room.

When Zoey came in, she was alone. “One of my friends offered to babysit instead of coming in. So, our plan is to line up all the floats we can. Anything else?”

Grace told her Bella’s answer to the next mayor question and about the sheriff’s press conference. “You’ll be in charge of keeping everyone upbeat and on task while I’m gone.”

“I can do that. When are you going to the gas station?”

“I’d forgotten about the gas station. I’ll go there after the press conference.”

“Do we have a script for the callers today?” Zoey asked.

“No, can you write it up for me? They will need to tell our float owners that sadly Mayor Daniel Reeves suffered a fatal heart attack, but we are continuing with the parade in his memory,” Grace said.

“Do we record the results just like yesterday?” Zoey asked.

“Do you think it slowed anyone down?”

“Not at all,” Bella called out from the conference room.

“Let’s stick with it then, but ask them to mark it as day two,” Grace said. “Bella is reviewing all the applications. Have our callers start with the applications that Bella approves.”

The callers from the previous day began trickling in. Nora brought a platter of apple cake, and another woman from the Bible study group brought cookies.

Zoey helped Grace settle everyone down and get to work.

Grace surveyed the room filled with women, each head bent, their voices a low murmur as they spoke on their phones while they recorded results. *We have about half the people from yesterday, but they're moving along faster.*

After a quick glance at the stack of completed calls, Grace picked them up and reviewed them. "Call back" was the most frequent comment.

When a woman in the conference room poured water from the jug into the coffee well to make a fresh pot of coffee, Grace watched her and then remembered. *Daniel had a meeting scheduled this morning with Ryan to talk about water.*

Grace went into Daniel's office and called the distillery.

When he answered, she said, "This is Grace."

"I heard about Daniel, Grace. Are you okay?"

Am I okay? "We're all working to make the parade a success in Daniel's memory."

"That was what I heard. What can I do to help?"

"Why was the St. Patrick's party canceled?"

Ryan snorted. "So much for the polite chitchat. When can we get together to talk?"

"My morning's booked. How about this afternoon?"

"Why don't you come here for lunch? Even project directors must eat lunch."

Grace's back tensed, and she gritted her teeth. "No, thank you. I need to stay close to the office in case anyone has questions."

"Makes sense. Willow and I will be there a little after noon with lunch."

A bell jingled in the background. "I have a customer. See you at noon." Ryan hung up.

Chapter Six

Grace glared at her phone. *At least Ryan sounded like we'd talk about why he canceled the party, and maybe he can tell me why Daniel wanted to talk to him about water systems.*

"Would you look at that? It's a cherry picker. I'll bet they're going to fix the sign." A woman peered out through the glass at the front door.

Grace reached her side ahead of a small group that left their seats still holding their phones to their ears.

A woman behind Grace said, "I called my brother who owns a land clearing business. He told me he'd take care of the sign."

When the cherry picker rolled away, the women spilled out of the building and into the street, solemnly gazing at the sign.

Zoey brushed a tear away, then led the way back into the building. Grace caught up with her. "Zoey, what if we change our script? Instead of asking them if they want to be in the parade, why don't we ask them a different question? One that assumes they want to be in the parade."

Zoey cocked her head. "Like what?"

Grace narrowed her eyes. "Like what would be the next question? The next thing we'd be doing would be creating the lineup so we could email the instructions to them, right?"

A smile crept across Zoey's face. "What if we asked them where they'd like to be in the lineup?"

Grace raised her eyebrows. "That's it."

Once the group was inside, the somber mood turned to all business as Zoey clapped her hands for attention and then asked the group. "What if we changed our script?"

Grace slipped out through her office back door to go to the sheriff's office for the press conference. Bile rose in her throat at the thought of cameras focused on her and reporters asking questions she didn't know how to answer.

By the time Grace reached the sheriff department's parking lot, her hands were shaking. She tightened her grip on the steering wheel until the tremor eased, then checked the rearview mirror.

Her face was pale and flat, and a knot tightened in her stomach. Grace pinched her cheeks, more out of habit than hope, then pushed the door open.

She stared at the lone, puffy cloud that drifted across the sky. *I don't like cameras, but I really don't like questions I can't answer honestly.*

Her footsteps crunched on the rough concrete sidewalk as she strode to the door. *But the parade matters to the town, so if that means I have to speak to the press to help steady things, I will.*

Inside, after passing through the security checkpoint, Grace took in the small lobby. It had the bland personality of a plain white cardboard box, with its gray speckled vinyl floor and a path worn smooth between the entrance and the hall.

The stark white walls bore the imposing seal of the sheriff's department; its sheer size was a silent testament to authority, while the fluorescent lights overhead emitted a low, cicada-like buzz.

She approached the information desk, which was secured behind thick glass. The deputy sheriff seated there smiled at her. She had reddish-brown hair pulled back into a ponytail, fire-engine red lipstick that refused to be ignored, and a long-sleeve brown deputy uniform shirt complete with a badge and nametag, Jackson. A wheelchair was tucked neatly beneath the counter, positioned with practiced precision.

Grace studied her face. "Leah?"

Leah's smile widened. "I didn't know if you'd remember me after almost twenty years, Grace. The sheriff told me to watch for you."

Grace returned the smile. "You haven't changed a bit. Isn't that the same color lipstick you wore in second grade?"

"As close as I could get." Leah tilted her head toward the hallway. "Second door on the left is the conference room. Press is already here."

Grace's shoulders tightened.

"We'll catch up later," Leah added gently. "After this part's over."

"I'd like that." Grace managed a smile and headed down the hallway, the quiet of the building slowly giving way with each of her steps to the low, restless murmur of voices waiting on the other side of the door.

She reached for the door handle and paused. *I'll talk about continuity, honoring the mayor's work, and keeping the parade on schedule.*

When she opened the door, the sheriff strode to her.

The rows of empty chairs behind him seemed to stretch endlessly, filling her vision.

"We got a lucky break," the sheriff whispered. "Something big broke in Atlanta, and the city press left ten minutes ago, so we have the regional news folks and a few independent journalists. I'll lead off, then you can talk about the parade."

The sheriff guided Grace into the room and positioned her slightly behind him as he stood at the wooden podium.

"Thank you for coming," he said, facing the cameras. "Earlier today, Mayor Daniel Reeves was found unresponsive at the city offices. At this time, there is no evidence of foul play. The investigation is ongoing, and we're asking the public to be patient while we do our work."

A few reporters leaned forward.

"Out of respect for the mayor and his family," the sheriff continued, "we won't be answering questions about the cause of death today."

A man with thinning hair three or four years older than Grace sat in the second row. His face bore a faintly irritated expression of someone accustomed to being ignored, and instead of a tablet, he clutched a spiral notebook, which he raised in place of raising his hand.

The sheriff continued, "I'd like to introduce Grace Callahan. She is our deputy mayor and parade coordinator. She has agreed to step in as acting mayor."

Grace moved forward to the podium and stepped up onto the sturdy wooden box nestled against the podium. When she lowered the gooseneck microphone to adjust a little more for her height, the cameras tracked her, and the room subtly recalibrated around her presence.

She relaxed her hands at her side as she surveyed the blank faces and pursed lips of the reporters before she spoke.

"Mayor Reeves cared deeply about this town," she said. "The St. Patrick's Day parade was important to him and to Briar Glen. After careful consideration, we are moving forward with the parade dedicated to his memory."

A hand shot up. "No changes at all?"

"No," Grace said. "The schedule remains the same as always."

"Isn't that rushing things?" another reporter asked.

Grace met the reporter's gaze and lightly placed her hands on the podium. "Honoring someone's work doesn't always mean stopping, and we're following the plan the mayor had already put in place."

The reporter's face softened, and she nodded.

The man with the notebook raised it again.

This time, the sheriff nodded to him.

"Caleb Morris," he said. "Independent."

Grace's palms grew damp, and she folded her hands together in front of her to resist wiping them off on her jeans. *Of course, it was.* His articles in the high school paper got people called into the principal's office.

"Ms. Callahan," Morris said, voice mild, "you were hired by the mayor yesterday, correct?"

The other reporters exchanged glances, then leaned forward to hear her answer.

"Yes," she said clearly.

"And now you're stepping into his role less than twenty-four hours after you were hired."

Challenge accepted. Grace made eye contact with Caleb and then strategically with other reporters in the room who were staring at her. "The mayor asked me yesterday to step in as deputy major to make sure the parade was successful and the town didn't lose economic momentum. I'm continuing in that capacity to honor his request."

Caleb scribbled a note in his notebook while Grace continued.

"As we have for years, Briar Glen will host its annual St. Patrick's Day parade, a celebration for everyone to enjoy and build their own family memories."

Morris tilted his head slightly. "Some might say that's a lot of responsibility for someone new to the position."

Grace lifted her chin. "Stability comes from follow-through and support from the community."

When she smiled, a few of the reporters returned her smile. "Come enjoy the parade with us."

The sheriff stepped forward. "That's all the time we have."

Cameras clicked, and chairs scraped on the wooden floor as people rose. The low hum of voices overlapped as reporters packed up. When the reporter who had asked the first question nodded, Grace returned the nod.

As the room cleared, Grace remained where she was, acutely aware of the fact that every word she'd chosen and every one she'd withheld would be replayed, dissected, and questioned.

When all the reporters had left the room, a shadow of a wry smile crossed her face.

The sheriff turned to her as she stepped down. "Well done. I loved your parting shot of inviting everyone to the parade."

"Thanks for your encouragement, sheriff."

As they strolled together out of the conference room, the sheriff said, "I assume you'll be using the same parade route. We'll send you a copy of last year's. If you have any adjustments, let me know before the end of the day. Send me your lineup schedule and the instructions for your parade monitors and participants when you send out the instructions to the float owners."

"When do you block off the streets along the parade route?"

"Everyone is used to the roads being blocked off by nine the night before. The cafés along the route close in the afternoon after lunch, and all the retailers and offices close by six."

"I can't imagine the amount of work to put together a parade without having the long history of previous years to follow." Grace headed toward the exit.

When Grace reached the information desk, Leah asked, "So how was it?"

"I was nervous, but I didn't hurt anybody."

Leah chuckled. "Do you remember that summer when you punched Trey in the nose because he said you could be his girlfriend because you were prettier than an elephant?"

Grace giggled. "I'd forgotten about that. It was the summer before third grade when you and I decided we would be artists when we grew up. We were sitting on a bench in the park, and you were drawing pandas, and I was drawing elephants."

"Do you suppose he remembers?" Leah asked.

"I have a meeting with him later. Should I bring that up?"

"I dare you."

When they snort-laughed, the deputy at the security checkpoint stared at them, and they laughed even harder.

After they settled down, Leah said, "My shift ends early; can you use any extra help?"

"I'd love it if you could review our lineup and instructions for the floats. Bella is thorough, and I can review the process, but I don't have the experience to give the details a decent review."

"Perfect. I'll be there around three."

"I appreciate it."

As Grace drove back to the office, she stared at the sky; a second puffy cloud had joined the first one. She growled, "If you're thinking about raining, do it today and be done with it for the rest of the week."

When she went in through the back door, she was greeted with silence except for the quiet murmuring of phone conversations. The three women working in her office glanced up and waved.

Grace stopped at Zoey's desk. Zoey pointed to Daniel's office. After the two of them were in the office, Zoey said, "We're doing phone call sprints. Bella is our timer. We make phone calls for thirty minutes with only potty breaks allowed, then we all take a five minute break for a stretch or more coffee."

"I have few things to catch up, so I'll work in here. I'm interruptible anytime."

Zoey left, and Grace turned on Daniel's computer. When it asked for a screen password, she opened the middle drawer on Daniel's desk and found an address book. She opened it and copied the password from the front page.

She searched his hard drive for spreadsheets, but he had only documents and photos. She changed the password and then logged out and rebooted. While the computer went through its rebooting process, she slipped the address book into her backpack and searched through the rest of the drawers. After she checked all the folders, she discovered all the papers were dated three or more years ago; she leaned back and glanced at the meeting table, then rose to check underneath it. *The shredder lid is off.* She put the lid back on the shredder.

She tapped the meeting table in thought, and then Bella called out, "Time."

When Grace opened the door, the silence had been replaced by conversations and laughter.

She met Zoey midway to the conference room.

Zoey bounced on her toes. "I was on my way to check in with Bella."

When they went into the conference room, Bella glanced at them and beamed.

"How are we doing, Bella?" Zoey asked.

"We have contacted fifty-two float owners so far and have forty-one floats confirmed." Bella's face flushed.

"We had four after making calls practically all day yesterday and forty-one today? What kind of magic have y'all pulled off?" Grace asked.

"Zoey's the magician. She came up with the idea to tell them we are finalizing the lineup today and ask them where they preferred to be: closer to the high school band, the dance team, or St. Patrick, and then confirm their email address."

Grace gaped at Zoey. "That is absolutely brilliant."

Nora joined them. "I had one person tell me he'd get back to me, and I told him I'd put him on the wherever was left list. He chose the dance team."

Grace hugged Nora. "Good choice on his part."

"We decided we didn't have time to play games," Zoey said.

"Especially any polite ones," Nora added.

Bella picked up a small stack of applications. “I've finished reviewing all the applications and pulled ten out for you to review, Grace.”

“Should we review them together?” Grace asked. “We could go into Daniel's office on the next sprint.”

Bella nodded as she handed the ten applications to Grace and called out, “Ready, everyone? Sprint.”

After they went into Daniel's office, Bella said, “Five have nonworking phone numbers, and three have no phone numbers listed. The other two are from Florida, so they were never contacted.”

“Why is that?” Grace asked.

“Mayor Dorsey did not allow out-of-state floats, so they were set to the side and never contacted. I chatted with both of them and promised to send them information for next year's parade. Is that okay?”

“I would have done the same thing. We'll have a list of this year's participants, which I assume we'll use to send an early signup notice next year. We could add them to the early signup list so we don't have to track them separately.”

Bella glanced at her phone. “At this rate, we'll be finished before lunch.”

“That's great. This afternoon we can organize the floats into groups, then establish a lineup. Leah from the sheriff's office will be here this afternoon and will help us with the lineup and our letter to the float owners.”

“Leah from the sheriff's office?” Bella pursed her lips.

Grace nodded. “What's wrong?”

"She hates me." Tears ran down Bella's face; she knocked over her chair as she jumped up and ran out of the office.

The automatic door slowly closed behind Bella.

Grace rose from her chair and picked up the overturned chair as Zoey came into the office.

"Is Bella sick? She ran into the restroom," Zoey said. "I came to tell you we finished. I want to give the final count, then you can give one of your pep talks before everybody leaves."

After they left Daniel's office, Zoey put her fingers up to her mouth and whistled.

A woman stage-whispered, "Show off."

Everyone laughed.

Zoey grinned. "Ready for our stats? Last year we had eighteen floats. This year, we started with seventy-eight applications. Ten of those were pulled out as invalid. We now have sixty-two floats confirmed for the parade thanks to y'all and Grace's brilliant nudge to close the sale. Don't you know how proud Daniel Reeves would be?"

There was a collective gasp of realization that was quickly overcome by whistles and cheers.

Nora hugged Grace and whispered, "I'm so proud of how quickly you've pulled the parade together."

"Thank you, Granny. Are you going to the animal shelter today?"

"I'd rather have a second opinion. Maybe you can get away tomorrow."

"I'll make time."

After everyone left, Zoey said, "Bella's still in the restroom."

"I'll check on her. Zoey, I told her Leah was going to be here at three, and she told me Leah hates her. Does that make sense to you?"

Zoey's eyes welled up. "Bella's brother was drunk and hit a sheriff's deputy cruiser head-on. He didn't survive. Leah was the deputy, and her recovery has been slow. She doesn't hate Bella."

"Why does Bella blame herself?"

"It must have been how she was raised because she does tend to assume everything is her fault."

Grace strolled to the restroom and tapped on the door. When there was no answer, her heart rate jumped, and she pounded on the door.

"What do you want?" Bella growled.

Grace's shoulders relaxed, and her heart rate slowed. "I want help with the instructions for the float."

Bella cracked the door open; her eyes were red and swollen. "I have a draft."

"Good; let's go over it after you throw some water on your face. Your allergies must have kicked into high gear."

After Bella splashed water on her face, she hurried to her computer and printed out three copies.

"It's almost noon," Zoey said. "How about a lunch break?"

Grace groaned. "Ryan and Willow are bringing me lunch. I have to talk to him."

"Yes, you do. We should disappear."

“That’s a good idea. Go to the café, have a delicious lunch, and bring the receipt.”

“Can we do that?” Bella asked.

“The deputy mayor said we could,” Zoey said. “I’ve never been to the café, Bella. What’s good?”

“I’ll drive,” Bella said.

“Smart choice. Crushed crackers have a way of appearing all over my car.”

After they left, Grace headed toward her office but turned around when the front door creaked, and Willow trotted inside.

Grace smiled. “Hello, Willow. How’s the girl?”

Willow’s tail went into high gear, and Grace opened the gate so she and Willow could say hello.

Ryan strode into the office, carrying a large white sack. “What food allergies do you have? Don’t say chicken or brownies because I have seen you eat both in the school cafeteria.”

“You did not. Granny packed my lunch for me. I lived on peanut butter sandwiches and chocolate chip cookies.”

Ryan cocked his head. “Really? I thought I was the only one who brought a sack lunch to school.”

“Let’s go into the conference room. It’s become our break room. Maybe you weren’t as much of an outcast as you thought.”

After Ryan set the sack on the table, he pulled out sandwiches, drinks, and napkins and arranged them as place settings. “Maybe I was in good company with the rest of the outcasts and didn’t know it.”

Grace sat at the table so she could see the front door, and Ryan inhaled as he sat next to her. While they unwrapped their sandwiches, Ryan asked, "What are we watching for?"

"Whoever comes through the door."

Grace lifted an edge of her sandwich. "This looks like homemade chicken salad." She took a bite. "Mmm. Delicious."

She swallowed her first bite. "Where did you get this? This is the best chicken salad I've ever had."

He raised his eyebrows as he reached into the sack with the flourish of a magician and pulled out a small plastic container. After he opened it, Willow politely sat, and he gave her a generous bite of plain chicken.

"I'm glad you like it, Grace. Cooking is my hobby."

While they ate, Ryan said, "Daniel told me yesterday he was going to invite you to our ten o'clock meeting. Did he?"

"Yes, and he gave me an envelope last night to bring to the meeting. It's in my backpack."

Willow followed Grace who went to her office and then returned with her backpack with Willow at her side. She pulled out the fat envelope and handed it to Ryan. Ryan read the first two pages. "Did he say anything about the papers?"

"He said there was an electrical problem with the water system because the pumps were overheating, or maybe he said they were running in emergency mode."

"Probably running in emergency mode."

"Anyway, he said he had a meeting on Wednesday with the water system manager except Sully wanted a list of problems. He said you could help him with the list, and he wanted me to go along because he didn't know anything about hydraulics."

"What do you know about hydraulics?"

"Nothing, and that's what I told him, but he insisted. And then he said since I was going with him, he'd just leave the papers with me."

Chapter Seven

Ryan flipped through a few more pages. "Have you looked at these?"

"I haven't had time."

Ryan pulled brownies out of the sack. Grace unwrapped her brownie and took a bite. "Did you make the brownies too? They taste homemade."

"Sure did." Ryan unwrapped his brownie. "Can I keep the papers? I need to spend some time on them."

"I'll copy a set for you."

Grace picked up the papers and took them to the copy machine with Ryan and Willow behind her.

"That's a cheap copy machine barely adequate for home use." Ryan was still as he peered over her shoulder at the machine while it whined and shuddered with each page it slowly ejected into its tray.

"No kidding. I reviewed this year's budget and checked the expenditures for the past two years, and the mayor before Daniel didn't update any of the equipment even though it was in the budget."

"Did the surplus roll over?"

"Not that I've found. It may have been absorbed back into the town budget, but I haven't had time to dig that deep."

After the document was copied, Grace handed the copies to Ryan. "Daniel said you knew hydraulics, and he knew budgets and how to spot a phony, and so did I."

Ryan tilted his head as he gazed at Grace. "I think Daniel was right. What are you doing this evening? Would you like to have dinner at the distillery? Willow and I could pick you up so you don't have to drive home alone."

"Granny would love it if you came to her house for dinner. We could take over the dining room for research, but..." Grace narrowed her eyes. *Granny would snoop.*

"What?"

"Granny would eavesdrop, then decide we needed help."

"We need an excuse for you to be at the distillery, but it has to be believable."

"I could use cooking lessons, but that seems pretty weak to me," Grace said.

"I suppose it's better than nothing."

"Maybe." Grace stroked Willow and cooed, "Pretty girl."

Prettier than an elephant. Grace chuckled.

"What's funny?" Ryan asked.

"I saw Leah today. Do you remember telling me I was prettier than an elephant?"

Ryan quickly covered his nose with his hand. "Vaguely."

He peered over his hand, and Grace laughed.

Ryan chuckled. "That's actually genius. Rekindling the old flame. Do you think Nora would buy it?"

"What? That I punched you in the nose again, and that's why I'm spending so much time at the distillery? Probably. What about your reputation?"

Ryan cocked his head and raised an eyebrow. "My reputation as a scoundrel? Enhanced."

Grace sniffed. "I'll be going home to Atlanta; you'll be stuck here in the aftermath."

Ryan was still then shook his head as he peered at her. "Heartbroken and crushed."

She gazed at Ryan's face, then narrowed her eyes. "I want to finish what Daniel started."

Ryan put his hand on the back of her hand, and she winced as her palm touched the table.

"What is it?" He lifted her wrist and turned her hand over as he slipped his hand under hers to support it.

He lifted my hand like it was a delicate butterfly.

Ryan frowned. "What happened to your hands?"

Willow put her head on Grace's knee and whined.

Grace whispered, "Thank you, Willow."

She met Ryan's gaze. "I crawled across the roof to get to Daniel because the wind gusts took away my breath and almost knocked me down."

As he supported her hand in his, Ryan leaned down to examine her palm and shook his head. "Some of those cuts are deep. Let me see your other hand."

Grace showed him her other hand. "They sting, but the throbbing bothers me the most."

He took her hands in his and inspected them more closely. "There might still be some slivers of gravel in there. We'll soak your hands this evening, and then I'll apply a salve and bandage them so you can sleep."

"I would really appreciate it."

Grace met his gaze. When a telltale heat crept up her neck, she self-consciously pulled away her hands. *I don't want to give him the wrong idea.*

She dropped her head and gazed at her hands. "It will be interesting to see how quickly Granny decides we're an item because as soon as she does, everybody in town will know."

"That will make it easier for us to take our time in analyzing Daniel's data. Do you have someone in the wings who will be brokenhearted about the news?"

"Dozens. What about you?" Grace asked.

Ryan carefully counted on his fingers on both hands, then shrugged. "About the same."

Grace giggled. "That's at least one less complication. I am really looking forward to having the time to do more research without someone looking over my shoulder. Did I tell you Daniel hid more documents in my office? I have those files in my backpack."

"In your office? That doesn't sound like Daniel."

"Really? At first, I thought he was a little paranoid because he told me he emptied his shredder every day."

"There are so many open questions, aren't there?" Ryan rubbed his jawline. "Do I pick you up after work so we can get started?"

"No, I'll call Granny and tell her you invited me to dinner, then I'll go home and change so she can grill me."

Ryan side-glanced at Grace. "I don't suppose you could break character and be nice to me, could you?"

Her voice was soft with a tinge of teasing. "Won't happen, and you know it."

"Let's go, Willow. I think you just witnessed the first of many rebuffs."

Ryan patted Grace's shoulder. "See you later, Gracie."

Grace cringed as Ryan and Willow left.

Will I regret this? Grace straightened her back and picked up her phone.

When Nora answered, Grace said, "Ryan invited me to have dinner with him at the distillery this evening."

"Ryan? Ryan Pearce? This isn't one of those pranks, is it?"

"I didn't think of that; it would have been a good one too. Did he miss making it onto your vetted list?"

While she waited for Nora to respond, Grace smiled at the memory of biding her time in the dark attic with Granny in silence waiting for the fairies to appear.

Finally, Nora said, "That silly list thing? I'd almost forgotten about it. Are you coming here to change first?"

"I thought I would. I'll see you around five."

After they hung up, Grace texted Ryan. "Granny has a mission."

He replied, "No surprise."

When Bella and Zoey came inside, Zoey said, "Thank you for lunch, Grace. What's our plan for this afternoon?"

Bella sat at her desk, waving a receipt. "I'll submit an expense report."

"While you're doing that, Zoey and I will go over the draft of the email to the float owners in the conference room."

While Grace and Zoey completed their review to hone the message, Bella brought in the applications that had been approved and set them on the conference table in their three piles. "What do we need to do after we finalize the parade lineup?" Grace asked.

Bella and Zoey exchanged a glance.

Grace sighed. "I forgot about the St. Patrick's float. We don't have a St. Patrick, do we? Who would be the most logical person?"

"Mr. Pearce," Zoey said.

"Ryan's grandfather?" Grace asked. "Don't tell me. I suppose the invitation should come from the deputy mayor."

"Maybe Nora or Ryan could introduce you so you could officially ask him," Zoey said.

"You're right." Grace pulled out her phone and sent a text to Ryan. "We need a St. Patrick to ride on the St. Patrick's parade float. Any ideas?"

Ryan replied, "Yes. We can talk at dinner."

You could have shared what you're thinking. Grace replied, "Thanks."

She put down her phone. "Ryan will help me."

Grace surveyed the three stacks. "So, let's spread out the applications by groups on the table, then we can talk about adjustments from there."

After the float applications were spread out on the tables in their groups, Grace stood back while Bella and Zoey discussed the floats, considering any personality conflicts or floats that were too similar in style. *They're used to working as a team. I didn't see it until now.*

When they reached the last float, Grace asked. "Do we have any reason to go back through the order one more time?"

"I'd like to just walk down the line from beginning to end," Bella said.

"What would we be looking for?" Grace asked.

Bella shrugged. "Floats with designs too similar."

Grace glanced back at the table. "They're all St. Patrick's Day parade floats. We could tweak and adjust for days, but right now we're at the point of being ready to go."

"We don't have to have the perfect lineup," Zoey muttered.

"Easy for you to say," Bella grumbled.

They're teasing each other. This is my cue to keep my mouth shut.

The front door opened partway, then slammed shut before it flung wide open. "Dammit."

"Leah's here," Zoey rushed to the front door.

"This door hates me," Leah said.

"I think you're right, Leah. Nobody else has any trouble with the automated front door," Zoey said.

"They are all just too polite to say anything," Leah grumbled.

"Are you getting warmed up to critique our email?" Grace asked.

Leah chuckled. "Exactly."

Zoey handed Leah a red pen and a clipboard with a copy of the email. "I have to leave in five minutes, Leah. Do your worst."

Leah read the email slowly, then quickly a second time. "I like you mentioned Mayor Daniel Reeves in your first paragraph."

On the third pass, she stopped at the last paragraph. "Well done, but you want this to sound like Grace, right? This doesn't cut it."

Leah read aloud. "If you have any further questions, please do not hesitate to contact me."

"Eww. I added that. Can I claim jet lag?" Grace asked.

"Throw in a lack of oxygen, and you're covered. I have a suggestion for your closing. 'Thanks to your support, the parade will be an enormous success for the families and friends of Briar Glen.'"

"Good enough," Bella said.

When everyone gaped at her, Bella smiled. "I've been hoping I'd find the perfect time to say that."

Zoey laughed. "Priceless, Bella. I'll see you in the morning."

After Zoey left, Bella said, "While you and Zoey were revising the email, Grace, I set up a mail merge to email the letters."

"So after you revise the last paragraph, you'll send out the emails. Is that right?"

"That's it. The emails will be in our float owners' inboxes before three thirty."

While Bella prepared the email, Grace said, "Leah, we need someone to ride on a float as St. Patrick. Who would you suggest?"

"Mr. Pearce. Is that who Bella and Zoey suggested?"

"Yes. I'm having dinner with Ryan this evening, and I'm hoping he'll help me."

"That was fast. How did you manage that?" Leah's glance was friendly, but a hint of suspicion colored her voice.

Grace smiled. "Well, Deputy, if you must know, he invited me, and I need a St. Patrick, so I decided to see if I could be nice for one evening."

Leah chuckled. "That's a bit of a stretch, but it's for a good cause. Since my work here is done, I'll be on my way. I'll check in with you tomorrow for a full report."

When Leah reached the door, she said, "Watch this." After she pushed the button, the door swung wide open. As she rolled out the door, Leah called out, "The door likes for me to leave."

Bella looked up from her computer. "She's right, you know. The door only works right when she leaves. What's our plan for tomorrow?"

"I'd like to go to the high school so I can understand the flow of the lineup. Maybe you could give me a walkthrough. Are you going to be available to work Saturday morning at the parade?"

"I always have been."

"Good. I could use your help with the parade, and I'd like to chat with the band director."

"I'll call the high school to schedule meetings with the principal and the band director."

I should have thought of that. "Thank you."

While Bella was on hold with the school, she handed a sheet of paper to Grace. "Here's a copy of the email for you. Are there any more changes you'd like to make?"

Bella hung up. "We have meetings scheduled with the principal at ten thirty and the band director at eleven, and I added the meetings to the office calendar. Is the email ready to send?"

"It's so perfect, it's good enough," Grace said.

Bella beamed as she sent the email. "Our new motto."

Grace glanced at the clock. "Granny wants me to go to the animal shelter with her. Are we ready to leave?"

Bella's hands tensed then she exhaled slowly while she straightened out her hands on her desk and released her tension. "Everything we can do today is done. We can leave whenever you say."

"Let's do it then. I'll take care of the lights and the security system."

Bella removed her purse from her desk drawer and stuck her coin in her coat pocket before she put on her coat. "I hope I'm not jinxing the parade, but I think we're on the right track."

That's high praise coming from Bella.

Grace secured the office, then hurried to her car.

Grace started her car and waited for the engine to warm up enough to turn on the heater.

Her phone rang. *Granny's calling me?*

Nora said, "I was halfway out the door to go to the shelter when I had a premonition that you needed to go with me."

"I'll be home in two minutes."

Nora replied, "I'll be on the porch ready to go."

Did Granny forget she told me when I was three that premonition is a big word that means fairies?

Grace pulled into the driveway, and Nora rushed to the car and jumped inside.

"It's getting colder, but we're supposed to have mild weather on Saturday for the parade. So, tell me about Ryan inviting you to dinner."

"I kind of wrangled the invitation after Bella and Zoey told me it was up to me to invite Mr. Pearce to ride on the St. Patrick float."

"I can only imagine how subtle you were," Nora chuckled.

Grace smiled. "My usual. You would have been proud. I'm looking forward to seeing dogs at the animal shelter with you."

"I think I might like an older dog. You know, one that's been overlooked."

Grace parked in the almost empty visitor lot at the shelter, and the two of them strolled arm in arm toward the shelter. Nora squeezed Grace's arm and grinned. "Hear the barking? I think they're talking to each other."

Nora elbowed Grace and discreetly pointed to the volunteer sweeping up tufts of dog hair from the gleaming white floor. Another volunteer quickly removed two kittens from a crate and set them in a box while she changed their drinking water.

The volunteer at the desk stopped typing on her keyboard and asked, "How can we help you?"

"I'm looking for an older dog to be my companion," Nora said.

The volunteer signed off her computer. “Follow me. We have our older dogs that are ready for their forever homes right this way.”

They followed her down a hall and through a door where individual kennels were lined up against the wall with outdoor access for the dogs. The kennel area was as clean as the waiting room but had more personality with yipping and barking canines and the musky aroma of dogs.

In the center of the row of kennels, a woman in gray scrubs was kneeling in a kennel with the door open. Her hands were steady as she leaned in, carefully examining a beagle's mouth and eyes.

“Are you here to see our dogs?” Another volunteer paused on her way out. “Look around. Dr. Higgins can help you.”

Nora surveyed the kennels, then immediately went to the kennel with a black labrador retriever with a slightly gray muzzle. The name tag over the door was Murphy.

Dr. Higgins joined them at the kennel and opened the door and then kneeled next to the dog and quickly examined him.

“He’s well-hydrated; his rear legs have a little arthritis, so stairs will be a problem for him.” She rose. “Older dogs adapt faster than people think.”

Nora approached the lab, and he wagged his tail; she cooed as she scratched his ear. “We’ll get along just fine, won’t we, Murphy?”

Murphy sneaked in a quick kiss on her hand, then leaned against her while she stroked his back.

Dr. Higgins peered at the two of them. "Grace, your grandmother is right. He's a good match."

Grace raised an eyebrow. *Does everybody know who I am in Briar Glen?*

Dr. Higgins continued, "If you're willing to meet him where he is, take him home."

Nora nodded, and a volunteer swooped to Murphy's kennel.

"As long as he eats, drinks, and gets his walks, he'll be fine. It's when one of those drops off that you have to act." Dr. Higgins returned to the beagle she had been examining when they walked in.

"Ready to go, old man?" The volunteer slipped a temporary leash around his neck.

Grace glanced back at Dr. Higgins who continued her methodical assessment.

The volunteer led the way to the main desk. "I'll take Murphy for a quick walk while you sign the paperwork."

The volunteer behind the desk handed Nora a folder. "Murphy is seven years old. These are the recommendations for food and care of a senior dog, and a sheet for what you'll need to get today."

Murphy and the volunteer returned, and Murphy wagged his tail when he saw Nora.

Nora chuckled. "I'm happy to see you too, Murphy."

Nora opened the back door for Murphy, but he backed up.

"If you get in the passenger seat, Granny, Murphy might realize you'll be with him in the car."

Nora sat in the front seat, then turned to face the back door. "Come on, Murphy. Let's go."

Murphy hopped in and put his head on the back of Nora's seat and then rested his chin on her shoulder.

"Murphy has definitely bonded with you, Granny," Grace closed the back door.

Grace climbed into the driver's seat. "The farm store should have everything you need, and you can take Murphy inside."

When they went into the farm store, Murphy stopped at the cash register and sat.

The cashier raised her eyebrows. "Is this your new dog, Nora? He's obviously well-acquainted with the benefits of shopping." She slipped him a doggie treat. "What's your name, good boy?"

"He's Murphy." Nora beamed.

"Nice to meet you, Murphy." The cashier slipped him another treat.

Grace left Nora and Murphy to wander around the store while she rolled a shopping cart to the pet section.

While she selected items that were on the list and put them in the cart, a woman who put a sack of dog food into her cart said, "I have an older German Shepherd. If it's not on your list, he'll need a soft doggie bed."

"Thank you." Grace added a large dog bed to the cart.

Grace returned to the front of the store. Murphy peered at her as he shook the blue dinosaur stuffed sturdy dog toy in his mouth.

"We found a toy he liked, and we picked out a green fish as a backup," Nora said.

"Nice dinosaur, Murphy. Granny, I have two collars so you can choose which one is right for Murphy." Grace held out the blue plaid and the red collar.

Nora glanced at Murphy. "We like the blue plaid. It matches his dinosaur."

The cashier snipped the price tag off the blue plaid collar, and Grace put the collar on Murphy.

"Perfect," Nora said.

When Grace rolled the shopping cart to her car, Murphy trotted alongside Nora carrying his dinosaur with his head up.

Murphy hopped into the backseat. Nora closed his door and then sat in the passenger seat and pulled out the folder while Grace put on her seatbelt. "What was the medicine you bought at the farm store?"

"It was arthritis medicine."

Nora pulled out the sheet with Murphy's information. "I see it here. One pill twice a day in his food. The only information in the section marked history is a trucker found him with no collar on the side of the road."

Chapter Eight

As they continued toward Nora's house, Grace glanced in her rearview mirror. "Granny, Murphy is stretched out on the backseat, relaxing with his paw around his new dinosaur."

"That's good, isn't it? You should have seen him. He stood stopped at the toy aisle then stalked the dinosaur. He gently lifted it off the shelf like it was a duck."

"I'll bet that was something to see. Murphy must have been an excellent hunting dog in his prime."

"I don't know what his routine is. Dr. Higgins said he needed walks. That's every day, right? Do you think walking to the dog park will be okay?"

"Sounds perfect, Granny."

"Good, and my backyard is fenced, so Murphy can go outside when he feels like it."

While Grace and Nora carried in the purchases, Murphy inspected the front yard, then laid down on the porch with his dinosaur and watched them.

Nora held the front door open. "Come on, Murphy."

Murphy stared at her and didn't move.

"He might not have been allowed in the house," Grace said.

Nora stood inside the house while Grace held the door. Murphy rose and peered around the corner, looking for Nora.

"Come on, boy." Nora took a step backward, and Murphy tentatively followed her in with his new blue soft dinosaur.

"Let's get you some water." Murphy followed Nora into the kitchen.

While Nora filled his water bowl, Grace said, "I'm going to take a shower and change, and then pack a few things to take with me."

Nora frowned. "You're not coming home tonight?"

"I might have a cocktail at dinner or be too tired to drive home."

Nora put Murphy's water bowl on the floor, then faced Grace with a scowl.

"You're making it complicated, Granny."

"It's my job." Nora put her hands on her hips."

"What if I promise Ryan I'll text him when I get home? Then he'll know I made it home safe."

Nora glared at Grace, and Murphy whined.

"Okay, Murphy said that will work if you text us when you get to the distillery."

Grace stared at Murphy, and he cocked his head.

She stroked his neck. "You're a good boy, Murphy, but you two are ganging up on me. I suppose it's a reasonable request. I'll do it."

"Good."

Murphy turned to Nora, and she rubbed his chin. "Let's see where your dog bed fits best in my bedroom, Murphy, and then I think I know where I have an old, soft braided rug we can put on the floor for you in the living room."

Grace stepped into the shower. While the almost too hot spray beat on her back, she hummed an old tune from twenty years ago. *It's the song Granny said the fairies sang when they were happy.*

While Grace dressed, Nora's voice carried from the living room.

"Now, Murphy, don't snap at the little lights. Those fairies will upset your stomach."

Grace covered her mouth to stifle her giggle when Murphy yipped.

"They annoy me too sometimes," Nora said, "but they're actually our friends."

Grace slipped a pair of warm socks and slippers into an old tote she found in her closet. After she dropped in spare toiletries, she added her favorite soft sweatshirt and a pair of sweatpants, and then went to the kitchen.

Grace found Nora and Murphy in the kitchen. Nora was stirring a large pot of soup on the stove.

Grace rubbed the side of Murphy's face. "Have a nice evening with Granny. I'll see you later."

Nora turned and glared at Grace as she pointed with her wooden spoon. "What do you have in that tote, young lady?"

"A see-through nightie and my lacy underthings." Grace tossed her hair.

Nora snorted. “Where did you get your sassy sense of humor from? See-through is not your style.”

“What’s my style?”

Granny cocked her head. “A peekaboo sweatshirt in camo.”

Grace giggled. “It does sound more like me, doesn’t it?” She kissed Nora on the cheek. “I’ll leave the tote in my trunk in case I need it and text you and Murphy when I’m at the distillery.”

“Pull an old blanket or quilt out of the hall closet and throw it into your trunk too.”

“Thanks, I will.”

“Murphy and I will pack a survival box for you if you can wait a few minutes.”

“I’m leaving before you call a security team to ride shotgun. I love you, Granny.”

Grace grabbed an old blanket, but before she reached the front door, Murphy growled softly, and then there was a knock at the door.

“Oh, good, Tristan’s here.” Nora hurried past Grace.

Grace returned to her bedroom with her tote, backpack, and the blanket with a sigh while Nora answered the door.

“I’m surprised to see you, Aaron,” Nora said.

Who is Aaron? Grace cocked an eyebrow as she left her bedroom.

Aaron’s voice reverberated down the hallway. “Who is this good boy?”

“This is Murphy.”

“Good boy, Murphy.”

“He likes you, Aaron,” Nora said.

"Dogs are my favorite people." Aaron chuckled. "When I heard Tristan and the boys were coming here to help you, I thought I'd come along so I could meet Grace."

Grace hurried to the front door and smiled at the man who almost filled the doorway.

"I'm Grace."

"I'm Aaron Wilson, the high school band director. We have a meeting tomorrow, but I thought I'd drop by and say hello in a less formal setting."

"I'm happy to meet you. I'm excited the band will be joining the parade."

"This will be our first year of being in the parade. We appreciate the opportunity to show off our talented musicians."

"That's thanks to Walt."

"My cousin's a good man to have at your back." Aaron continued to scratch Murphy's ears.

"Ah, Grace. It's nice to see you again." Tristan interrupted as he joined them in the hall. "Too bad about the problems with the parade."

Tristan glanced at Murphy and took a step back.

"Which problems?"

"Still being brave." Tristan chuckled. "I admire how strong you are through all of this. The latest is the downtown merchants' petition to re-route the parade."

"Where did you hear that?"

"In the hallway at school. A teacher heard it in her yoga class last night."

Aaron gave Murphy one last pet. "Check with Walt, Grace. He'll help you if there's a problem with some of the downtown merchants."

"Thank you. I'll do that."

Grace hurried to the kitchen. "Bye, Granny." She kissed Nora's cheek, then leaned down and stroked Murphy's neck. "Good boy, Murphy."

She hurried to her car. *Who fired up the merchants into wanting the parade rerouted at the last minute?*

A lone car idled in the parking lot ahead, its engine a low rumble against the silence of the abandoned Briar Glen Feed and Seed warehouse. After she passed the building, the dark sedan pulled out of the parking lot toward downtown.

As she drove down Main Street on her way to the distillery, Grace admired the St. Patrick's Day decorations on the storefronts. *When I was six, Mom and I helped the bookshop decorate, and the owner told me, "Now you're a part of the parade too."*

She slowed down as she passed the bookshop, glancing at the window display with sparkling shamrock necklaces draped over the books. *I need time to think.*

She glanced in her rearview mirror at the car that was half a block behind her.

Grace pulled into the gas station and stopped at the pump to fill up. When her tank was full, she moved to park in front of the store.

When she went inside, Walt was behind the counter and pointed at her receipt he had already printed. "Good to see you, Grace. How are you doing?"

"Not bad except I heard the downtown merchants were circulating a petition to stop the parade or re-route it because it's hurting their bottom line."

"That's nonsense. Who said that?"

"Evidently, it was repeated in the teacher's lounge at the high school."

Walt snorted. "I have an idea which teacher it was. Her husband is that one merchant every town has who is never satisfied with any idea that wasn't his."

"I'd still like to have a meeting with the merchants right after the shops close for the day tomorrow. Would five o'clock catch most people leaving for the day?"

"Make it five thirty, so they'll have time to close up. Where were you going to hold the meeting?"

"I'm hoping we can use the sheriff's press room."

"If that doesn't work out, let me know and I'll contact the churches for you."

Grace's eyes welled up. "Thank you, Walt."

Before Grace opened her car door, she scanned the surrounding area. A black car with dark tinted windows was parked next to the air compressor for tires, but she couldn't see the driver.

Grace shook her head as she climbed into her car. *Next I'll be seeing shadowy vehicles lurking behind trees.*

As she turned onto the highway to go to the distillery, she glanced in her rearview mirror at the vehicle that followed her. Grace accelerated to the speed limit, and the sedan behind her stayed two car lengths behind her. *The car is pacing me.*

When the vehicle turned at a side road, Grace exhaled but kept checking her rearview mirror until she reached the distillery.

While Grace parked, Ryan and Willow came out of the distillery and waved. She sent a quick text to Nora and then grabbed her backpack and hurried to the door.

"We were hoping we wouldn't have to start happy hour without you." Ryan and Willow led the way past the shop to the living area. "I found a new appetizer recipe a few weeks ago, and you're my guinea pig."

"Is the new appetizer for the St. Patrick's Day party?" Grace asked.

Ryan lowered his head; his tone was flat. "That's canceled."

Grace caught up with him. "Why?"

Ryan continued walking but didn't answer. When she stopped, he turned and glared at her, but she held her gaze.

Willow laid down at his feet and whined.

"Should I leave?" Grace asked.

He went still, then met her gaze. "We'll talk over appetizers."

When he opened the door, Grace strolled past him, and Willow followed Grace into the living room.

Grace called out, "So, when does happy hour start in this joint?"

"How did you learn those strong-arm tactics?" Ryan asked.

"I'm a natural born thug."

"Always were." Ryan tried to hide his smile, but Grace giggled at him.

Ryan dropped a large ice cube into each of two short, wide glasses and then poured a shot of whiskey into each glass.

"This is Grandad's legacy whiskey. It's a bourbon blended from local heirloom grains. Take a sip for the full flavor, then bring your glass into the kitchen. We can talk while I finish preparing our appetizers," Ryan said.

Grace took a tiny sip, and her eyes widened. "This is much smoother than I expected."

Ryan smiled. "I've always thought that too. I'm hoping mine will be as smooth as his, but it will be a few more years before we'll know."

Grace and Willow followed Ryan into the kitchen.

Grace was mesmerized by the massive commercial gas range, with its multiple burners and grills, and she could almost smell the delicious meals a talented chef could create.

Grace set her glass on the massive bar that faced the range and climbed up on a bar chair. "This is impressive. Is this like a chef's table?"

Ryan smiled. "Exactly. I haven't opened the table to the public yet, but Grandpa's chef loved having company while he cooked."

"I didn't know there was a chef at the distillery."

Ryan chuckled. "I didn't either until Grandpa asked me to take over the operation when his chef retired."

"What are your plans?"

"I don't know, which is why I canceled the party." Ryan glanced away and put his fingers over his lips.

Grace raised her eyebrows.

He continued, “I’m just not ready to dive in full steam with the distillery operation, including the shop and a bar with appetizers.”

“How long have you been operating the distillery?”

“Almost two years. Grandpa helped me at the beginning and then slowly stepped back, so it’s technically been less than a year.”

Ryan placed a plate of cheese and bacon-wrapped dates on the bar, then sat next to Grace.

While they sipped and munched, Grace asked, “Do you mind being here by yourself?”

“It’s not bad, but if I want to open the retail and hospitality side, I’ll have to find someone to take over the retail and manage the hospitality.”

“St. Patrick’s Day is pushing for a decision, isn’t it?”

Ryan put down his glass and stared at his plate. “Exactly.”

“And I suppose the party has to be at the distillery.” Grace pulled a notepad and pen out of her backpack and began doodling.

Ryan tilted his head, staring at her. “What are you thinking, Grace?”

Grace sipped her drink. She picked up a bacon wrapped date. “I don’t know yet.”

She took a bite of her appetizer. “Yum. This is delicious, Ryan.”

Grace’s phone rang, and she showed the number to Ryan.

He peered at her phone. “It’s a local number.”

Grace answered.

"Grace, this is Gordon Thompson. I'm Briar Glen's city manager. I'm sorry I didn't think of this earlier, but the city council would like to meet with you tomorrow. Would ten o'clock work for you?"

"I already have meetings scheduled tomorrow morning; I can meet in the afternoon. What is the agenda?"

Grace wrote "Gordon Thompson" on her pad.

Ryan raised his eyebrows and picked up her pen. "Caution."

Thompson's chuckle was thin. "No agenda. More of a get acquainted."

"That's even better because we won't be conducting city business. I was planning to meet with the town merchants tomorrow. Bella will make sure everyone is invited. Shall I pull together an agenda? I'd hate to waste the merchants' time. Is there a meeting hall we can use? The conference room will be too small. I know the sheriff's conference room would be large enough, but I'm not sure if it would be available. I'll call him tomorrow."

Ryan smiled and gave Grace a thumbs up.

"I'm looking forward to it." Thompson hung up.

Grace sent a text to Leah. "Gordon Thompson & city council plus town merchants. Maybe five thirty tomorrow. Possible to meet in sheriff's press room?"

Leah replied, "Brilliant. I'll talk to the sheriff."

Grace showed Ryan her phone.

"You must have worked with some real doozies, Grace. You went straight to the core."

"I have. I'd give Bella a heads up about inviting the merchants, but she'd go straight to the office and start working on it."

"Like you wouldn't, but you can't because you're already working on another project tonight. I'll grill our pork chops, and we'll have chocolate bourbon pecan pie for dessert."

Grace put another date on her small plate. "What do you think about a St. Patrick's Day party in the park? You provide whatever you usually provide, and we'll invite the local merchants to take part. What do you think?"

Ryan went still then glanced over his shoulder. "It sounds like a lot of work."

"For you?"

"No, for you. All that coordination of the merchants, getting approval for the park, and whatever else I have no clue about."

"Bella and Zoey are dynamos. We'll handle it. Now, what do you usually provide?"

"Usually, a beer and a bourbon, and something to munch on."

"What about gallons of limeade instead, and can you make green popcorn?"

"I could do that."

"Then the party will be one of our agenda items. I'll clear everything with Bella in the morning because she knows all the speed bumps. I'll talk about the parade, and you can talk about the party."

"Will this work?" Ryan rubbed the pork chops with spices.

"Not as well as it sounds in my head, but not as bad as it sounds in yours."

Ryan snorted while Grace daintily ate the other half of her date, playfully holding up her pinky.

Placing a large shallow bowl in front of Grace, Ryan said, "Soak your hands for a bit. It's just warm water with Epsom salts, but it will reduce the inflammation and ease some of that pain."

Grace rolled her eyes. "I guess I don't have a choice. Is this the recommendation of the chef or the chemist? Do I have to do this, or I won't be allowed to have dinner?"

Ryan chuckled. "The chemist in collusion with the chef."

When Ryan dropped their pork chops into the hot cast-iron skillet, the sound of the sizzle and the aroma of the seared meat filled the kitchen, and Grace's mouth watered.

After he slid the cast iron skillet into the oven, Ryan deftly sliced potatoes, then fried them in hot oil.

While the potatoes cooked, Ryan gave Grace a clean hand towel. "Pat dry."

He removed the bowl, rinsed it, and put it in the dishwasher along with his knife.

When the potatoes were done, Ryan put the pork chops and fried potatoes on plates.

While they ate, Grace said, "I'm not saying I agree with you or anything, but I'm having second thoughts about dropping the work of a new event on my team at the last minute."

Ryan chuckled. "But you have an alternative in mind because you are Grace."

"Of course." Grace smiled. "All the stores in town are decorated for St. Patrick's Day, and most of them are advertising St. Patrick's Day specials. What do you think about a coordinated campaign with the slogan, "Come for the Parade and Shop the Specials'?"

"I think it has huge possibilities. All you have to do is pitch the idea, which all the businesses will love, and step back."

"I'll talk to Bella and Zoey tomorrow, but I think this would work."

After they had eaten their dinner, they carried their desserts into the living room. Ryan had set up a desk for Grace to use for any computer work, and she pulled out the papers.

"I think we should read the papers in the envelope first because this is what Daniel planned for him and me to go over with you," Grace said.

"Let's sit on the sofa, eat our dessert, and read." Ryan motioned toward the enormous, overstuffed green sofa with its beautiful rustic wood coffee table in front of the bookcase.

After they sat together on the sofa, Ryan said, "Kick off your boots if you like and put up your feet."

"I'm fine." She handed Ryan the top sheet of paper from the stack and picked up the next one, and started reading while she ate her dessert.

After five minutes of trying to decipher the data on the page, Grace said, "I don't know what I'm reading."

"I do," Ryan said. "These are technical hourly reports of the city's water pressure, volume, and other data that measure the quality and quantity of water and its flow. I'll need these sorted into date order so I can see what the trends are."

"I can help sort."

After the documents were in order, Ryan said, "I'm ready to dive in. Why don't you relax and pick out a book to read?"

"I'd love to, but I have the files Daniel locked up in my office desk. I'll just start reading to see what I have."

Grace pulled out the files and took off her boots so she could sit cross legged on the sofa to read.

At eight o'clock, Ryan said, "Break time. Willow and I are going outside for a walk. Are you interested?"

Grace rolled her shoulders, then stretched. "I might complain about the cold, but I'd love some fresh air."

While Grace put on her boots, Ryan said, "Are you going to be warm enough? I have a spare coat. It might swallow you, but it will be warm."

"Thank you. I think I'll be okay, and if I'm not, I'll come right back in."

When they went outside, Grace gazed at the clear sky. "The stars are beautiful. I never see them in Atlanta because it's impossible to get away from the lights."

"What do you know about the constellations?" Ryan asked.

Grace peered at the sky and then pointed. "The big dipper, Orion's belt, and that's about it for me."

Ryan inhaled as he gazed at Grace. "Sometime when we're not under any deadlines, I'll give you a cheat sheet for you to study, and then we'll come outside for a tour. The winter and summer skies are different."

She returned his gaze and smiled. “Two tours. I’d like that. How did you learn about constellations?”

Ryan glanced away and shuffled his feet. “When I was a kid, my dad and I would go for a walk every evening and talk about anything and everything. We talked about constellations and why sometimes it was easy to catch fish and sometimes it wasn’t.”

“That sounds heavenly. Did you ever come to a conclusion about fishing?”

“Never did and never cared.”

“I don’t know anything about fishing.”

“We’ll have to talk about that sometime.”

Willow trotted to the door.

“Supervisor says get back to work,” Ryan said.

“She’s not wrong.”

As they went inside, Ryan asked, “So what are you finding in the files you have?”

“I’m about a third of the way through, but from what I’ve seen so far, I have copies of unrelated contracts, deeds, and bank accounts. I could sure use a table of contents.”

The two of them settled down with their documents and continued in silence.

Ryan broke the silence. “It’s ten o’clock, Grace, and I think my eyes are fried.”

“Along with my brain. I’ve read this page at least three times and can’t make any sense of it.”

"Shall we quit for the night and resume same time tomorrow, or do you want a break and work longer?" Ryan asked.

"I hate saying this, but we should quit." Grace covered her yawn, then groaned as she rose to her feet.

"You're welcome to stay here, Grace. I'm not sure you won't nod off while you're on the road."

"I might have to drive with the windows down," Grace yawned again. "I'll text you when I get home, so you'll know I'm not in a ditch."

"I have two bedrooms. The guest bedroom isn't big, but it's comfortable."

"Really?"

"Want a tour of the guest facilities at the distillery?"

"I'd love it. A short walk may be what I need to perk me up so I can drive home."

When they strolled down the hall with Willow between them, Ryan stopped and opened a door to a short hall.

"The guest bedroom is the first door on the right, and the guest bathroom is next to it."

He opened the door and flipped on the lights.

Grace sighed. The queen-sized bed, with its handcrafted patchwork quilt of pale pink, blue, and cream, floated like a fluffy cloud ready to deliver sweet dreams.

"We could have a nightcap," Ryan said.

Willow whimpered.

"I'd love it too, Willow, but tomorrow promised to be a rough day." Grace exhaled as she turned to leave the room.

"I'll follow you," Ryan said.

Grace shook her head. "Then I'd sneak behind you to be sure you got home okay."

Ryan narrowed his eyes. "What if Willow and I wait on the porch, ready to dash to my truck if we think you're taking too long to text or trying to cheat and text before you get home?"

"Fair enough. I'll leave all the papers with you so we can pick up where we left off." Grace wrinkled her brow. "I should have asked, do you already have plans for tomorrow?"

As Grace strolled toward the door, a bright sparkle flashed in front of her nose, and she had a brief vision of the black car.

She gasped and stopped so abruptly that Willow crashed into her, and Ryan caught her before she hit the floor.

Grace shuddered at the memory of her frightening vision of a car. "I'll take that nightcap after all. I have a bag with a change of clothes in my trunk."

"Willow and I will run out and grab it for you."

Grace gave him her car keys.

Ryan and Willow rushed back inside. "It's getting colder."

Grace said, "I'll change after my clothes warm up. Did you say something about a nightcap?"

"It will cost you. I need to hear what caused your abrupt change of mind."

As they headed toward the guest bedroom, Grace groaned. "I should leave. I have only a change of clothes, but no hairbrush or toothbrush."

Ryan smiled. "I have a gift shop. Drop off your tote bag, and then we'll go shopping."

While they strolled to the shop's small storeroom, Ryan said, "So tell me what changed your mind."

"Did I ever mention Granny's fairies when we were kids?"

"Only once. You told me to stop bothering you, or you'd tell the fairies to burn my nose."

Grace arched an eyebrow. "I'd forgotten about that. Was I always that mean to you?"

"Not answering. Tell me about the fairies."

Grace told him about the black vehicle. "I'm sure it wasn't really following me, but it made me nervous. Then, when a sparkle popped up in front of my face, I instantly recalled the car."

"No wonder you stopped so abruptly." Ryan opened the storeroom door. "Our inventory is limited, but these are yours to use when you stay here." He handed her a gift bag of toiletries.

"Thank you. I'm going to change so I can wear these clothes to work in the morning. Shall I meet you in the kitchen?"

"Meet me in the living room. We'll have regular hot chocolate with whipped cream and pretend we're at a ski lodge."

Grace changed into her sweatpants and sweatshirt and sent a text to Nora. "Working late. Staying here."

Nora replied, "Thank you."

When Grace strolled into the living room, Ryan smiled. "We have hot chocolate with whipped cream and crushed peppermint cookies from the bakery in town.

Ready to talk trash about the other skiers before we call it a night? I'll put some salve on your hands before we go to bed."

"Absolutely." Grace stifled a yawn, then ran her hand through her hair.

While they sipped their hot chocolate and ate cookies, Grace leaned back. "You're calmer than I remember."

Shrugging, Ryan said, "Atlanta rewarded panic. I got tired of that."

Grace nodded. "I never looked at my job like that, but I think you might be right."

Ryan's mouth twitched. "I've graduated to might be?"

Peering over her cup of hot chocolate, Grace said, "Almost."

They talked about fishing and fairies until Grace said, "Bedtime for me."

Wrapping her hands with gauze after applying the salve, Ryan smiled. "Thank you for humoring me."

Grace returned his smile, then padded off to her bedroom and immediately fell asleep.

Chapter Nine

An earthy, alcoholic aroma with notes of sweetness swirled around Grace when she woke at five thirty. She inhaled deeply and hugged her pillow. *I'm safe here.*

Clothes in hand, she padded to the guest bathroom for a hot, relaxing shower.

Before the beckoning aroma of coffee could entice her to the kitchen, she straightened her room and tucked her dirty clothes into the tote she'd brought from Nora's.

When she stepped into the kitchen, Ryan had his back to her.

She smiled at the familiar cowlick and the slight shuffle of his feet that was exactly the same as when he stood in the lunch line twenty years ago.

"Good morning," he said without turning.

"Good morning. I thought I was being sneaky."

Ryan gave a quiet huff. "You can't sneak past Gracie soap."

She froze. "What?"

He waved the spatula vaguely. "I'd know that smell anywhere. Grab yourself some coffee."

She stared at his back as she poured a cup of coffee then sat at the breakfast bar and exhaled. "What's your schedule for today?"

"Nothing time critical. What do you need?"

"I have a meeting at the high school at ten thirty with the principal and the band director. I'd like to visit the downtown merchants along the parade route for their feedback about the parade."

Ryan glanced over his shoulder. "Will you have handouts?"

"We'll create flyers about the parade and the stay and shop promotion."

Ryan plated two omelets. "Take a breath, then after breakfast you can hyperventilate."

"I don't have time for that, but it's on my list."

Ryan chuckled. "I believe you."

"Do you think I was being overly cautious last night?"

"Not at all. I'm glad you stayed. In fact, I think you should stay here until we understand what Daniel was focused on. How do you feel about Nora being alone?"

"I forgot to tell you about Murphy."

"Eat first, then we'll have one relaxed cup of coffee while you tell me about Murphy."

"You're right, and you didn't hear me say that."

"Sure didn't."

While they sipped a cup of coffee after they'd eaten, Grace said, "When we went into the kennel area at the animal shelter, Granny beelined to a black labrador retriever with a gray muzzle, and he immediately wagged his tail."

"Talk about instant bonding," Ryan said.

"It was. When Granny cooed at him, he licked her hand and leaned against her. I don't think I could have dragged Granny out of there without Murphy."

"How is he adjusting?"

"Like he's been at Granny's forever. He gave a low growl before Granny's visitors knocked on her door yesterday. He liked Aaron Wilson but was a little wary of Tristan Sharpe."

"He's an excellent judge of character. Now I understand why you aren't worried about Nora being alone."

Grace nodded. "It's a little before seven. I need to dash."

"Don't leave on my account," a man behind Grace said.

She turned and smiled at the man who had the same crooked smile with a dimple that Ryan had.

"Good morning, Mr. Pearce," Grace said.

"Good morning to you, Grace. You've become a lovely young woman."

"Thank you."

"I understand there's an opening for St. Patrick on a parade float. Are you accepting applications? Walt tells I might have an inside advantage."

"I would love for you to be Briar Glen's St. Patrick." Grace beamed.

"Consider it done. I've already talked to Mack, who owns the St. Patrick's Day float. With your permission, we'll come up with something that will wow the crowd."

"You have carte blanche. We line up at the high school on Saturday at eight in the morning, and the St. Patrick's Day float is our grand finale," Grace said.

"I'll confirm everything with Mack, and we'll get busy."

"Thanks, Granddad," Ryan said.

Ryan walked out with Mr. Pearce and then returned.

"Walt is a treasure." Grace peered at Ryan. "You called your granddad and told him I was here."

"Sure did. Seemed like the easiest way to go."

"Thank you for your help, and for the record, you're right again. I have to go to the office and knock out some of my tasks."

"I have a few things to do, and then I'll come to your office. If you aren't there, I'll find you."

Grace carried her tote and backpack to her car. As she drove into town, her hands were damp as she frequently checked her rearview mirror for signs of anyone following her.

When she parked behind the building, she scanned her surroundings and froze at the sound of a car's engine starting on the street near the front of the building. She waited until the car drove away, and then went inside and turned on the lights.

Deadly quiet greeted her. Shadows faded as she went from her office to the conference room. She rolled her shoulders, then exhaled. *Relax.*

After she started a pot of coffee, the coffee maker gurgled into life, lifting her spirits. She began a task list for the day on the whiteboard in the conference room. Before she was finished, her phone rang.

When she answered, Nora asked, "Where are you?"

"I'm at the office. Why?"

"You haven't seen today's paper, have you? I'll be right there." Nora hung up.

While Grace worked on the first draft of the stay and shop letter, Bella came in.

"Have you seen today's paper?" Bella asked.

"No, but Granny's bringing me a copy."

"Caleb Morris wrote a horrible article about the parade and its effect on the local economy."

"Let's go in the conference room. I have a list of our tasks for today, but we need to list what else we have to do before Saturday so we'll be more organized."

While the two of them examined Grace's list, Bella said, "Shouldn't we have a flyer for the parade and another one for the stay and shop."

"I like it. What do we need for sidewalk sales if that's what the merchants want to do?"

"Sometimes the merchants would talk to the city manager, but Mayor Dorsey always took care of it."

"Good. Which means a permit, right?"

"Yes, I'll pull together a permit for you to sign."

"If we're missing anything, we'll add it to the board, but I think this is a decent task list for this morning."

"I can do the flyers for the stay and shop and for the parade," Bella said.

"Thank you. We'll go together. I'd like to leave here by nine so we can at least talk to the merchants who open at nine. Ryan may go with us, but he agreed to take over when we go to our meeting at the high school."

While Grace and Bella were working on their projects, Nora and Murphy came in through the front door and went straight to the conference room.

Nora's eyes were red-rimmed as she handed the newspaper to Grace. Grace's eyes widened at the headline.

"Bad Luck or Bad Timing? Briar Glen's Parade Ignores Setbacks. Moves Forward."

Grace raised her eyebrows as she read the article and then reread the headline.

Nora put her hand on Grace's shoulder. "Are you okay?"

"I'm okay. He didn't get the byline, but this article has Caleb's fingerprints all over it."

Grace read the article one last time.

She handed the newspaper back to Nora. "We don't need poison in here."

Caleb didn't call me out directly, but he certainly was pointing at incompetence.

"What do we do?" Bella's face was tight.

"We shake it off and follow our plan."

"That's my girl," Nora whispered as she hugged Grace. "Let me know if I can help."

Murphy nudged Grace's hand, and she rubbed his ear.

"Thanks, Granny."

"Anytime." Nora and Murphy left.

Zoey rushed into the conference room. "Did you see what that scum posted on social media? Check your phone."

Grace pulled up the newspaper's social media headline for the post. "Some traditions exist for a reason. Ignoring them doesn't make the risk disappear."

After she read the headline, Grace set her phone face down.

"Aren't you going to respond?" Zoey asked.

Grace shook her head. "No."

Zoey swallowed hard. "But, Grace, people are talking."

"I'm sure they already were," Grace said. "Any comment we make just invites more conversation, and Caleb will love that he diverted us."

She pointed to their whiteboard. "We'll stay focused on our tasks."

Bella's lips were tight.

Grace examined the board. "We are missing one important task."

She picked up a green marker and wrote "St. Patrick" in large letters and then turned to Bella and Zoey who groaned as they looked at the board.

She put a large checkmark next to the name. "This morning, Mr. Pearce agreed to be our St. Patrick in the parade."

Bella and Zoey applauded, and Grace curtsied.

After they settled down, Zoey examined the board. "What do I do?"

"The stay and shop flyer could use your flair, and what about social media?" Grace said.

Zoey popped her forehead with her fingertips. "I should have thought of that. I'll get my Moms group to help."

"The notes are on the conference table," Bella added.

Bella returned to her desk to create the flyer for the parade. She moved with her usual efficiency and focus as she revised it. After she printed it, she studied it and then crumpled it and threw it into the trash.

"What's wrong with your flyer?" Zoey asked.

"The title was off center," Bella growled.

"What happened to good enough?" Zoey asked.

"Doesn't apply to off center," Bella grumbled as she returned to her desk to rework the flyer.

Grace joined her with the draft letter to the merchants. "Bella, my opening paragraph seems weak. Would you look it over?"

Bella glanced up at Grace and exhaled.

As Grace returned to her office, Zoey raised her eyebrows, and Grace shrugged.

After Bella read the draft, she marked up a few sentences and drew an arrow to move the bottom paragraph to the top.

Bella took the revised letter to Grace's office. "This may be what you're looking for."

Grace read it and nodded. "It is. Thank you. You good?"

Bella glanced away from Grace and toward her desk where her coin lay next to her keyboard. "Just making sure we don't miss anything."

"Will you have a draft for us to review in fifteen minutes?"

"Yes." Her gaze flicked to Grace's phone, face down on the table, then back to Grace.

"If anything changes," Bella said, "call me. Doesn't matter what time it is."

"I will." Grace raised an eyebrow at the firmness in Bella's tone. "If you'll promise you'll do the same."

Bella stared at her then clenched her jaw. "I promise." She hurried back to her desk. *Something is definitely bothering Bella.*

Grace called out, "Zoey, will you have something for us to review in fifteen minutes?"

"Ten minutes."

Grace asked, "How many copies will we need?"

"We'll be okay with twenty-five of each," Bella said.

When Zoey finished her flyer, she went into Grace's office and handed her the flyer, and then flopped down in the visitor chair.

Grace studied the flyer. "I love it. Let's check with Bella."

Grace and Zoey watched Bella closely as Bella scrutinized the flyer. "I would remove the words sponsored by and make Briar Glen at the bottom a little larger."

"Thanks, I'll do it." Zoey rushed back to her desk, made the quick change, and printed a final copy.

"Bella, would you pull together the packets for the high school principal and band director? I'll be back at fifteen minutes after ten so we can go to the high school in my car."

Bella nodded.

Ryan came into the shop as Zoey was copying the letter to the merchants. "I'm looking forward to working with you, Mayor."

Zoey giggled, and Bella tried to maintain her stern look, but a smile crept across her face.

"Don't even start." Grace glared at him as she put on her coat.

Zoey handed three folders to Grace and a copy of the two flyers and the letter to Ryan.

"We've got time for you to look over the flyers and read the letter, Ryan," Grace said.

After Ryan reviewed the flyers and the letter he nodded. "Well done. Are you ready to go, Your Grace?"

When Grace burst out laughing, Zoey giggled, and Bella's smile widened.

"How's your nose feeling?" Grace asked as they went out the front door.

Ryan chuckled. "In virtual pain."

"Most of the shops on Main Street open at ten, but we can still go to the coffee shop, bakery, drugstore, grocery store, and gas station," Grace said.

"Let's start with the gas station. Walt can be our guinea pig. My truck is around the corner."

On the way to the gas station, Grace said, "I'm glad you're going with me to get me started this morning. I've been worried people would see me as an outsider."

"You aren't an outsider, Grace. Your tribe is here." He glanced at her with his lips pressed, and his gaze unwavering.

He turned back to focus on the road ahead. "I saw the article in the paper. Are you planning to respond to it?"

"No. I do expect to be asked about it at this afternoon's meeting. My only response would be I was surprised to see an opinion piece as the lead article in the newspaper."

"That's good. What do you actually think about it?"

"Caleb Morris has never had an original idea in his life. I'd like to know who is behind him telling him what to say."

Ryan nodded as he tapped his thumb on the steering wheel. "I hadn't thought about it like that, but you're right."

Ryan parked at the gas station, and Grace pulled the three sheets for Walt out of the folders.

"I'll follow your lead," Ryan said.

When they went into the bustling gas station, the smell of bacon and scorched coffee mixed with gasoline filled the air.

Walt was behind the counter with a line of people with their steaming morning coffee or large cold drink cups in one hand and prepackaged egg and bacon wraps from the warmer in the other.

When the line cleared, Walt raised his eyebrows. "You aren't serving me with eviction papers, are you, Grace?"

"Oh, no. Do I look that official?" she asked.

"Yes."

Grace stared at him, then went outside and returned with a smile. "Is this better, and who tipped you off?"

Walt laughed. "You did with that serious face, but you really got me when you walked out. I thought you were angry."

Grace narrowed her eyes. "So, do you want to hear my spiel, or do I serve these papers?"

Walt laughed even harder, and so did the customers who had gathered around to listen.

He wiped his eyes. “Spiel away.”

Grace gave him the parade flyer, then explained the stay and shop promotion. She invited him to the meeting in the sheriff’s press room at five thirty and gave him the letter.

“What’s your agenda for the meeting?”

“I’ll hand out the flyers and the letter, and then I was thinking about an Ask Me Anything session.”

“That sounds brave.”

As the customer dispersed, Walt lowered his voice. “I’ll bet you have a plan so that no one can monopolize the question time, and everyone will have a chance to ask a question.”

Grace nodded. “You’d be right. Thank you, Walt.”

On the way back to town, Ryan said, “Grace, you haven’t changed a bit. You have killer instincts for defusing a situation.”

“Thank you. We were at the gas station longer than I expected, but I really needed it. Walt reminded me I was peddling my wares, not going to the gallows.”

“Peddling your wares?”

“Sure. Let’s start two blocks away from the mayor’s office and see how far we can get.”

“Sounds good. We’ll be starting at the café.”

After the café, Ryan said, “Let me take the next one. I won’t be as smooth as you are, but I’ll feel more confident with you as my backup.”

On the way out of the drugstore, Grace asked, “How are you feeling?”

"Like I mumbled, but the pharmacist was a friend of Dad's, so he didn't toss me out of his store. I call that a win."

Grace giggled. "You did great, but I understand what you mean."

When it was time for Grace to return to the office, she asked, "Do we want to ask Zoey if she'd like to go along with you?"

"If she's willing, I'd feel more comfortable. What about the office?"

"Bella will put a sign on the door that we're closed until eleven thirty or noon. It's your preference."

"What time will you be back?"

"A little after twelve thirty."

"Put me down for twelve thirty."

Grace nodded.

When they went into the office, Zoey asked, "How was it?"

"It really worked out well to have two people. Would you like to go with Ryan?"

Zoey's eyes widened in surprise. "If that's okay, I'd really enjoy talking to our town merchants."

"Bella, would you put a sign on the door that says the office is closed until twelve thirty?"

Bella nodded as she pulled out a permanent marker and created the sign. While Zoey put on her coat, Bella taped the sign to the door.

Ryan held the door for Zoey. "When we go into our first store, I'll talk to them so you'll have the perfect example of what not to do."

Zoey burst out laughing as Ryan closed the door.

Bella put on her coat and then locked the front door. "I have our copies for the high school in a folder."

Bella followed Grace out the back door and waited next to Grace's car while Grace locked the back door.

On the way to the high school, Grace glanced at Bella who held her coin tightly in her hand. "How do you think things are going?"

Bella rubbed her coin. "I don't want to bring bad luck down on the parade, but I'm surprised at how much progress we're making in such a short time."

"You are doing an amazing job. I'd be really floundering without the knowledge you have of all the processes. I really appreciate you."

Bella turned her head away and nodded.

I'll have to be careful. Bella's not used to being complimented.

"I'm not sure I've ever seen a coin like yours."

"My dad and I went hiking in the Grand Canyon when I was a kid. He bought me a coin at the gift shop and told me it would always remind me of him and the good times we had. He left not long after that, and nothing was the same."

Grace found a spot in the visitor parking lot. After they climbed out and she locked the car, Grace scanned the surroundings. "The high school has expanded since I went to elementary school in Briar Glen. Where do we go?"

Bella pointed. "The main door."

After they checked in with the woman behind the thick glass window, they strolled down the hallway to the principal's office.

The aroma of sweat mixed with the sharp chemical bite of the institutional cleaner permeated the walls, and the muffled classroom sounds of instruction echoed in the hall.

When they entered the administrative assistant's office, a middle-aged woman smiled and nodded when they entered but returned to her computer screen.

Her desk had stacks of forms squared at the corners of the desk, paper clipped and color-coded, and was decorated with a row of brightly colored trolls arranged with surprising precision.

Even the whimsy is controlled.

Bella took a seat in the chair near the door with her back straight and leaning slightly forward with her hands folded in her lap.

Framed certificates and district commendations filled the walls; their glass catching the fluorescent light just enough to glare. Grace examined each plaque and certificate like a fine arts critic in an exclusive gallery.

A man burst into the office. "Hi, Bella. Nice to see you."

She nodded as she rose. "You too."

"I'm sorry to keep you waiting. I'm Henry Gallegos." He put out his hand.

"Grace Callahan."

After they shook hands, the three of them went into his office. He gestured toward his cluttered desk. "Busy week."

Bella glanced at Grace, who smiled and nodded.

Bella stepped forward and handed him the file folder she had prepared for him. "We've included the flyers for the parade and a Stay and Shop promotion for the local businesses."

Mr. Gallegos glanced at them before setting them aside, and Bella flinched.

Grace raised an eyebrow. *We won't count on his support.*

"We'd like to review the plan for staging the floats in the high school parking lot," Bella continued.

She stared at the clutter on the desk, then carefully laid the map out on the corner of the desk, smoothing it flat with one hand. Colored blocks marked each staging position, with arrows showing the traffic flow.

Mr. Gallegos leaned over it, studying the layout for a moment. "This looks fine to me."

Grace raised an eyebrow.

"We'll have security onsite," he added. "Someone to unlock the gates and help direct the floats into position."

Bella jotted down a note.

Grace nodded. "That will help keep things moving. We'd like to have security's phone number so we can coordinate."

"I'll have my assistant send it to you."

"Thank you." *I'll ask her for it.*

There was a tap at the door, and Aaron Wilson stepped inside.

"Ah, our band director is right on time," Mr. Gallegos said.

When Mr. Gallegos introduced him to Grace, Aaron winked, and Grace stifled a smile as they shook hands.

"Can you show me where the band will stage?" Aaron asked.

"We'd love to. Bella, would you lead the way?"

Bella collected the map and slid it back into her folder, her movements precise and satisfied.

While Bella and Aaron left the office, Mr. Gallegos rearranged his papers back into uneven stacks, already moving on to whatever came next.

Grace stopped at the admin's desk. "Mr. Gallegos said you'd give me the phone number for your security officer."

The woman neatly printed a number on a notepad and smiled as she handed it to Grace.

"Thank you." Grace strode down the hall and caught up with Bella and Aaron before they reached the front door.

Bella handed both of them the map for staging, then led them outside to the road near the visitor parking lot.

"The band stages here, and will go out of the parking lot that way." Bella pointed to the nearest exit.

"This is good." Aaron examined the map. "It looks like the floats can drive straight in, and if they miss their spot, they can continue, go out, and come back in the entrance. Very well thought out. Is there anything you need from us?"

Bella nodded. "To keep down congestion, we'd like the band to continue marching back to the high school. All the floats have instructions to follow you here."

"We'll be happy to do that because the band students can put away their instruments before they leave the school, which is definitely my preference. I'll send the parents an email this afternoon."

After they were in the car, Grace backed out of the parking space. "Do you know where the dance studio is?"

Bella frowned. "It's close to the vet's office."

"Let's drop off a parade flyer at the vet's office after we visit the dance studio."

Bella turned her head and swiped at her cheek while she stared out her side window.

She's worked hard for this. I'm worried too.

When they reached the dance studio, the parking lot was empty, and the lights were off. Grace hopped out of the car and read the posted hours on the front door. "Wednesday through Friday 3:00 PM-6:00 PM. Saturday, 9:00 AM-Noon."

She climbed back into the car. "The dance studio opens at three this afternoon. Do you know how to contact the dance director?"

"I'll call and leave a message," Bella said.

"Next up is the vet's office."

While Grace backed out of the parking space, a scowl crossed Bella's brow.

Not a fan of the vet's office?

Chapter Ten

Barking dogs sharing the day's news greeted Grace as she parked at the animal shelter. She turned to Bella. "Would you like to wait in the car while I go in?"

Bella glanced up at the building, then stared at her clenched hands in her lap. She exhaled and relaxed her fingers. "You shouldn't go in alone. I'll go in with you."

Grace opened the door, and the distinct aroma of disinfectant and wet fur enveloped her with a promise she'd carry the lingering odor away with her.

A volunteer stood at the desk with a couple and their toddler. The man held a hard plastic cat carrier with a kitten side. The woman held a toddler who looked at Grace and then pointed at the carrier. "Kitty."

"That's a nice kitty." Grace smiled.

"Nice kitty," the toddler echoed.

After the family left, the volunteer said, "Hi Grace. Are you here for another dog?"

"No, we have flyers for the parade we'd like to leave with you."

"That's great. I'll leave a few on the counter and post one on our bulletin board by the front door."

While Grace handed the flyers to the volunteer, Bella said, "The breakroom is just past the treatment area. I'll leave a few there."

A sharp bark from the back distracted Grace, and she nodded. Bella rushed toward the hallway and then shrieked as her foot vanished into the gleaming, freshly mopped floor.

Bella went down hard, instinctively throwing out her hands. Her shoulder clipped the edge of a rolling stainless-steel utility cart as she fell, landing on her elbow and hip, and sending the cart careening into the wall and crashing to the floor.

"I'm okay." Bella struggled to push herself up to a sitting position. Her face was pale, but her voice was steady.

A tech dropped her mop with a clatter and rushed over, mortified. "I'm so sorry, I just finished mopping, but I could have sworn I put the sign out."

The yellow caution sign stood crooked against the wall, half-hidden behind the overturned cart.

Bella rolled her shoulder experimentally and winced. "I was just startled." She cradled her elbow.

Grace crouched to help gather the fallen items. One of them, a heavy duty stapler, had landed inches from where Bella's head had been.

Too close.

"I'll take you to your doctor to be checked," Grace said.

Bella forced a slight smile as she shook her head. “No need. Occupational hazard, right?”

As Grace moved closer to help Bella to her feet, a shimmering gold speck flashed near the wall.

Valerie appeared in the doorway, pulling on exam gloves. “Let me see.” Valerie paused and then reached for an item in the corner.

Bella's coin.

Grace deftly snatched up the coin, then stepped back.

A frown crossed Valerie's face as she turned to Bella who froze when Valerie kneeled close. Valerie's movements were brisk and practiced as she rotated Bella's arm once, twice, and Bella winced.

Valerie rose and removed her gloves as she turned away, already motioning for a tech. “No swelling. No loss of motion. You're fine. If it were serious, you'd know.”

Grace's face tightened as she stared at Valerie's back.

As Bella slowly limped toward the door, Grace joined her and took her non-injured arm to help steady her.

After Bella was in the car, Grace handed Bella her coin. “You dropped this when you fell.”

Bella paled as she clutched her coin to her chest. Her voice cracked. “Thank you. I don't know what I would have done if I'd lost it. It's all I have to remember Dad.”

Grace started her car in silence. As she backed out of the parking lot, she said, “You may want to ice your shoulder and maybe your elbow. If you want to take the rest of the day off, it's fine with me.”

“I'm okay. I'd rather be working, if you don't mind.” Bella lowered her head. “There's nobody to listen to me complain at home, and structure keeps things from getting messy."

Grace nodded. "Complain all you like, and Zoey and I will respond appropriately."

Bella mumbled, "Zoey will tease me to make me laugh."

"Sounds like her. If you change your mind, feel free to go home and rest."

Bella stared out her side window the rest of the way to the office.

When Grace turned the corner to go to the back of the building, Bella continued to gaze out her side window. *Is something more than her fall bothering Bella?*

After Grace parked, she picked up their folders and unlocked the back door. Bella walked into Grace's office and continued to her desk. Grace ran her fingers across the now-familiar deep scratches in her wooden desk. *My desk.*

She followed Bella past Zoey's desk and through the wooden railing's gate.

"Could you call the security person to arrange a meeting tomorrow?" Grace asked.

"Right away."

"I'll add the meeting to our list on the whiteboard and on the calendar."

Before Grace reached the conference room, Ryan and Zoey came in through the front door.

"How did it go?" Grace asked.

"I carried the folders, and Zoey talked. It was perfect because she's a natural."

Zoey chuckled. "We talked about taking turns, but then Ryan told me he'd buy lunch for Bella and me."

"What about you?" Ryan cocked his head.

Grace said, "I'm glad we went. The high school has a security person who will have to unlock the gates, and we have his number so we can coordinate in advance."

Zoey held up a large white sack. "Do you want to eat in the conference room, Bella? We can take an actual break like normal office workers and complain about how overworked we are."

"We aren't overworked." Bella rose from her chair.

"Then you can pick the subject." Zoey carried their lunch to the conference room.

"We'll be at the café if you need me," Grace said.

After Grace put on her coat, Ryan inhaled as he opened the door and then followed her outside.

As they strolled to the café, Ryan asked, "Did you have any problems?"

"Not at the high school, but Bella slipped on a wet floor at the animal shelter and injured her shoulder. Dr. Higgins checked her and said it was nothing serious."

"Was it her right shoulder? She seemed to favor it."

"Yes. It might not be serious, but it must be painful. I couldn't talk her into going home. Do you know Dr. Higgins? She seems very matter-of-fact."

"Willow goes to a different vet in the town south of here, so I don't really know Dr. Higgins all that well."

As they continued toward the café, Ryan said, "I was really impressed with Zoey. Her enthusiasm was contagious when she talked about the parade and the Stay and Shop promotion to the merchants. I asked them about changing the route or canceling the parade, and no one was in favor of it."

"Are they going to come to the meeting?"

"Quite a few said they would because of the rumors flying around about the parade being jinxed."

"Is that the latest rumor? That the parade is jinxed?"

"The parade being jinxed has been around for a lot of years."

"Granny told me stories don't need to be true to stick."

"She's got a point."

When Ryan opened the door to the café, they were greeted by the familiar aroma of hot oil from the fryer and grease from the grill, which likely hadn't been changed since the first time Grace went to the diner with her dad.

She cringed but resisted covering her ears, which were assaulted by the clatter of melamine dishes being tossed into bins by servers clearing tables as fast as they could for waiting customers, the shouts as each group of diners raised their voices to be heard over their neighbors, and the cook's booming voice that overrode them all, "Order up!"

Ryan leaned close so Grace could hear him. "Do you want to go somewhere else?"

"Let's get our order to go," she said.

"Do you feel brave? I'll order for both of us."

"I can eat anything you can eat."

"Was that a challenge?" Ryan raised his eyebrows.

Grace shook her head. "Only a dare."

Ryan chuckled and maneuvered through the waiting crowd to the cash register. When he spoke to the cashier, she nodded, and he stepped back as she hurried to the kitchen.

When the doorway became crowded, Grace was pushed against Ryan. He covered his nose with one hand and put his arm around her to keep her from being crushed.

Grace laughed as she gazed into his eyes; Ryan grinned. *I didn't know he had gray-blue eyes.* The surrounding noise faded into the background as his scent, a mix of soap, deodorant, and something uniquely him, enveloped her, and she relaxed.

When the cashier motioned to Ryan, Grace pushed her way to the door so she could go outside.

She inhaled the fresh, cold air; the street noises were almost whispers compared to the roar in the café.

Ryan came out of the café with a large sack and two bottled colas.

"It's cold; let's go to my office," Grace said.

"I'll race you." Ryan strode away.

Laughing, Grace ran past him, then waited at the door.

He chuckled as he strolled to join her and opened the door. "Warmer now?"

"Meany." Grace laughed as they went inside the office.

Zoey glanced up. "Why didn't you tell me lunch was supposed to be fun? What are you doing back here already?"

"I wanted to stay in the diner, but the mayor insisted you needed close supervision," Ryan said.

Bella cleared her throat. "It's an office rule, the mayor is always right."

Grace chuckled. "You must be feeling better, Bella."

"Zoey told me to say the first thing that popped into my head."

"You're my star student, Bella." Zoey beamed.

Bella winced when she turned towards the computer screen, and a sympathetic twinge shot through Grace.

"I'm starving." Ryan waved the sacks.

"Very subtle." Grace headed toward the conference room, and Ryan followed her.

Ryan pulled out their food, while Grace pulled out the napkins, then a plastic knife.

Grace unwrapped a sandwich and looked at her fingers.

"A greasy cheeseburger. This is perfect, and thanks for the knife." She cut her cheeseburger in half.

While they ate, Grace said, "I have another project for this afternoon."

Ryan choked on his drink, then cleared his throat. "I don't know why I was surprised. Of course, you do. What now?"

"Daniel had scheduled a meeting with Sully this afternoon. Did you find anything in Daniel's data that would suggest we should go ahead with the meeting?"

Ryan gazed at her. "How do you come up with this stuff? I actually did."

Grace called out. "Bella, what time was the Mayor's appointment with the water and waste manager today?"

"Two thirty."

"Call him for me and tell him I'm keeping the appointment."

"Will do."

"I have a few things I need to do," Ryan said.

"Will you have enough time to pick me up, or do you want to meet me there?" Grace asked.

"I'll pick you up."

"I'll see if we have anything in the water permits that might help," Grace said.

After Ryan left, Grace strolled to Bella's desk. "Are the float owners posing any questions that raise concerns for us?"

Bella exhaled. "All the questions they've asked are ones that were answered in the email we sent them. Zoey is replying to them."

"Glad to hear it. So, I'd like to understand our permit process. Do you have time to walk me through all the different permits we issue and who has approval authority?"

Zoey said. "That's like asking a grandmother to tell you all about her grandchildren."

"It's not that bad," Bella said. "But I'll admit it might be close."

Bella pulled out two large notebooks from her largest desk drawer and a third notebook from a different drawer. She pointed to the chairs for visitors. "Pull a chair up next to my desk."

After Grace was seated next to her, Bella pointed to the notebooks. "I keep the original permits in my notebooks."

“Who approves the permits?” Grace asked.

Bella flipped through the notebooks like favorite photo albums. “Each department has signing authority over its permits, but technically, the mayor can approve all the permits.”

“Can we search them online?”

“Which type of permit would you like to see first?” Bella asked.

“How about land use?”

“Sure. Are we looking for anything special?”

Grace shrugged. “I don’t know enough to say. I’d just like to get an idea of the permits that are issued.”

As Bella scrolled through the permits of the last year and then the year before that, Grace pointed to the screen. “These were all signed by Mayor Dorsey. I would have guessed the city manager would sign permits.”

“The mayor liked to be involved in all the planning. He said it was the city manager’s job to manage operations. The city manager calls me when he has questions.”

“He doesn’t have view access?”

Bella shook her head.

“How long has Gordon Thompson been city manager?”

“Almost two years. I have his application file.”

“Can I see it?”

Grace followed Bella who strode to the supply closet and unlocked one of the filing cabinets, then removed a file.

“Who has keys to the filing cabinets in here?”

"Only me. Mayor Dorsey left his keys behind. I should have given those to you earlier, but I forgot about them. I'll get them for you."

As Bella headed toward her desk, she said, "You have access to all the permits if you ever want to learn more."

"That's great. I really am interested in how everything works. Maybe I'll have time after this weekend."

Grace went to her office and pulled up her resume from her personal cloud, removed a few lines, and printed it.

Strolling back from the printer to her office, she paused in the doorway and stared at her resume. *Did I forget my last day of vacation is nine days away? I don't have any business making plans here.*

When a tear slipped down her face, she angrily brushed the tear away. *Save it for next week.*

She picked up her phone and called Gordon Thompson as she dropped her resume into a folder.

When he answered, she said, "This is Grace Callahan. I'd like to chat with you if you have a few minutes."

His voice was a dry monotone. "I've got all the time in the world."

"I was hoping I could drop by your office later this afternoon. Will four o'clock work for you?"

"Four? Sure. Is there an agenda?"

Grace smiled. *Same thing I asked him.* "Sure. Getting acquainted."

He paused, and then his tone brightened. "Without the city council? I like it. See you at four."

She pulled out a notepad to take notes for the five thirty meeting. Instead, she doodled mindlessly, then stared at her notepad where she had drawn a crude outline of a chicken coop. *The old poultry processing plant that Daniel referenced in his notes.*

She opened the permit system and searched for records of the old poultry processing plant and discovered it had been purchased three years ago by Fair Valley Manufacturing, LLC. She checked the Georgia state LLC records and couldn't find it.

She leaned back and sighed. *They organized their company in another state.*

Grace strolled to Bella's desk. "Do you know how to research an LLC when you don't know where the LLC was registered?"

Bella took her hands off her keyboard and sat back. "The only way I know to do it is to create a list of likely states and search each one. Is there a company I can search for you?"

"No, it was a question someone asked me, and I told them the same thing. I was worried I'd misled them."

Bella's face reddened.

When Grace headed back to her office, Bella cleared her throat. "Can I talk to you for a minute in your office? You know, just in case someone comes in. It's personal."

"Of course."

Bella followed Grace to her office.

"Shall I close the door?"

Bella shook her head, and then while Grace sat in her chair, Bella gripped the arms of the chair as if she were on a roller coaster and her seatbelt had failed.

"I'm concerned I might have spoken out of turn, but anyway..." Bella's hands shook as she pulled her coin from the Grand Canyon out of her pocket and clutched it in her fist tightly against her body.

"We can talk later if you like," Grace said.

"No, I need to tell you while I can." Bella opened her hand and stared at her coin. "I got a call from someone on Tuesday who asked me what was going to happen to the town since Daniel was gone and the parade was canceled. I told her what our plan was."

"I'm sure everybody in town knew we'd have a plan."

"I know, but I told her exactly what we planned to do, and what if she told the person who tried to flood us with worthless information?"

"It could explain how that happened." *But there's more to it.*

Bella stared at the ceiling. "But she might be the same person who told me about the insurance because she said it was really awful about the parade being canceled then asked what we were doing..."

Might be? "Who was that?"

Bella studied her coin and shook her head, then slowly shuffled to her computer with her head down.

Grace narrowed her eyes. *I almost wish she hadn't said anything if she was going to backtrack and try to cover up what she'd done.*

Grace turned to her computer and logged into the permits and licenses system. She was deep into checking for more information about the company that bought the former poultry plant and discovered it wasn't the owner of record on the tax rolls. She exhaled. *Another brick wall.*

She tapped her pen on the notepad and glared at her screen.

Ryan burst into the office a little after two o'clock, bringing the fresh air from outside in with him along with his big grin that brightened the office. "Ready for your waterworks education, Grace?"

She smiled. *Just what I needed: a cheerful man popping in.*

She turned off her computer and grabbed her coat and backpack. "I'm looking forward to it."

After they were in the truck, Grace said, "Bella explained the licensing and permit system to me. Did you know Mayor Dorsey, not the city manager, approved all the permits and licenses?"

"I didn't know that, but I guess I'm not surprised. The mayor was a real control freak."

"Is the city manager competent?"

"He must be. Walt interviewed him and said Gordon Thompson was an excellent candidate."

"So why did you say caution?"

"The city council is pushing him to take over."

Grace tapped her fingers on her backpack. *That might explain his attitude.*

She said, "I don't think Daniel worked out to be quite what the city council expected, and they certainly didn't expect him to ask for help with the parade."

As they continued to the water plant in silence, Grace stared at the passing landscape. *I don't think I can trust Bella.*

Ryan parked at the waterworks. Behind the faded gray concrete building was the town's water treatment system, enclosed by a tall chain-link fence.

When they approached the building, a man opened the door.

"Haven't seen you in ages, Ryan, and this here must be Nora's granddaughter. You look like your mama, Grace." He held out his hand, which engulfed Grace's as they shook hands.

"It's nice to meet you, Sully."

"Come on in. Daniel wanted to talk to me, but he wasn't sure why. Do you know?"

"I think so," Grace said. "I don't know anything about water systems, but analyzing data is my specialty. Have you seen anything unusual in yours?"

Sully raised his eyebrows. "You like data? I've got facts and figures that would make a numbers geek swoon. Come into my office, and I'll show you not just a statistical outlier, but a major shift."

Chapter Eleven

Ryan nudged Grace and put his hand over his heart when they went into the office.

Sully's office was a command center with closed circuit TV screens on one wall with dials and gauges under them and a computer with four active screens on his oversized metal desk. His leather desk chair was padded and could have doubled as a comfortable recliner.

"Our systems monitor everything. It's a classic set it and forget it system, except when it isn't." He swept his arm in a grand gesture, nearly knocking over his coffee mug.

He leaned forward and lowered his voice. "It started nine months ago when somebody must have bought the old poultry plant. There was a sudden, steady increase in the water being used there."

"I thought the plant was abandoned," Ryan said.

"So did I." Sully pulled up a chart on one of his screens and pointed. "This was seven months ago, and we had a sudden drop for a week, and then see this spike in consumption between ten at night and six in the morning?"

Grace narrowed her eyes. "They shifted their operation to run at night?"

"That was my guess, but their water usage has skyrocketed in the last month. Now look at this."

Sully pointed to the next screen. "This is a comparison. Between ten and six, they're guzzling down four times more than the entire town does from six in the morning until ten at night."

Ryan spread a chart out on the desk. "Like this?"

"That's the chart Daniel gave me," Grace said.

Sully squinted at the chart. "No, that chart shows almost no water usage after ten o'clock at night until a slight increase a month ago. You got this from Daniel? It looks like a city printout."

"He gave it to me the day before he died," Grace said.

"Maybe that's what he was talking about when he told me he wanted to go over a critical list." Sully rushed to his desk.

Grace and Ryan both reached for the chart. When their fingers touched, Ryan paused and then slowly withdrew his hand. Grace quietly exhaled, then picked up the chart.

"Look at this." Sully tapped on his keyboard, then pulled up a report on one of the computer screens.

He motioned for them to come closer. "Here we have the surge, and this is the source data from the water system. It feeds its data straight to the city system."

"I don't mean to change the subject, but something's been bothering me. What happens to all that water after they use it?" Grace asked. "Wouldn't that much water all at once flood the city's sewer system?"

Sully raised his eyebrows. "The simple answer is the building was an abandoned poultry processing plant and probably had its own septic system. But as long ago as it's been since production was in process there, I doubt if the septic system would be large enough even if it was still operational."

"There's a small creek downstream from that plant," Ryan said.

"Get me a sample of that creek, and I'll check it out."

"I'll get you a sample today," Ryan said.

Grace tapped her fingers on the desk. "My next question is wouldn't a seven month lag mean the city data was useless? Could you run a few reports on the source data over the past nine months similar to the city's report? I could pick it up tomorrow."

"I could email it to you and save you a trip," Sully said.

"I don't know how secure my office email is." Grace bit her lip.

Sully stared at her. "I'll download it to a flash drive from my local server. Can you meet me at the gas station tomorrow at eight?"

Grace side-glanced at Ryan.

"I will," Ryan said.

"Even better."

Grace rose. "Thank you for everything, Sully. Let me know if there's anything I can do for you."

"This system has been building up pressure close to the danger point for a while, Grace. I'm glad you're on it."

As they headed back to Grace's office, Grace said, "Thanks for going with me and for volunteering to meet Sully at the gas station. He's safer if he's not connected to me. I'll be at the sheriff's office a little after five for the meeting."

"I could pick you up."

"I don't want to leave my car in the parking lot with no one around, and I want to run by Granny's early to pick up a few things so I can stay at the distillery." Grace cocked her head. "Or is there a reason to change our plan?"

"No reason to change. You can search the permits without too much interruption, and we can brainstorm without being overheard."

"I was thinking the same. Thanks."

When they reached the edge of town, Grace said, "Drop me off in the back."

After he pulled close to the back door, Ryan said, "I'll won't leave until you're inside."

"I knew that." She waved as she went inside, and Ryan nodded.

Draping her coat over her chair, an off-key tune drew Grace toward Bella's desk.

Humming under her breath while she referred to her yellow notepad, Bella checked off an item with a flush rising on her face.

Glancing up at Grace, Bella's eyes brightened. "There you are. I cleaned out the file cabinets in the storage room and called the document people to pick up the boxes tomorrow so they can shred them."

What on earth? Grace exhaled. "A little housecleaning?"

Cringing at the sound, Grace resisted covering her ears as Bella tapped decisively on her notepad with her pen. "That's right. I have a list of all the systems and the new passwords. I changed your password too. It's right here." She tapped on her list.

Changed my password? "Changing passwords regularly is always a good idea. So what brought this on?"

"I almost forgot this." Pointing at an item in the middle of her page, Bella circled it. "Oh, we've been so busy with the parade I'm afraid I let a few things slide, and security is important. I'll have everything organized by the end of the day."

"That's good. Is this the only list of all the passwords?" Grace craned to see the list.

"It is the complete list, and for now, the only copy. I'll get them into the system tomorrow." I still need to go through my files. I'll probably have at least another two boxes for the document company to pick up tomorrow. Most of my files are online, anyway. Do you want me to go through the files in your desk drawers too?"

"Do you have a key to the drawer? It's locked, and I don't have a key."

"Oh. I'll call a locksmith tomorrow." Bella added a note to her list.

"Have we missed anything she said to do?"

Flinching, Bella scanned her list. "I'm pretty sure I've covered everything, so I think this is it."

Confirmed, but who is she?

"Do we need to empty the shredder?" Grace asked.

"Do we have a shredder? Daniel had one, but he emptied it every day. She didn't mention it, but that's a good idea to check."

While Bella rushed to the conference room, Grace pulled out her phone and snapped photos of the new passwords and Bella's list.

Returning with a satisfied smile, Bella added shredder to her notepad and checked it off. "I confirmed don't have one in the conference room, but she'll be impressed I checked. She told me we had a serious security breach, and I needed to act today."

"That's wonderful that she gave us a heads up. Was it Leah from the sheriff's department?"

Bella snorted. "Leah's a nice girl, but she wouldn't know anything about security."

"Is there anything I can do to help?" Grace asked.

After considering her list, Bella shook her head. "Not really. I only have one more thing to do."

"Let me know if there's anything you need me to do, but it looks like you'll have everything on your list completed by five o'clock today."

Bella beamed. "I'll be done in ten minutes."

"That's wonderful. You can wrap up and go home then, can't you?"

Bella's eyes widened. "That's right. I should leave as soon as I finish because we're working on Saturday."

Grace went into her office and changed her password, the system administrator password for the server, and then continued down the list.

Bella announced, "Well, that's it. All my documents are packed up, and I even called the locksmith. He'll be here tomorrow at nine."

Grace strode out of her office. "That's great news. I'll see you in the morning."

Carefully folding the password list, Bella slipped it into her purse, and then put on her coat while she held onto her coin. She smiled as she rubbed her coin then dropped it into her coat pocket and patted it.

After Bella left, Grace locked the door behind her and changed the security code. She carried the boxes out one at a time and stacked them in her trunk until it was full, then she put the last one in her backseat.

She turned off the office lights, turned on the security for the building, and left.

While her car engine warmed up, Grace put on her gloves. "I'm not sure if I'm paranoid or savvy." She snorted. *Either way, I feel better.*

Grace parked on the street in front of the old building near the courthouse, which had been converted into a suite of six offices.

Grace opened the door and coughed at the musty smell in the short hallway lit by buzzing fluorescent lights. The directory of the occupants in the building hung on the wall inside a framed message board with removable letters behind a glass cover, and she found the listing "City Manager, Suite 103".

She tapped on the door, and a man opened it. "I'm Gordon Thompson. Nice to meet you, Ms. Callahan. Come in." He offered his hand, and they shook.

"Call me Grace."

"Grace," he repeated.

The large window brightened the office with natural sunlight. The aluminum desk had a computer, keyboard, and a notepad that was nearing the end of its pages.

Two metal filing cabinets with chipped paint acted as sentries for a small table with a coffee maker and an oversized coffee mug on it. On top of one filing cabinet was a framed snapshot of a smiling woman who was a few years older than Grace, with a toddler in her arms and a beagle standing next to her.

Grace sat on the cracked, padded seat of the aluminum chair. Gordon's desk chair creaked when he sat down and looked at Grace expectantly. "What can I do for you?"

Grace pulled the resume out of her folder and handed it to him. "Would you hire this person?"

Gordon raised his eyebrows then accepted the resume. He scanned it, then read it carefully.

"If I had a complex project, I'd hire him in a heartbeat."

He studied Grace's face then read it again. Gordon cleared his throat. "Is this your resume?"

"I read yours, so I thought you would like to read mine."

Gordon stared at her then softly chuckled. "I guess everything I've heard about Grace Callahan must be true."

"I think Briar Glen is underutilizing its city manager. I'd like to rectify that, but if you don't like my idea, no one will ever know."

He studied her face. "I'm listening."

"Good. Daniel hired me to make sure the parade was successful. When the parade is over, my project ends."

His eyes widened. "I didn't know that."

He picked up the resume and read it again. "Of course. You're a project director. Routine small town government operations would bore you, wouldn't they?"

"Absolutely, and you don't know how relieved I am you understand."

He nodded. "I could probably manage a small project, but thinking about all the things that could go wrong would keep me awake at night."

"I think it's time for you to take over the reins of being the city manager."

He gaped at her. "What do you mean?"

"You're a highly qualified city manager with stellar recommendations. I was shocked when I found out you didn't have access to any of the systems to manage the operations."

"So, I'm not fired?"

"Not at all. From what I've seen in the short time I've been the deputy mayor, Mayor Dorsey neglected the duties of his office. Daniel Reeves was the first mayor Briar Glen has had in a long time."

"I guess I better get busy."

"Yes. The staff should report to the city manager, and you need training and access to all the systems so you can do your job."

Gordon exhaled. "This isn't what I expected at all, but when you first became deputy mayor, Walt told me to expect the unexpected."

"When can you move into the office next to mine? Can you pack up and be there tomorrow?"

Gordon rose and opened the top drawer of one of the file cabinets. He pulled out a file folder. "Can you loan me a sack for my files?" He opened the rest of the drawers, which were all empty, and grinned.

Grace smiled with him.

He continued, "My computer is old, but there are files on it I want, so I'll bring it along. I can move in one trip in my car. What time do you want me there?"

"I'll be at the office at seven, so any time after that."

"Are you going to announce my move at the meeting this afternoon?"

Grace leaned forward. "Let's talk about that. Should I?"

Gordon cleared his throat. "I think you should focus on the parade, so no, don't announce it."

Grace nodded. "That's what I was thinking. We can talk about any announcements later. For now, it's all about the parade, but you'll be there today, right?"

"I wouldn't miss it for the world."

"Good. I need all the friendly faces I can get." Grace rose from her chair.

"Wait. I have to ask you about the Sponsors' Float."

Dropping back down into her chair, Grace said, "I don't know anything about a Sponsors' Float."

"I guess you wouldn't because Daniel would have expected Bella to tell you, which she wouldn't."

"Why not?"

"The Sponsors' Float was always Mayor Dorsey's project, so Bella was never involved. The sponsors of the parade donate money to the local children's summer program."

Grace rubbed the back of her neck and then exhaled. "How do I pull together a Sponsors' Float?"

Gordon strode to his closet door and opened it. "You don't have to. I have all the flags and signs for the float right here."

Grace rose to peer into the closet. Lifting the corner of a flag, she said, "These are good quality. I see how they have lasted from one year to the next."

"The Sponsors' Float has been my responsibility for past two years." Gordon beamed.

"Do the sponsors know they're supposed to donate?"

"Yes. It won't be a surprise to them. Just mention the Sponsors' Float when you talk about the parade later, and everybody will know what you're talking about. The truck follows the St. Patrick float. That's how everyone knows it's the end of the parade."

"I am really glad I came to talk to you. I'm just sorry I didn't do it earlier."

"You couldn't have. The meeting I called you about was for the city council and could have easily turned into an ambush, so we never would have talked."

"That makes sense."

Gordon opened the door for her. "It was nice working with you, Grace."

"See you at the meeting."

Grace climbed into her car, checked the time, and headed toward Nora's house.

After Grace parked in the driveway, Nora and Murphy met her on the porch. Grace hugged Nora and rubbed Murphy's chin.

"I'm here to pack. I probably will be at the distillery through the weekend."

Following Grace to her bedroom, Nora sat in the rocking chair, and Murphy flopped down on the rag rug while Grace packed.

"How much of this is strategic for the parade, and how much of it is personal, and when are you going to resign from your job in Atlanta?"

"Granny, I'm not resigning my job. I need to focus on the parade, and Ryan has been helping me."

When Grace added her warm flannel pajamas to her bag, Nora said, "Flannel, Grace?"

"I don't like to be cold."

"Or sexy either," Nora mumbled.

"Granny, I'm not telling you again this isn't that type of weekend."

"That's too bad because my friends think Ryan is perfect for you."

"Well, he isn't." On a whim, Grace tossed Rosie into her small suitcase before she slammed it shut.

"Okay, then. Let me know if you need any help tomorrow. My Bible study group is on standby."

"Thanks, it's nice to know. I'm really sorry I snapped at you, Granny." Grace hugged Nora and kissed her on the cheek before she picked her suitcase up and headed toward the front door.

Following Grace to the front door, Murphy nudged her hand, and Nora said, "You're under a lot of pressure, Grace. I won't mention Ryan until after the parade."

Giggling, Grace stopped. "I bet you can't."

Nora crossed her arms as Grace hurried outside and dropped her suitcase on the passenger seat. "I refuse to accept that bet."

"Because you'd lose." Grace hopped into her car, and Nora slammed the front door.

Grace smiled as she drove toward the sheriff's office. While she was stopped at a light, she glanced at the time. *I can't show up forty-five minutes early especially with one of Bella's boxes in my back seat.* She turned right and parked in a fast food parking lot.

She sent Ryan a text. "Where are you?"

Her phone rang.

Ryan said, "I'm at the distillery. What's up?"

"I'm ready to go to the meeting, but it's too early."

"Well, then why aren't you on your way here?"

Grace shrugged then hung up.

When the turn to the distillery driveway was ahead, she glanced in the rearview mirror. *A vehicle is following me, and it's coming fast.*

She slowed for the driveway. After she turned, Grace exhaled. *Beer truck.*

Ryan and Willow waited at the front door.

She hopped out of her car and grabbed her backpack and computer while Ryan opened the back door of her car. "What's that box?"

"Bella boxed up all the documents in the office and called a company that shreds documents to come get them tomorrow. I rescued all the boxes and filled my trunk. This box didn't fit."

"Do you want to empty your car before we leave?"

"I'd like to if we have time."

"Unlock the trunk, and I'll carry boxes inside."

Grace handed the keys to Ryan and picked up her small suitcase.

While she struggled with her backpack, computer bag, and small suitcase, Ryan carried in a box then returned with a cart and hauled in the rest of the boxes.

When she was inside, Grace carried her suitcase to the guest bedroom and set her computer bag down in the living room.

Ryan left the boxes on the cart in the living room.

He rubbed Willow's face. "Goodbye, sweet girl. We'll be back later. You're going to stay home this time."

Willow circled her favorite rug then flopped down.

After they were in the truck, Grace asked, "Did Willow understand what you said?"

"Sure. She knows I'll be gone for a while, and I'll be back."

Grace leaned back in the seat and closed her eyes. "I snapped at Granny. I think I'm a little wound up."

"I'm sure she understood."

"She did. I went to Gordon Thompson's office, and he told me about the Sponsors' Float. I had no idea."

Ryan groaned. "I should have thought of that, but at least you know. Is he driving the truck this year?"

"Yes, and I asked him to move into the mayor's office so he can have access to the systems and manage the staff."

Ryan was silent as he focused on the road.

When he turned at the sheriff's department parking lot, he said, "I suppose this means you haven't considered staying."

"Briar Glen already has a city manager, and it's definitely not a job that I would want."

"Makes sense, I suppose."

Even though they strolled across the parking lot together, Ryan avoided eye contact and was focused intently on the building ahead with his arms close to his sides.

Before they reached the door, Grace grabbed his forearm, and Ryan instantly stopped.

She didn't remove her hand. "What's wrong?"

Ryan looked at her hand then met her gaze. "What do you mean?" He gently placed his hand over hers, holding eye contact a second too long.

When a car parked and two people started walking toward them, he lowered his hand.

Releasing his arm but staying close to his side as they strolled inside together, Grace whispered, "We'll talk later."

When they went into the press room, Leah was waiting for them. "Come with me to the sheriff's office. It's our version of the celebrity green room except it's not fancy or comfortable."

She rolled out of the room and led them down the hall. "The sheriff's waiting for us."

When they went into his office, the sheriff rose from behind his desk. "Have a seat, Grace. You'll be on your feet long enough. We don't know how many people will show up, but I suspect most of them will be your supporters. I thought I'd introduce you then open the floor to you. If you want me to step in and stop the meeting, just give me or Leah a wave, and it will happen. I'd like to talk to you after the meeting. Ryan, you're included, of course. Do you have any questions for me?"

"Who do we work with during the parade?" Grace asked.

"We've been supporting the parade for a lot of years, so we're relatively independent, but Leah is your contact."

"We'll get together tomorrow," Leah said.

"Gordon Thompson will move into the mayor's office tomorrow. He will have access to all the systems to manage the operations and the staff."

The sheriff raised an eyebrow. "That is a brilliant move. Are you announcing that tonight?"

"No, Gordon and I decided my focus tonight is the parade. Anything else will be a different discussion."

"Good idea."

"Did you turn Zoey loose on social media?" Leah asked. "Briar Glen is all over the place."

"Zoey said her Moms club would help."

"They're doing a great job," Leah said. "Mention your social media campaign when you talk about the Stay and Shop promotion. Do you have an outline for your opening?"

"Yes. Talk about the parade and don't maim Caleb Morris."

Laughing, the sheriff shook his head as he opened the office door. "You're all set then. I'll be back when it's time for our grand entrance."

Rising from her chair, Grace rolled her shoulders and shook the tension out of her arms.

"Are you nervous?" Leah asked.

"No, just getting ready for the ring."

Chuckling, Leah said, "You'll have 'em spinning like a top."

A few minutes later, the sheriff came into the office, smiling. "Let's go."

As they strolled down the hall, the sheriff whispered, "Your fans came early and claimed all the seats on the front row."

"Poor Caleb," Leah said.

Chapter Twelve

The sheriff opened the door to the pressroom, and Grace flinched and took a step back. All the seats were taken, and people were standing along the wall.

Ryan placed his hand on her shoulder and whispered, "Look for friendly faces, Gracie, especially mine. The rest of them are just bourbon barrels of whiskey waiting to be aged."

Relaxing her shoulders at the warmth of his hand, she rolled her eyes at his outrageous comment, then strode to the front of the room with the sheriff.

As the sheriff spoke, Grace scanned the room for people she could use as focal points. Gordon nodded, and Melba waved with enthusiasm. Grace finger-waved in return.

Granny, the women from her Bible study group, Zoey, and her Moms club members along with several toddlers occupied the entire front row. Aaron stood with his arms crossed in the back on her left like a sentry, and Tristan was in the last row. Ryan was her anchor in the back on her right.

He grinned and pointed to his face, and she suppressed her giggle with a smile.

After the sheriff concluded his introduction with "Grace Callahan," a toddler in the front row squealed, "Hi, Grace," and laughter filled the room.

Grace paused for a quick peekaboo with the toddler, and then stepped up to the microphone and waited until the audience settled down.

"Thank you, everyone, for being here and for your support for the Briar Glen St. Patrick's Day parade, which is this Saturday beginning at ten o'clock. Our weather will be sunny with no rain allowed."

She paused for the cheers, then continued, "Our parade will be led by our high school marching band and will include our local dance team and our St. Patrick's Float, and will have over sixty floats, which is three times as many as we've ever had."

Grace nodded at the gasps and murmurs.

"My heart is touched by the outpouring of support as the community honors the memory of Mayor Daniel Reeves."

She paused at the outburst of applause.

"This year we created a promotion honoring our faithful downtown merchants to encourage people to stay after the parade and shop. I'm sure you've seen the flyers and our viral social media posts, Stay and Shop."

She motioned toward the moms on the front row and led the appreciative clapping for the promotion.

"I hope I covered any questions you may have had, but I'll open up the floor. Ask me anything."

"What about the money?" Caleb blurted out.

Grace scanned the audience. "Was that you, Caleb? Where are you?"

Caleb slowly rose as he glared at Grace.

"Thank you so much for your question. Our sponsors, who are members of the city council, will present their donations to the Briar Glen children's summer program at the appreciation dinner, as they do every year."

Caleb hesitated, then tightly pressed his lips together and furiously wrote in his notebook as he sat down.

Sitting in the middle row with a leather folio on her lap, a woman politely lifted her hand. She wore a black turtleneck, the perfect background for her solid gold disc necklace engraved with a single initial P.

As she rose, her fingers briefly touched the pendant, pressing it flat against her chest before she spoke. "I'm Piper Franklin, the regional vice president at the bank. Grace, thank you for keeping things moving during a hard week."

She gave a small, courteous smile. "What contingencies are in place if something disrupts the parade schedule? Our merchants are counting on this weekend."

Grace nodded. "Yes, they are. We've been working closely with our local businesses, schools, and community leaders to make sure we can adjust quickly if anything unexpected comes up. The goal is to keep things moving safely and smoothly for everyone."

Applause broke out from the back of the room.

Piper's fingers returned briefly to the necklace as she inclined her head and sat while the clapping continued.

Grace's gaze drifted across the room. Valerie Higgins sat halfway back, hands folded neatly in her lap, her expression calm and attentive. She gave Grace a small nod, the polite kind shared between acquaintances in a small town.

Grace nodded back before moving on as the room quieted. After scanning the room, then glancing at Gordon, who gave her a thumbs up, Grace said, "If there's nothing else, thank you everyone for all your support."

The sheriff stepped up to the microphone while everyone rose to give a standing ovation as Grace strode to the back.

When Tristan rose with his arms outstretched, Ryan stepped in front of him and put his arm around Grace. "Let's go."

He ushered her out of the room where Leah waited in the hall. She led them to the sheriff's office.

After Grace dropped into the chair, Leah said, "The sheriff and I decided you would have been mobbed, and Ryan agreed. I loved how easily you caught the pompous banker's foul ball."

Grace exhaled and leaned back in the chair. "I've spoken to much larger groups than that, but I always had the data and charts to back up every word. This was hard."

"Next time, I'll ask Zoey to make you a chart," Leah said. "You know what set the mood for your talk?"

Chuckling, Ryan said. "I do. Hi, Grace."

Leah laughed, and Grace smiled. "That little guy was such a delight when the army gathered to make calls. His mom said, 'Hi Grace' when she came in, so that's what I heard the rest of the day when he saw me."

When the sheriff came in, he said, "You did a great job, Grace. Everyone is pumped up about the parade and the Stay and Shop promotion. How are you feeling?"

Grace's shoulders slumped. "Glad it's over. Caleb played his part well, but the banker was a wild card."

"I don't know what her point was, but your answer really highlighted that the parade is a community project," Leah said.

The sheriff exhaled. "The reason I wanted to talk with you after the meeting is I have news about Mayor Dorsey, and it's not good. A citizen reported a car submerged in a lake in Alabama about four hours west of here. The sheriff ran the license plate, and the car belonged to Dorsey. The state has taken over and is searching the lake. There probably won't be anything on the news before next week unless they find a body."

Ryan inhaled and put his hand on Grace's shoulder as she leaned forward, but she didn't push his hand away.

Narrowing her eyes, Grace asked, "What about Daniel Reeves? Has the medical examiner determined the cause of death yet?"

The sheriff glanced at Leah. "No, but it's still early, and the medical examiner's office doesn't rush. They're very thorough."

Grace glared at the sheriff, but he didn't drop his gaze.

Leah rolled between them, not facing either of them. The soft squeak of her wheelchair tires was the only sound in the room. "Two days before the parade. Focus."

"We're on the same side, Grace. We're just on different paths," the sheriff said.

"It's still early," Grace leaned back as she quoted him. "Okay, Sheriff. You're right."

Leah exhaled. "Call us if you need us, Grace."

Grace's eyes softened as she smiled at the sheriff, who returned her smile.

"Are you ready to go?" Ryan asked.

"Yes. I need to focus," Grace said.

As they strolled to Ryan's truck, Grace said, "Can we run by Granny's house on the way to the distillery?"

"Sure."

Grace called Nora, who answered immediately. "I was so proud of you. It's been a long time since people were this excited about the parade. So, what can I do for you?"

"Can I have copies of your utility bills for the past year or two years, if you have them. I need them as a reference."

"It will take me two minutes, and you don't need to get out of your car. I'll run them out to you."

"That's great. I'm with Ryan."

"Good." Nora hung up.

When Ryan pulled into the driveway, Nora and Murphy raced out, and Nora handed Grace a manila envelope.

"Thanks, Granny."

"Let me know if there's anything else I can do." Nora hurried into her house with Murphy at her side.

As he backed out of the driveway, Ryan asked, "Why did you ask for her utility bills?"

"I wanted an example of the water and sewer costs for a household. A family might have been better, but I can use Granny's bills as a baseline."

Heading toward downtown, Ryan asked, "What do you think about having a quiet dinner at the restaurant?"

"I don't really want to be around people right now."

He nodded. "Then we'll have a quiet dinner at the distillery."

"We could order something from the restaurant and take it with us," Grace said.

"You can keep me company by sipping on a glass of my finest bourbon and telling me what you've been doing for the past fifteen years while I cook, and then you can work after dinner. You know you need a break, Grace."

Grace crossed her arms and stared out her side window.

When they were close to the distillery, he asked, "Are you okay?"

"Don't rush me. I'm still trying to come up with a snappy reply to your insinuation that I need a break."

Ryan chuckled. "Ouch. That was a really sharp comment."

Grace giggled. "Thank you."

"What irritated you so much when the sheriff told us about Mayor Dorsey?"

"He told us about the car in the lake as a distraction. There is something about Daniel Reeves he doesn't want me to know."

Ryan parked at the distillery and rubbed his chin. "The medical examiner should have known within an hour if Daniel died of a heart attack."

"That's right, and the sheriff led me to assume Daniel had had a heart attack. Now I think something else killed him."

After Ryan unlocked the distillery door, Willow bounded to him with her tail wagging at full doggie speed. "Let's go, Willow."

Laughing as the two of them left her standing in the hall to race down the driveway, Grace carried her backpack into the living room. "Hello, books."

Ryan and Willow dashed back into the house and passed her on their way to the kitchen.

When Grace joined them, Willow leaned against her for pets, and Grace petted her neck."

While Ryan dished up Willow's food, Grace glanced down at her dress shirt. "I'm not dressed properly for fine dining at the distillery. I'm going to change into my sweatpants."

"I always knew you were smart. You caught onto our strict dress code right away."

Hurrying to her bedroom, Grace pulled her sweatpants, sweatshirt, and a T-shirt out of her suitcase. After she changed clothes, she stared at her clothes in her suitcase, then opened the small closet and frowned. *Would it look like I'm being pushy and trying to move in if I hang my clothes in the closet?*

She called out, "Hey Ryan, can I hang up a few things in the closet?"

"In my favorite closet?"

She wrinkled her nose and hung up her clothes. *I should have known not to ask.*

Strolling into the kitchen, Grace inhaled the aroma of searing chicken mingled with the distillery's distinct underlying scent of grain and oak. "No, your second favorite closet."

"Well, in that case, it might be okay." Smiling, he pointed at the breakfast bar. "Your whiskey on the rocks and appetizers."

Holding up her glass for inspection, Grace sniffed her drink and then took a tiny sip of bourbon. "This tastes smoky."

"Good. I bought a new smoker. Is it too much?"

She climbed up on the barstool. "I don't think so, but I'm not an expert."

Ryan set a glass of iced tea on the bar. "Try that."

Grace sipped the tea. "Raspberry tea?"

"Excellent. I've been experimenting with different flavors for sweet tea."

While she nibbled on the apple slices and smoked gouda cheese, the sizzle of the chicken and the click of Ryan's knife on the cutting board as he chopped vegetables echoed through the distillery dispelling its stony silence.

Sipping her tea, Grace quietly slid off her barstool. "This has been a relaxing break. Can I bring a box in here and go through it?"

Ryan exhaled. "Of course, as long as you talk to me while you're doing it. You actually took a longer break than I expected."

Grace carried in a box and put it on the small kitchen table. As she went through the contents, she began separating the papers into blueprints and contracts. "I suspect this is Bella's box. I don't know why she didn't shred this ages ago."

As Grace glanced through the papers, she came across a sealed manila folder marked 'Notes' and set it aside on a chair.

When she was about halfway through the box, Ryan said, "Are you at a point where you can stop and eat?"

She returned all the blueprints to the box, then set the contracts on top of them. "Yes. I think I need to ignore the boxes Bella packed for now and go through the files Daniel left for me."

"We're having chicken fried rice." He set their bowls down on the bar, then sat on the stool next to Grace.

While they ate, Grace asked, "Do you miss your Atlanta job?"

Ryan set his fork down and leaned back, the faint drip of condensation from the back of the distillery breaking the silence.

"In Atlanta, if a line in the lab backed up, alarms screamed and set off red lights, warning buzzers, and panicky people waving their arms and yelling about contamination. You'd have thought the place was about to explode." He nodded toward the back. "Here, the still gurgles at me like it's clearing its throat, and I adjust a valve."

His mouth twitched. "Same issue. Easy fix with no panic required."

Grace examined his face. "You don't like noise, Ryan. You like listening."

After Grace ate another bite, she said, "There are people who enjoy the arts and city culture and would find life in small towns too slow."

"True. Is that how you feel?" Ryan went still, then dragged his fork through the rice and stabbed a piece of carrot.

She shrugged. "I thought I did."

He tilted his head as he gazed at her. "What's changed?"

"I don't know. Maybe seeing what I do makes a difference? Or maybe it was the difference between friendly faces and everyone else." She gazed at Ryan. "That hit home harder than I would have expected. I work with barrels in Atlanta. Does that make sense?"

"I understand exactly what you're saying."

After they finished eating, Grace hurried into the living room and sat on the sofa with Daniel's files.

She pulled out a sheet of paper with hand-drawn boxes and arrows like a workflow, and recognized Daniel's tight, neat handwriting. The top boxes were labeled Buyer, KS; Owner, AZ; Operations, SC; and Distributor, MO from top to bottom with two boxes to the side each labeled simply Supplier. In the top left corner was a box labeled Controller, BG.

She shifted to Bella's boxes, searching for the permit for Fair Valley Manufacturing Company, LLC, the company that purchased the poultry processing plant.

After an hour, she found it and groaned as she stretched then hurried to the desk Ryan had set up for her computer.

"Daniel made me a key." she muttered, powering up her computer.

Ryan strode to her side and leaned close. "What did you say?"

She turned, and his face was inches away.

He went still.

His head tilted slightly as his eyes met hers, and he unconsciously drew in a slow breath through his nose.

The air shifted.

He exhaled, his lips parting just a fraction...

"Daniel made me a key." She turned and pointed to Daniel's drawing. "The LLC for the purchaser listed on the permit must be registered in Kansas."

Ryan scrubbed his hand over his face and returned to the sofa while she searched for the state office in Kansas that issued LLCs.

When she flopped down on the other end of the sofa, Ryan asked, "No luck?"

"I found the LLC, but the agent listed with the state is a lawyer's office."

"So, what now?"

"I don't know. I might be overthinking this. I should take a break from it like you said."

"If you're going to say crazy stuff like that, I recommend fresh air. Want to bundle up and take Willow for a short walk?"

Willow danced while Grace zipped up her jacket. When Ryan opened the door, Willow dashed into the dark.

"Did she see something?" Grace asked.

"A rabbit, but that was last week. She's just hopeful."

"I really feel like Daniel was trying to tell me something, but am I just mired in wishful thinking and seeing something that was never there?" Grace shivered. "It's cold out here."

"Go inside. We'll be there soon."

Grace stepped closer to him. "I'll wait with you."

When Willow reappeared, she dashed to the door while Grace and Ryan followed her.

Opening the door, Ryan went still as Grace passed him. "It's getting late."

"I feel like I'm getting close, but..." Grace ran her hand through her hair.

"You're so tired you just might miss it entirely," Ryan said.

"Exactly. What makes you so smart?" Rising slowly, she picked up the notes envelope and shuffled off to bed.

Chapter Thirteen

Buzzing sounds circled Grace's head; she flailed at the air to shoo away mosquitoes. When the buzzing didn't stop, Grace sat up. *My phone.*

Fumbling for her phone, Grace answered, her voice still barely coherent and weak from sleeping. "Hello? Is something wrong, Bella?"

"Yes." Bella's voice was panicky. She disconnected.

Instantly energized by the terror in Bella's voice, Grace threw her sweatpants and a sweatshirt over her pajamas and pulled on a pair of socks. Willow whimpered at her door, and Grace opened it.

Nudging her hand, Willow whimpered again; Ryan appeared in the doorway.

"What's wrong? Why are you dressed?" Ryan wore sweatpants but was bare chested.

"Bella called me. Something's wrong."

"Give me one second to throw on some clothes. I know where she lives."

Grace pulled on her boots and picked up her backpack. She hurried to the living room, but Ryan and Willow caught up with her.

"Put on your coat. It's cold."

Grace threw on her coat, and the three of them hurried to the truck. While Grace climbed into the truck, Ryan opened the back door for Willow, who sailed inside.

As Ryan sped down the driveway, Grace called Bella, but her phone rang around to voicemail. She dropped her phone into her pocket.

"What did she say when she called?" Ryan asked.

Putting on her gloves, Grace said, "She's in trouble. What time is it?"

"A little after three."

"I told her she could call me anytime," Grace said. "She doesn't have anyone else."

Ryan glanced at her. "You keep doing that."

"Doing what?"

"Making sure people aren't alone."

Grace blinked, surprised. Before she could answer, a glow lit up the dark sky.

"Is that a fire?" Grace leaned forward to get a better look.

Ryan said, "One more block. You're carrying, Grace?"

Grace patted her backpack. "I've had a weird week."

Ryan nodded. "You keep your skills up to date?"

Grace side-glanced at him. "I have a range partner."

"Good."

When they turned at a driveway, sparks and ash shot into the sky. Grace called 911. When the dispatcher answered, Grace said, "This is Grace Callahan. Bella Davis's house is on fire."

Ryan slammed on the brakes and parked off to the side of the driveway before they reached the house. He jumped out of the truck. "Stay here."

Grace jumped out behind him as he raced toward the front door.

She dashed around to the back of the house where gray smoke leaked out of the eaves and dark black smoke and flames rolled out of the open back door and the toxic fumes from burning plastic stung her eyes and her lungs.

The explosive pops and crackles from electrical arcing were frightening, and the intense heat from the house burned her nose and throat with every breath the closer she got.

When a sudden small spark flashed in the dark near the door, Grace pulled her sweatshirt over her mouth and ran to the back door and coughed. Bella was sprawled in the middle of the kitchen, surrounded by deadly flames creeping toward her.

Grace took in a big breath, then was snatched away from the door and tossed onto the grass, landing face down, her singed hair in her mouth. She sputtered and pulled her hair away from her mouth as she struggled to her feet. Ryan ran into the kitchen and disappeared in the flames.

She raced to the door that was filled with dark, stinging smoke. She tucked her chin and pulled the neck of her sweatshirt over her mouth and stepped inside.

Ryan had lifted Bella up and had her back cradled against his chest, but a fallen rafter across her hips had pinned her. Grace dropped down and crawled under the smoke. She rolled onto her back and then pushed the rafter away from Bella with her legs.

Ryan roared, "Get out!" as he pulled Bella free. Grace crawled out the door and onto the grass.

With one hand, Ryan lifted her by the back of the jacket, his nose inches from hers, and their angry eyes met. He gritted his teeth. "Never scare me like that again."

She pushed him away and picked up Bella's feet. They carried her to the front yard where there was no smoke and laid her on the ground.

Grace dropped to her knees and leaned over Bella. "She's breathing."

Bending over, holding onto his thighs, Ryan nodded as he caught his breath.

Willow was barking wildly in the truck and throwing herself against the window. Running to the truck, Grace opened the back door, and Willow leaped out. She sniffed Grace then raced to Ryan and sniffed him.

Still coughing, Ryan kneeled next to Willow and hugged her. Willow's tail, which had been tucked, wagged in big circles.

Grace picked up her phone and called 911 again. "Ryan pulled Bella out of the house. She's breathing, but unconscious."

"Do you need two ambulances?" the dispatcher asked.

Grace glanced at Ryan. *It would serve him right.* "No, only one for Bella."

Suffocating smoke rolled across the yard toward them as firefighters shouted over the roar of the flames and the even louder din of the fire engines.

After the ambulance crew brought their stretcher and quickly lifted Bella onto the stretcher, they rushed her to the ambulance.

Grace stared at the flattened grass where Bella had laid. Catching the gleam of a small object on the ground from the strobing lights, Grace kneeled down and picked up Bella's coin. She gazed at the coin lying in her hand then stuffed it into her pocket.

Adding to the chaos was the surge of the water pumps and the angry hiss of steam when a solid stream of water knocked down yet another growing hot spot.

Bella was on a stretcher near the ambulance, oxygen mask over her face, her chest rising in shallow, uneven pulls. The crew quickly loaded her, then the ambulance sped away with its sirens slicing through the silent neighborhood and setting off the howls of once-sleeping dogs for blocks around.

Grace paced in the grass, coughing, her eyes burning from smoke and her own fury.

Ryan came toward her with soot streaked across his forehead, his sweatshirt damp with sweat and water.

Crossing her arms, she snapped. "What was that?"

Ryan blinked. "What?"

"You threw me! You literally picked me up and threw me into the yard like I weighed nothing."

"You were about to run into a burning house!"

"She called me for help!"

"So you die for her?" he shot back.

The words hung there, louder than the sirens.

Grace froze.

Ryan's jaw tightened like he wished he could pull them back.

Fire crackled behind them.

The cacophony of roaring engines, desperate shouts, and the ominous groans of the failing structure diminished, becoming mere whispers beneath the overwhelming weight of their words.

"I wasn't going to die." Her voice was shaky.

"You don't know that," he said, low and fierce. "You don't get to make that decision like it doesn't matter."

Her eyes flashed. "You don't get to grab me like I'm a child."

"You were acting like one."

Staring at each other like strangers, they faced off, breathing hard.

A firefighter pulling a hose passed them as someone shouted for more water.

Grace looked away first.

"I had to help her," she said.

Ryan's voice dropped. "I know."

The sheriff strode toward them. He glanced at them, then audibly exhaled before he approached Grace.

"Tell me what happened, Grace."

She told him about the phone call. "So, Ryan, Willow, and I came here. I went around to check the back, and the door was open. I saw Bella on the floor with flames all around. Ryan went into the house first and pulled her out, then we carried her to the front to get her away from the smoke."

"Did you see anyone else?"

Grace shook her head.

"Did she tell you why she needed help?"

"No."

At the whomp-whomp sound of an approaching helicopter, everyone on the scene paused and gazed at the sky.

"They are flying her to the burn unit in Atlanta," the sheriff said. "There's no reason for you to stick around. Will you be at work later this morning?"

"Yes."

The sheriff's face softened. "Get some rest if you can, Grace."

Grace headed toward the truck, and Ryan strode past her with Willow in the lead. After Willow hopped in, he waited for Grace. He offered his hand to help her in, but Grace ignored him and climbed into the truck.

They drove back to the distillery in chilly silence. Willow lay flat and quiet on the back seat.

After Ryan parked, they walked to the distillery door. Ryan strode ahead, followed by Grace with Willow at her side.

Without their usual banter and energy, the distillery was stuffy and quiet when they walked in.

Once inside, Grace shut the door harder than she meant to and stood there for a second, staring at nothing. *Nothing feels right.*

She followed Ryan into the kitchen who went straight to the sink and turned on the water without looking at her. After drying his hands with a towel, he wiped down the breakfast bar.

The still hummed softly in the next room, steady and indifferent.

Grace tugged her sweatshirt over her head and tossed it onto a chair. "I smell like a chimney."

She glanced down. *I'm still wearing my pajamas.*

Ryan didn't answer.

She opened a cabinet, then another, not sure what she was looking for. A glass. A distraction. Something to do with her hands.

Behind her, the rhythmic sound of a damp cloth wiping the bar broke the silence.

She turned. "What are you doing?"

Ryan paused, towel in his hand. "Cleaning."

Grace rubbed her eyes. *They still burn.* "You don't get to throw me around like I'm a sack of grain."

Ryan's jaw flexed. He folded the towel and set it down, carefully and aligned with the edge of the bar. "You don't get to scare me like that."

She glanced away. "I wasn't thinking."

"I know," he whispered. "That's what scared me."

That took the heat out of her anger, but she refused to let it show.

She moved to the living room. Ryan slowly followed her.

She sat down hard on the sofa, wrapping her arms around herself.

Ryan stayed in the doorway for a long moment, then leaned back against the wall with his head cocked, watching her.

"Stop watching me," she muttered.

"You almost ran into a fire."

"I told you, I wasn't thinking."

"That's the problem, Grace."

Silence settled between them, thick and tired.

Ryan remained still as he stared at the floor.

For once, it didn't irritate her.

She rose. "I need a shower."

"Good idea," Ryan said. "So do I."

Grace pulled her spare pajamas out of her suitcase and slipped into the guest bathroom.

When the hot water poured over her head and down her back, her tears flowed for Bella, for Ryan, and for herself. They mixed with the shampoo and the shower soap Ryan insisted on calling *Gracie soap*.

She smiled faintly. *I forgot to be mad at him for that.*

As she rinsed, the weight of the night settled on her shoulders.

Maybe we'd all be better off if I went to a hotel.

Grace stepped out of the bathroom in her fresh pair of pajamas, toweling her hair dry.

Ryan was sitting on the edge of the sofa. His hair was damp, and he'd changed into an old T-shirt and jeans.

He looked up when she came in.

For a moment, neither of them spoke.

Grace cleared her throat. "I was thinking... maybe I should get a room at the hotel for a few days."

Furrowing his brow, Ryan examined her face. "Why?"

"So I'm not underfoot. And so if this thing with Bella turns out to be what we think it is, I'm not bringing it here. Or to Nora's."

Ryan watched her for a long beat. Head tilted slightly. Listening.

She almost smiled at the familiarity of it.

"You're not underfoot," he said.

"That's not the point."

"Then what is?"

Grace hesitated. "You shouldn't have to worry about me running into burning buildings in your own place."

Ryan exhaled through his nose, slow and controlled. "Grace."

She braced herself for another argument.

"You don't leave," he whispered.

She blinked. "Ryan..."

"You don't leave," he repeated, softer but firmer. "Not tonight. Not because of this."

His fingers brushed across his forehead as he held her gaze.

"I can handle the worry," he said. "What I can't handle is you not being here."

Grace stared. *He just stole my entire argument away from me.*

The room felt small again, but not in the same way as before.

Grace folded her arms. "You're still bossy."

Ryan's mouth twitched. "You're still reckless."

She walked past him toward her room, then paused.

"Thank you," she said without turning around.

"For what?"

"For not letting me run into that house alone."

Ryan didn't answer.

But she heard the soft exhale he let out after she closed her door. She turned off the light and climbed into bed. *No way will I be able to sleep.*

Grace woke before the alarm on her phone ever had a chance. Wincing at the tightness in her chest, she paused in confusion until the sharp, chemical odor of the still-present smoke in her discarded clothing brought it all rushing back.

She dressed quietly and padded into the kitchen. Ryan was already up.

He sat at the breakfast bar with a mug of coffee in front of him, staring toward the still in the next room like it might say something back if he waited long enough.

He glanced up when she came in. "Morning."

"Morning."

Her mug sat on the counter beside the coffee pot. She poured herself a cup and carried it to her seat at the breakfast bar.

As she set it down, Ryan reached out and turned the mug so the handle faced her without looking at it.

Grace stared at her cup. "Have you heard anything about Bella?"

"I called the sheriff who told me she's in a burn unit and her condition is guarded."

Grace nodded and wrapped both hands around her mug. "I keep thinking... what if you hadn't grabbed me?"

Ryan's jaw tightened. "I keep thinking what if I'd been ten seconds later getting to her?"

They looked at each other as if for the first time. All the anger from the night before was gone; what was left was softer and honest.

Grace swallowed. “You were right.”

Ryan shook his head once. “I wasn’t trying to be.”

A natural silence stretched between them.

Ryan’s gaze dropped briefly to her mouth, then back to her eyes. Leaning forward like he was about to say something, Ryan remained silent.

Meeting him halfway, Grace was unaware she’d moved.

Their lips touched softly, almost by accident; for a second, neither of them reacted. Then Ryan’s hand came up to the side of her face, nestling it with his thumb near her cheekbone, like he needed to make sure she was real.

The kiss deepened, not hungry, not urgent, just certain.

When they finally pulled apart, they stayed close.

Blinking, Grace whispered, “Well.”

Ryan’s mouth twitched. “Yeah.”

Leaning back but still studying his face, she said, “That was probably a bad idea.”

“Probably,” he agreed. “You should try to get some rest.”

Narrowing her eyes, Grace asked, “If I go to bed, what are you going to do?”

“Same.” Ryan met her gaze.

Grace petted Willow. “You’ll come tell me if he doesn’t, right, girl?”

Willow licked Grace’s hand.

Ryan chuckled. “I know when I’m outnumbered. Two hours tops?”

Grace nodded as she rose.

She stopped at the door and glanced over her shoulder with a small smile. "Well."

Ryan returned her smile. "Yeah."

***

Grace woke to a tap on her door. "Two hours tops, Grace. It's after six, and I have coffee."

Grace stumbled into the kitchen and picked up the cup on the breakfast bar, and took a big gulp. After she had drained her cup, she put it down. "I'll be back for more coffee after I'm dressed."

"Our clothes from the fire should be washed separately from other clothes. I'll throw yours in with mine."

"I didn't think about that. I'll take them to Granny's and pick up clean clothes later today."

"Are you being weird about laundry?" he asked.

"Yes, and leave me alone until after I've had another cup of coffee."

Ryan turned her cup so the handle would be on her right when she sat at the bar.

Glancing at her cup, then sneaking a peek at Ryan, Grace smiled as she went to her bedroom to change.

While she was dressing, Nora called her.

Grace held her phone against her ear with her shoulder to listen while she pulled up her jeans.

"Caleb is at it again, Grace. Check the paper. Call me later."

Nora hung up.

Grace hurried to the kitchen but stopped at the anger on Ryan's face.

"Granny called me. Is it terrible?"

"I just now pulled it up, so I haven't read it other than to look at the heading." Ryan straightened a potholder next to the stove, then poured her coffee. He handed Grace his phone.

Grace read the headline twice before the words settled into meaning.

"Bad Luck Parade: Is Briar Glen's New Deputy Mayor in Over Her Head?"

Don't scroll.

She scrolled anyway. With every line, her mouth pressed thinner. Not anger. Not yet. Something colder.

The article didn't accuse her of anything, which was the worst part. It simply laid out the week like a list of unfortunate coincidences and let the reader draw the conclusion themselves.

Daniel's death. Bella's fire. Parade complications.

All gently arranged into a pattern with her name in the center.

Grace swallowed and read the quotes.

"We all appreciate enthusiasm, but running a town event takes more than energy. It takes experience."

Tightening her jaw; she continued reading.

"I'm not saying anyone is to blame, but at some point you have to ask whether the stress of all this is affecting decision-making."

She stopped and read the quote again.

She stared at the screen until the words blurred. *They aren't calling me incompetent. They're saying I'm unstable.*

Grace set the phone down on the counter with deliberate care, like it might explode if she didn't.

She'd faced angry people before with their accusations, suspicion, and grief.

This is different.

Someone was quietly pulling the floor out from under her reputation one board at a time and smiling while doing it.

Not fighting me. Erasing me.

She exhaled slowly.

Ryan had been watching her face while she read, so he didn't interrupt her to ask what it said because he already knew it wasn't good.

"What?" he asked quietly.

She returned his phone to him; Ryan read in silence.

His expression didn't change at first, but then his jaw tightened.

He read the quotes twice and then read the one about stress affecting decision-making a third time.

Ryan's fingers rested on the breakfast bar for a moment, flat, like he was holding himself in place.

"This is deliberate," he said.

Grace nodded. "I know, but the thing is, Caleb's not this smart. Someone else wrote it and gave it to him."

He set the phone down more firmly than she had; not a slam, but just enough to make the point.

"They're trying to make you look unstable," he said.

"Not just unstable," Grace corrected softly. "In over my head."

Ryan gazed at her. "They're wrong."

She gave him a thin smile. "That's not the problem."

He didn't ask what the problem was because he already understood.

Grace drained her cup of coffee, and then she and Ryan reached for the coffee pot at the same time. When their hands brushed, they exchanged a look.

Ryan poured her coffee. "I have biscuits in the oven that will be ready in two minutes. Do you want a fried or scrambled egg?"

"Whichever one is faster."

Ryan nodded as he cracked three eggs into the skillet. "I know you'll come up with a Gracie scheme. Just don't do anything without me. Although it might be a good idea if you called Nora and told her it was time to activate the fairies."

Grace giggled and called Nora.

"Are you okay, Grace?"

"I'm fine. Ryan suggested it was time to activate the fairies. What do you think?"

"I think Ryan is a genius. Consider it done. If they aren't available, I'll call the Bible study group."

"Thanks, Granny. That's a wonderful idea."

"What's a wonderful idea?" Ryan put an egg and a biscuit on a plate for Grace.

"Granny's going to call her Bible study group."

"What will they do?"

"I have an idea." Grace called Nora back.

"What's our plan?" Nora asked.

"How did you know I had a plan, Granny?"

"It's you. So what's the plan?"

Chapter Fourteen

"Whoever wrote the article for Caleb tried to make it personal, but they got a little too fancy and mentioned the city. Maybe we need to rally people to support Briar Glen and the Briar Glen St. Patrick's Day parade," Grace said.

"Ooo. That's great. We'll get the word out. Tell Ryan to talk to Mr. Pearce, Senior. He has a lot of clout, and you should stop by and talk to Walt. He's a Grace fan. I'll call Tristan. Maybe I can catch him before he leaves for school." Nora hung up.

"Your Grace plan is brilliant. I'll fill Granddad in on what's going on and how he can help," Ryan said.

"That's great, and I'll talk to Walt on my way in. Zoey should be in the office later. She'll spread the word in the Mom's group."

"Will you and Zoey be able to manage the office alone?"

"Yes. Oh, no. I just remembered I told Gordon Thompson I'd be at the office at seven." Grace shoved the rest of the biscuit in her mouth.

Ryan stared at her. "I'm meeting Sully at the gas station at eight anyway, so I'll go a little early and talk to Walt. I know it might be too soon, but maybe Sully will have a report on that water sample."

"Thank you." Grace finished swallowing as she stroked Willow's neck. "Have a good day, girl. See you later."

"Thanks for breakfast and the pep talk." Grace grabbed her backpack and rushed out the front door, then hurried back in. "I forgot my dirty clothes."

Ryan handed her two grocery bags. She shoved her clothes into the bags and hurried to her car.

Driving into town, Grace checked the time. *I have time to drop off my laundry at Granny's.*

Grace parked in front of Nora's house and grabbed the two makeshift laundry bags. When she stepped onto the porch, Nora opened the front door, and Murphy rushed to greet her.

While Grace scratched Murphy's ears, Nora said, "Murphy told me you were here. Come on in."

Wrinkling her nose before Grace stepped any closer, Nora said, "Hold it. You don't have to tell me why you're here. Give me your clothes so I can throw those smoky ones into the washer before they stink up my house."

Grace handed the sacks to Nora. "Thanks."

Motioning with one hand for Grace to leave, Nora said, "Go. Be righteously indignant all day over that horrible article that is ruining Briar Glen's reputation."

As Grace headed toward the office, she smiled. *I have my word for the day.*

After she flipped on the lights, the fluorescent buzz filled the room, too loud in the quiet. The steady whir of the printer sounded mechanical and out of place.

Bella's desk sat exactly as she'd left it, the dark computer screen, the keyboard pushed back, a coffee mug with a faint ring in the bottom.

It looked abandoned.

Grace swallowed and turned away before the image could shift into something else. Bella framed by flames, smoke curling toward the ceiling.

She crossed to the conference room and started a pot of coffee, needing the familiar routine more than the caffeine.

A tap on the front door cut through the silence.

Hurrying to the front door to unlock it, Grace sighed in relief. *Gordon's here.*

When she opened the door and beckoned him to come in, Gordon picked up a large box and strode inside. "I didn't know if you'd be here or not after what was in the paper this morning. How are you doing?"

"Battle ready."

Chuckling, Gordon came inside. "Not what I expected to hear, but I'm right there with you. What are we battle ready for?"

"The newspaper's attack on Briar Glen's reputation and the disparaging remarks about the St. Patrick's Day parade."

"Excellent. After this arduous move, I'll have to take a break at the café and grab myself a cup of coffee, with your permission, of course." Gordon chuckled at his own jokes, and Grace rolled her eyes.

Glancing around, Gordon asked, “Where do I set my box?”

“The office next to mine is the city manager’s office.”

Gordon narrowed his eyes as he passed Grace’s office. “How can your door be open?”

“I hated being shut off from everybody else, so I removed the automatic door closer.”

Gordon laughed. “I’ll see if anyone knows why the newspaper has turned against Briar Glen.”

Brushing his hands together as he strolled out of his office, Gordon asked, “What’s my plan for today?”

“Training on all the systems after Zoey arrives. They aren’t complex, but you’ll need to know how to log on and find what you need.”

“Sometime I’d like to go over my responsibilities with you. I’ve essentially done nothing since I was hired, and I’d like to buckle down and get to work. Driving the sponsor float for thirty minutes once a year just wasn’t cutting it for my self-esteem.”

“If you have a copy of the city manager job description, we can review and revise it this afternoon or first thing tomorrow.”

“I’ll give you a copy before I leave for the café.”

While Gordon took down the automatic closer, he muttered, “Never knew why Mayor Dorsey wanted these in the first place.”

Grace’s phone rang. When she answered, Zoey was sobbing.

“Grace, my sweet husband is being an absolute bear, and I can’t come to the office. I am so sorry. I won’t be any help to you at all.”

"You can work from home, right?"

Brightening, Zoey said, "Of course. What can I do?"

Grace explained the indignation on behalf of Briar Glen.

"My moms group will love it. What else?"

"Gordon needs training on all the systems. Is that something you could do over the phone?"

"Oh sure. I can log in here while he logs in..."

Grace interrupted. "Wait. Bella changed all the passwords late yesterday..."

"She did what? Why did she do that?"

Grace ran her fingers through her hair. "I don't know. I snapped a photo of all her new passwords, but I changed them after she left because she was acting so strange. I'll text you both sets in case I missed something."

"I'll get them into the password safe right away."

"We'll need a schedule to change them, but we can talk about that later," Grace said.

"I'm still shocked about Bella. It's hard for me to believe she changed all the passwords without talking to you first. If you hadn't caught it, we would have been completely locked out of all our systems."

"I'm just glad I was there before she left."

Zoey exhaled. "So am I."

"I just thought of one more thing. Do you know anyone who is friends with Caleb?"

"Not really what you and I think of as a friend, but one of our moms talks to him occasionally. Why?"

"I don't think Caleb wrote the article. It's the first time I've seen him have a byline. I think someone else wrote it and gave it to him. I'd like to know who it was."

Zoey exhaled. "That is huge, but now that you say that, it makes sense. We'll see what she can do."

"Done." Gordon called out. "Where do I put it?"

"Trash or in the storage closet," Grace said. "Your choice."

"Trash. What time does Zoey come into the office?"

"Nine o'clock, but she's working from home today and probably tomorrow. She'll train you on all the systems. Call her after you get back from the café. Here's her number." Grace scribbled the number on a notepad and gave it to him.

Smiling, Gordon saluted her with two fingers. "I put the city manager position description on your desk, and now I'm off to the café and a soul-satisfying stirring of the pot."

He stopped at the door. "Seriously, Grace. Thank you for what you're doing. I was ready to leave Briar Glen."

The door clicked shut, and Grace snapped her fingers. *The sponsor float.*

She sat down at her computer and typed an email. After correcting a few typos, she emailed it to Zoey, asking her to edit it.

A few minutes later, Zoey called her. "I made a few corrections so you would sound more like a stuffy official bureaucrat and not so project director cool, which is your normal tone. You're inviting a company to sponsor the parade that is the day after tomorrow?"

"Sure. Do I apologize for leaving them out?"

"No. You'll see what I added. You mentioned their business will become the talk of Briar Glen for the rest of the year if they don't sign up as a sponsor."

"I like that."

"Good, I just sent it to you. I haven't heard from Caleb's friend yet. She told me she might offer to buy him lunch. I told her you would reimburse her. That was okay, wasn't it? Gotta go. The boy just went quiet." Zoey hung up.

Chuckling, Grace copied Zoey's version into her email and then sent it.

The front door opened, startling Grace, then slammed shut. It opened again. "Dammit."

Leah. Grace hurried to the door.

"I hate that door. Zoey called me and told me about our newest outrage. I told the sheriff, and he said he had a little business at the gas station, so Walt will know too. Where's Gordon?"

"He went to the café for a cup of coffee and to ask if anybody knew why the newspaper hates Briar Glen and what it has against the parade."

"I brought Mardi Gras beads so we can clutch our pearls. They are green and gold." Leah pulled a green necklace and a gold necklace out of a sack, then tossed the sack to Grace.

"Perfect." Grace copied Leah and put on two necklaces.

"Zoey gave me the idea. She said her group had St. Patrick's Day jewelry and T-shirts they wore every year, so they're spreading the word for everyone to wear green to show their support for Briar Glen."

"That's brilliant. I'll call Granny."

When Nora answered, Grace said, "Zoey's group is wearing their St. Patrick's costume jewelry and T-shirts."

"That's a brilliant idea. I'll let my ladies know. I bought you a shamrock T-shirt for the parade as a surprise. Do you want me to drop it off on my way to the grocery store?"

"I'd love it."

Nora hung up, and Grace rolled her eyes.

"Everything okay?" Leah asked.

"Granny loved the idea and will be here in two minutes unless she gets stopped for speeding. She has a shamrock T-shirt for me."

"I'm here to help, Grace. What's my assignment?"

"Really? There's isn't anyone to answer the phone, and I expect we'll be inundated with calls. If you'll sit at Bella's desk and answer the phone, that would be a tremendous help."

"Do I have to be nice?"

"Just today, and tomorrow if you're here. Anything after the parade ends is out of my realm of caring."

"Two days is probably my max." Leah rolled to Bella's desk while Grace carried Bella's chair to the conference room.

Gordon strolled into the office, whistling.

Returning from the conference room, Grace said, "Must have gone well at the café."

"Sure did." He glanced at their necklaces. "I was going to tell you about the brilliant idea somebody had to support Briar Glen and the St. Patrick's Day parade, but I think I'm looking at the source. Everybody wears green, right?"

"Only a genius would have thought of that," Leah giggled.

Gordon chuckled. "You wouldn't believe how many people are taking credit for the idea."

"That's great news," Grace said. "That tells me how well received the idea is."

"Somebody asked me if the bank was still going to be a sponsor this year," Gordon said. "They've always been a sponsor, so I said yes. Grace, I've actually never heard from the bank for this year. I have the banner the bank used before the new crowd bought it out, but now I don't know if I should put it on the truck or not."

Nora came into the office. "I brought your shirt, Grace. Murphy's waiting for me in the car. We have a playdate at the dog park. I'll see you later." She handed Grace her shirt and left.

Peering at Gordon's face, Grace asked, "Are you going to call Piper Franklin?"

"In person would be best, but I thought the subject should be coming from you since you are managing the parade."

"Is there an issue Grace needs to know about?" Leah asked.

"Piper has the reputation for calling in loans and shutting down businesses. Half the café said to leave her alone, and the other half said no one is above the rules especially with supporting the children's program."

"What did Mayor Dorsey do?" Leah asked.

"He ignored it."

"What brought all this on?" Grace asked.

"At the end of your meeting yesterday, someone asked if the bank was sponsoring the parade this year after all, and her answer was a flat no."

"Who asked?" Grace narrowed her eyes.

"I didn't see it, but those who did said it was Caleb."

Grace and Leah exchanged a glance.

"What do you want me to do?" Leah asked.

"Call Zoey. Her friend needs to know." While Leah was on the phone, Gordon asked, "Are you going to see Piper, or let it drop?"

"I think I have to go."

"Go where?" Ryan strolled into the office.

"To the bank. Gordon, give me the sponsor list, and do you have a copy of the agreement the city council members signed stating they will be sponsors?"

"I can dig, but according to Mayor Dorsey, the signed agreement was optional."

"How long will it take you to check?"

Rushing to his office, Gordon said, "Give me two minutes."

Tapping Leah on the shoulder, Grace said, "I need to talk to Zoey."

"Grace wants to talk with you." Leah handed the phone to Grace.

"Zoey, do you know if we would have online records for the city council?"

"Yes, their formal meeting notes, their charter, all of that is online. What do you need?"

"I need to know whether a city council member signs an agreement to be a sponsor for the parade, and specifically whether Pipe Franklin signed one."

"I'll check." While Grace waited, Leah broke the silence with repeated clicks of her pen.

"Grace, I have three signed agreements, but Mayor Dorsey wrote waived at the top of the Piper Franklin's agreement and initialed it."

"Thanks." Grace handed the phone back to Leah as Gordon came out of his office.

"I don't have anything except meeting notes for the city council, but here's the sponsor list for this year. The bank isn't listed."

"She didn't sign the agreement, but I'd like to make a courtesy call."

"We can go in the truck," Ryan said.

The truck tires hummed along the road.

Grace stared out the passenger window, watching the bare trees blur by.

"You still do that," Ryan said quietly.

"Do what?"

"Look out the window when you're planning how a conversation will go."

Grace blinked. "I do not."

"You did it on the school bus too."

She glanced at him, surprised, and then looked back out the window, hiding a small smile.

Ryan parked near the front door, and they went inside together. The bank lobby smelled faintly of cleaner and the distinctive chemical scent of new construction plastics and paint. Their footsteps squeaked on the slick vinyl floor. Two metal chairs sat against one wall beside a narrow island with chained pens and a rack of bank brochures. Three customers stood in line at the lone teller window.

Ryan nodded toward the hallway on the right.

A brass nameplate on the closed door read: Piper Franklin, Regional Vice President.

Grace tapped twice.

"Come in." Piper didn't bother to hide the irritation.

Ryan opened the door and followed Grace inside, leaving it ajar behind them.

The office was carpeted and neat, blinds half-drawn, striping the room with narrow bands of light. There was no visitor's chair.

Piper removed her reading glasses and looked up. "Yes?"

Ryan stood beside Grace as she laid the parade sponsor list on the desk.

"I think there's just been a minor oversight," Grace said lightly. "I don't see the bank listed this year."

"That's not an oversight," Piper pressed the gold disc pendant on her necklace flat, and then leaned back with her fingers steepled. "We're choosing not to participate."

Ryan shifted slightly. "Is there a reason?"

Piper tapped the edge of a spreadsheet on her desk like numbers mattered more than conversations.

Her eyes slid to him. Cool. Assessing. "Mr. Pearce, this is technically a city council matter. Would you mind giving us a few minutes?"

Grace started to object, but Ryan touched her elbow.

"It's fine. I'll be right outside."

He stepped out, closing the door. The click sounded louder than it should have.

Piper waited a beat.

"You're new," she said.

Grace smiled politely. "I understand you are too. It's been a tradition for council members to sponsor the parade. Optional, of course, but expected."

"Traditions become flexible when circumstances change."

"Like what circumstances?"

Piper's gaze sharpened. "Like a deputy mayor creating waves in places she doesn't understand."

Grace felt the air shift. "I'm not sure what you mean."

"I think you do," Piper said calmly. "And I think you'd be wise to let certain things go. The parade. The questions. The curiosity."

"The sponsor list isn't curiosity," Grace said. "People are asking about it."

"Policies matter," Piper said smoothly. "Until something more important comes along."

"Such as?"

"The stability of local businesses."

A cold thread slid down Grace's spine.

"The bank reviews its portfolio of outstanding loans regularly," Piper continued. "Including the one on the distillery."

Grace went very still.

"I'd hate for an unnecessary review to create stress for Mr. Pearce. He's worked very hard to build that place."

"Are you threatening him?" Grace asked quietly.

"I'm suggesting you focus on the parade," Piper said. "And let the rest sort itself out."

A knock sounded.

Ryan's voice. "Everything okay?"

Piper's pleasant smile returned instantly. "Just fine."

Grace raised an eyebrow. "Let me know if you change your mind."

She stepped into the hallway and closed the door behind her.

Ryan was waiting. He didn't speak. He studied her face.

That was enough.

"What did she say?" he asked quietly.

"Later," Grace said, walking toward the lobby.

"Grace."

"Let's go."

Grace set the sponsor list on the console. Ryan adjusted the edge so that it lined up perfectly.

She noticed. Of course she did.

"She's not sponsoring the parade," Grace said.

Ryan frowned. "That's it?"

Grace shook her head.

Ryan waited.

"She mentioned loans," Grace said.

Ryan went very still. "What about loans?"

"She said the bank reviews outstanding loans regularly." Grace swallowed. "Including yours."

The air inside the truck felt thinner.

Ryan's jaw tightened.

"She threatened you," he said.

"She threatened you."

He held her gaze for a long moment.

"That means we're close," he said quietly.

Grace blinked. "What?"

"If she's nervous enough to go after my loan, we're close to something she doesn't want found."

I hadn't thought of it that way.

Ryan's voice softened. "You okay?"

She nodded. "I didn't expect her to go after you."

Ryan's mouth twitched faintly. "Grace. I've been on your side since second grade. I knew what I was signing up for."

That almost made her laugh.

Chapter Fifteen

The heater kicked in, and Grace stretched her legs toward the vent to warm her toes. The sky outside was a hard, cloudless blue that only made the cold sharper.

Rhythmically thumping his fingers on the steering wheel on the way back, Ryan side-glanced at Grace. "I don't have an update on the water sample, so actually, that is my update."

Giggling, Grace said, "Eloquently put. Now, what did you say?"

Ryan chuckled. "It's simple. Sully didn't have the results back this morning and hopes to late this afternoon. If he does, we'll run out to the waterworks to pick them up."

"What if I'm busy?"

"Then we'll go when you aren't busy."

"What if..."

Relaxing his hands, Ryan said, "If you go with me, I'll let you help with dinner."

"Cooking lessons? You aren't just teasing me, are you? I'd love a cooking lesson."

"Then that's what we'll do."

Ryan drove around to the back and stopped next to Grace's car. "I have a few errands to run. I can return with lunch, if you'd rather skip the café."

"That would be great. See you later."

When she went inside, Gordon asked, "Any luck?"

"No. I'm glad I walked in there knowing about her exemption to being a sponsor, or I might have taken a completely wrong direction. She didn't change her mind, but I let her know people were talking."

"How did she take that?" Gordon asked.

"She didn't seem to care."

"Interesting stance for a banker in a small town," Leah said. "I have a question for you. Who is working with Dr. Higgins?"

"What do you mean?" Gordon asked.

"A friend of mine is one of the long-time volunteers for the parade..."

"There are volunteers?" Grace asked.

"You didn't let me finish. Dr. Higgins called a meeting of the volunteers this morning and told them the city wasn't interested in working with them," Leah said.

"What a sneak." Grace asked. "I never heard of volunteers before. What do they do?"

"They're like a hospitality crew, making sure the visitors leave with a good feeling and come back another day to spend their money."

"Gordon, are you taking notes of all these things?" Grace asked.

"I started a list this morning."

"Gordon, didn't Valerie pitch the old Baxter Feed building as a volunteer center last month?" Leah asked.

"Yes, but the city council turned it down."

"Sounds like I should talk to Dr. Higgins. Does Dr. Higgins have family in Briar Glen?"

Furrowing his brow, Gordon said, "Now that you mention it, I don't think so. Maybe she saw an opportunity to provide a service to a small town."

Leah snorted. "Not the Dr. Higgins I've seen. I think she found an opportunity for leverage."

Grace paused.

"In that case," she said slowly, "I'd prefer talking in person."

Placing a call to the animal shelter from her office, Grace was initially put on hold. When the eager front desk volunteer finally answered, she reluctantly forwarded Grace's call to Dr. Higgins' office manager. Grace and the office manager settled on a five o'clock meeting in a library reading room.

She sent a text to Ryan. "Call when you have time."

Her phone rang.

"I pulled over on the side of the road. What happened?"

"It wasn't urgent. I only wanted to tell you I have a meeting this afternoon at five at the library. We'll talk at lunch."

"Tell Gordon and Leah I'm grabbing sandwiches for them too. See you later."

Grace pulled out Bella's notes manila folder. After skimming the first twenty pages, she slumped in her chair and then slammed her fist on her desk. She marched into Gordon's office and dumped it on his desk.

"What's wrong?" he asked.

Gritting her teeth, Grace said, "This was in Bella's desk drawer. I found a list like we're talking about making for the parade and a few other things that could have helped if we'd had it even yesterday. This is a comprehensive training manual for a city manager, with a special section for parades."

"Don't you want to go through it yourself first?"

"Maybe later. Right now I'm in no mood to read. I'm going for a walk."

Grace grabbed her coat and pushed out the door.

A soft whir followed her. She turned just as Leah rolled up behind her.

"You sure can move fast for a short gal when you're hacked off."

Grace threw her hands up. "I can't believe how much time we've wasted worrying and scrambling to figure things out when Bella had the answers all along. We wouldn't even be dealing with this volunteer mess if she'd shared that manual. It was sitting inside her desk drawer the whole time."

"Maybe the answer to why is in those papers."

"Maybe." Grace shoved her hands into her coat pockets and picked up her pace, the bitter cold tightening her chest with every breath. "But come Sunday morning, it's not my problem anymore. I'm thinking I should go home on Monday."

"That is not the best idea you've ever had," Leah said, keeping pace beside her. "What about Ryan?"

Grace exhaled hard. "It's complicated."

"Slow down. You're wearing my arms out."

Grace eased her pace and glanced at the bright St. Patrick's decorations fluttering from the light poles.

"That's better," Leah said. "Complicated sounds right up your alley."

"Not this time, Leah."

They returned to the office in silence.

Grace went straight to her office and closed the door gently to keep from slamming it. Sitting down and crossing her arms on the desk, she dropped her forehead onto her arms, fighting tears.

She raised her head and glanced at the closed door. *Why is everything so hard?*

She exhaled, then consciously slowed her breathing.

Maybe Leah's right. But it's done. I have to move forward.

She straightened up and walked into Gordon's office. Concern tightened his face.

"The walk did me a world of good," she said. "What have you found?"

Gordon tapped his finger on Bella's notes. "You were right about the volunteer details being in there."

"What's our involvement?"

"Probably not what Dr. Higgins is expecting. I've marked a page for you so you can tell her what we'll do instead of her telling us what she wants. According to Bella's notes, the city gave gifts to the volunteers, and that's it. I'll check with Zoey. She can help me check how much the city spent for the gifts last year so we'll know the expected price range."

Smiling, Grace said, "I dreaded that meeting, but now I'm looking forward to it. Speaking of a meeting, don't we need to go over Saturday's plan?"

"Lunch is here," Leah called as the front door opened.

"Right after lunch?" she added.

"Sure do."

Grace hurried out of Gordon's office, then slowed when Leah raised her eyebrows.

"Conference room?" Ryan asked, smiling as he looked at Grace.

She met his gaze.

The only sound in the room was the hum of the copy machine.

Gordon broke the silence. "I'm on the phone with Zoey. I'll be there in a minute."

Leah took the sacks from Ryan and rolled past Grace. "You coming, or not?"

Ryan took a step toward Grace.

She turned and walked to the conference room. He fell into step behind her.

As Leah unpacked the food, she asked, "Are all the sandwiches the same?"

"Yep."

Joining them at the table, Gordon asked, "Does the distillery have a banner, Ryan?"

"Quite a few. Why?"

"In my research this morning, I've discovered the sponsors' float isn't limited to the city council, even though the city council members have traditionally donated to our children's summer program to show their support of the local charity at the St. Patrick's Day parade. Since the bank opted out, I have a big space that should be filled, and thought maybe you'd help me out. If the distillery donated a dollar to the summer program, the spot would be yours."

"The distillery has donated to the children's summer program every year, so that's already in our budget. What size banner are we talking? I'm pretty sure the distillery has a St. Patrick's Day banner, but I can't remember how big it is. It might be close to the length of the truck bed."

"That would be fine," Gordon said. "Can you get it to me today? I'll be working on the float tomorrow."

"I can do that right now. Do you want to go for a ride, Grace?"

"Can't. Gordon and I have work to do so he can focus on the float tomorrow."

"I'll be back before five."

After they went over the three pages of instructions for Saturday, Grace said, "So much of this is common sense, but by Saturday morning my brain cells will be fried."

Frowning at the list, Gordon said, "You won't be alone. We'll need high visibility vests." He added them.

"Hey, Leah. We're going to need vests on Saturday while we're working the parade. Can you take care of that?" Grace called out.

"Gotcha. I'll have them tomorrow."

Checking vests off his list, Gordon tapped his pen on the paper. "While we were eating lunch, I remembered the city council turned down Dr. Higgins' proposal for the city to donate the Briar Glen Feed and Seed warehouse on the edge of town to the hospitality volunteers so they could host events."

"Could that be what she was talking about? Is that something the mayor could approve?"

"It would take an override, but that's just paperwork."

"Maybe she's counting on my sweet nature to sign off on it to make the volunteers happy."

Sitting at Bella's desk, Leah snort-laughed, then called out, "Funniest thing I'd heard all day, Grace."

Glancing down at his list again, Gordon cleared his throat. "That's pretty much all I've got."

Returning to her desk, Grace opened her email, discovering a reply from the Fair Valley Manufacturing lawyer's office. One sentence in particular jumped out. "While our client enthusiastically supports local charities, she has expressly instructed us to ignore solicitations."

The owner of Fair Valley Manufacturing is female.

Strolling into her office with his list in his hand, Gordon said, "Things are looking up. I got a call from the owner of the dealership where Daniel worked. He's going to provide a driver for the sponsors' float so I can be free to help with the parade on Saturday. The driver and I will set up the banners in the morning, so I'll be here before lunch tomorrow."

Grace exhaled. "I didn't expect you at all tomorrow and had hoped you'd help with the lineup as long as you could on Saturday. That really takes away a lot of pressure."

Peering at the list, she asked, "Is there anything on the list for tomorrow that we can do today?"

"It would be nice to know how many volunteers there are. Zoey told me that last year there were twenty-seven volunteers, but I've heard there are more people interested in getting involved with all the publicity the parade has been getting. Zoey's looking for items in our price range and how quickly we can get them. My wife will shop for us if Zoey can't get away."

"I'll ask Valerie how many she has, but I'm not confident that we'll get an accurate number from her. Let's double last year's number to be safe and count on fifty-five or sixty. If we've overestimated, we'll have award and donation items on hand."

"We'll get on it right away. I came across a few pages in Bella's notes that were torn out of a notebook, and they read more like a diary. I'll set them aside so you can decide later what you want to do with them."

As Gordon turned to leave, Ryan burst into the office. "I found our St. Patrick's Day banner, and it isn't as big as I thought."

He handed the banner to Gordon, who held up the colorful banner of the Hearth & Barrel's wooden sign surrounded by shamrocks, a pot of gold, and a dancing leprechaun.

"This is perfect." Gordon chuckled.

"I love it," Grace said as Leah applauded.

While Gordon carefully rolled the banner, Ryan said, "Are you ready to go to the library, Grace?"

Grace rushed to her office and picked up the leather portfolio she'd found in the storage closet, then put on her coat. "Now I am."

On the way to the library, Grace told Ryan what she'd learned about the volunteers from Gordon.

"This is going to be a really interesting meeting. Where'd you get that portfolio? I don't remember seeing it before."

"I found it in the storage closet. I think it makes me look more professional."

"I would have said formidable." Ryan chuckled.

When Grace stepped into the library, she paused just inside the door. The usual hush was replaced by the indistinct murmur of voices as small groups gathered around tables, papers spread out between them. The place felt alive in a way she hadn't expected, the quiet space humming with purpose instead of silence.

As they approached the main desk, the librarian who was chatting with a young reader paused, then pointed toward a hallway. "Your meeting is in the first room on your right, Grace."

The meeting room was small but had a whiteboard at the front, and a rectangular table in the middle of the room with two chairs pushed in on each side and a chair at the head of the table facing the door. The windows overlooked the side parking lot and beyond that, a dog park.

Grace plopped her portfolio at the head of the table and removed her coat, then draped it over the back of the chair.

She strolled to the window and gazed at the dog park; a father watched while a preschool girl threw a ball for their attentive German shepherd. After the shepherd snatched up the ball from the ground, the little girl laughed while the dog ran around the fenced-in perimeter and then dropped it at her feet with its tongue lolling in a semblance of a grin, and waited for her to throw it again.

Ryan remained near the door. "It's after five."

"I expected her to be late," Grace said.

Ryan joined her at the window, close but not crowding her. "Power move, but you claimed the power seat. This is going to be an interesting meeting."

"I doubt if she expects me to be prepared." Grace turned toward Ryan, a half step closer. "How long has the distillery been in your family?"

Ryan chuckled. "I come from a long line of chemists. My great-great-grandfather was a bootlegger in the hills of Georgia. My great-grandfather built the original distillery along with living quarters for his family. The distillery became a success thanks to all he had learned from his father."

"That's much farther back than I realized. Where did the name come from?"

"According to family legend, my great-grandmother often quoted an old Irish proverb that translates to there is no hearth like your own hearth, so Hearth & Barrel was the natural choice for the distillery."

Grace smiled. "I knew there had to be a story."

When Valerie entered the room, Ryan resumed his spot near the doorway and quietly closed the door.

Valerie glared at Grace's portfolio, then pulled a chair around to the end of the table.

She scanned the room and sniffed, then set a thick binder on the table like evidence at a trial.

After Valerie rested her gaze on Grace, Grace smiled politely. "Thanks for coming."

Valerie remained standing. She studied Grace first, measuring.

Ryan leaned against the wall, arms folded, watching without speaking.

Valerie finally took her seat. "I only have a few minutes. Volunteers don't manage themselves."

"Of course," Grace said easily. "I don't think we'll be very long."

Valerie opened the binder but didn't look down at it. Her eyes stayed on Grace.

"Even though you are at the mayor's office before everyone else, there are several items you may not be aware of that have been standard procedure for years."

Grace met Valerie's gaze. *How do you know when I go to work?*

When Valerie glanced down at her binder with its pre-checked items, Grace opened her portfolio and nodded, pen poised.

"I'm certain there is a policy list at your office if you are interested, which includes welcome baskets, meal vouchers, and parking passes. All the standard courtesies that may seem old-fashioned to your generation, but the rest of us see them as respectful."

"I'm aware of the policy, Valerie. I approved it."

Valerie leaned back and studied Grace, recalculating.

"We have twenty-two volunteers this year," she said.

Grace tilted her head slightly, her pen hovering over her portfolio.

Silence stretched.

Valerie's fingers tightened on the binder before she snapped it closed with crisp finality. "I have another meeting."

Grace glanced at Ryan. His hand dropped from his folded arms to his side, ready without looking ready.

Grace stood. "Thank you for coming."

Valerie paused at the door and looked back. "You seem very calm for someone who just inherited a logistical disaster."

Grace smiled. "I find things usually make more sense once you have all the information."

Valerie held her gaze a second too long, then closed the door behind her.

Ryan exhaled softly. "She was feeding you garbage."

Grace nodded. "She was, wasn't she?"

"Why?"

Grace clicked her pen. "Because she doesn't want me looking somewhere else."

Ryan's expression changed. "Where?"

"I don't know, but I have a feeling it has something to do with the volunteers." Grace picked up her portfolio.

Ryan opened the door. "Let's go see Sully."

On the way, Grace said, "I think I messed up Valerie's original intent."

"How is that?"

"The city council turned down Dr. Higgins' proposal for the city to donate the city-owned abandoned building on the edge of town to the hospitality volunteers so they could host events. Gordon told me the mayor could override the decision."

"I was certain she was about to say something then had a sudden change of mind when she announced she had another meeting."

"I think I understand. The claim of standard policy was supposed to put me on the defensive."

"Right, then she could follow up by offering to let you rescue the volunteers by approving the donation."

Grace stared out of her side window. "Hopefully Sully's report will be just as easy to explain."

They didn't speak the rest of the way; Ryan quietly hummed and Grace leaned back in her seat, relaxed.

The water treatment plant sat low beside the river, all concrete and chain-link fence and the constant hum of machinery. It smelled faintly metallic in the humid late afternoon air.

Sully met them at the door before they could knock; his usual serene smile was missing.

"Come on," he said quietly.

He didn't take them to his office; instead he led them into a small side room with a metal desk and no windows. He motioned for Ryan to close the door behind them.

Ryan stood stiffly at the door.

Sully laid a thin report on the desk like it weighed fifty pounds.

"This is preliminary," he said. "The lab called me as soon as they saw it."

Grace looked at the paper with its columns of numbers and chemical names she recognized from warning labels and environmental articles: Lead, Mercury, Cadmium, Arsenic. The words were all highlighted.

"All far above safe limits," Sully said.

Grace's stomach soured, and bile rose in her throat.

"How?" Ryan asked.

"That's what we don't know yet."

Sully rubbed the back of his neck. "I called the lab back, and they re-ran the samples. Same result."

Grace looked up. "Who else knows?"

Sully hesitated. "I was required to notify the EPA."

Ryan swore under his breath.

Sully nodded. "They told me to keep this quiet because I stumbled across one of their highest priority investigations."

Grace's mind raced. *Highest priority.* "They think it's deliberate, don't they?"

Sully looked away. "They asked for historical records, discharge reports, and industrial permits on everything upstream."

Ryan and Grace exchanged a look. *Upstream.*

"I told them I was required to report it to a supervisor. They balked and argued with me."

"Have you reported it?" Ryan asked.

"When I suggested reporting my findings to the mayor so there would be no official record, they agreed. They made it very clear, though. Don't say a word about this to anyone," Sully said.

Ryan and Grace exchanged a glance, and he half-reached for her but pulled his hand back.

Grace met Sully's gaze and nodded slowly, but pieces were already shifting into place. *Volunteers. City resistance. Parade logistics. Now poisoned water.*

Someone is desperate to keep certain things from being looked at too closely this week.

Sully exhaled. "I'm glad you're here, Grace. I would have been stuck between losing my job or being arrested."

"I'm glad I could help."

"Let us know if you need us," Ryan said.

As they headed back toward town, Ryan asked, "Are you going to leave your car at the office and ride home with me?"

"No, I've got a few things to do, and I suspect Gordon might still be there. I'll have to chase him out the door."

Ryan chuckled. "He's turned into a real dynamo, hasn't he? You gave him permission to be the city manager, and he has run with it."

"I might be a little late, so you don't have to wait for me to eat."

"Have you forgotten? I owe you a cooking lesson."

"Really? We're still on? I didn't want to push. I'm looking forward to it."

After Ryan dropped her off in the back, he waited until she went inside before he left.

Grace shook her head as she removed her coat, remembering when the school's biggest bully and two of his buddies trapped her in a corner at school the day before Christmas break when she was in the second grade. Ryan pushed past them and grabbed her hand, and they walked away together as the bully and his friends taunted them. *Ryan told me he'd always watch my back.* Grace giggled. *And I told him I didn't need another stalker.*

"Is that you, Grace?" Gordon called out.

"Sure is. What are you working on?" She strolled into his office.

"Zoey's a genius. She found discontinued St. Patrick's Day tea towels for only two dollars each and bought all seventy-five of them because she didn't want anyone else to have any like ours. She sent her husband to pick them up, and he'll be here with them in a few minutes. What about you?"

"Ryan dropped me off to pick up my car, but I saw the lights on and was worried you'd lost track of time."

Gordon smiled. "We'll have a busy day tomorrow, but in a good way, for a change."

"Good night, Gordon. See you in the morning."

Chapter Sixteen

Grace stepped into the distillery and stopped. It smelled... different. Warm. Savory. Rich.

Not the usual sharp bite of grain and alcohol that clung to the air back here. This was deeper. Heavier. The smell that belonged to kitchens and long wooden spoons and something left to simmer on purpose.

For a moment, she simply stood there and breathed it in before she went to the kitchen.

Ryan stood at the small stove with a cast-iron pot, sleeves rolled up, wooden spoon in hand. Willow lay on the floor nearby, nose on her paws, watching him like this were a normal part of the evening.

Grace dropped her backpack on the chair. "I don't even want to talk about today."

"Good," Ryan said without turning. "Because I'm not asking."

He stirred the pot slowly and steadily.

"What are you doing?"

"Making gumbo."

Grace blinked. "You cook gumbo?"

"I cook a lot of things. Sit."

She obeyed before she thought about it.

Ryan slid a cutting board a fraction so it sat square on the counter, then handed her a knife and an onion.

"Chop."

She stared at it. "I don't cook."

"You do now."

Grace sighed, but started cutting. Uneven pieces. Too big. Too small.

Ryan didn't correct her. He just kept stirring.

After a minute, he said, "Come here."

She stepped beside him, shoulder brushing his arm.

He tipped the pot slightly so she could see.

The flour and oil had turned a deep caramel color.

"That's the roux," he said. "This is where people mess up. Too fast and it burns. Too slow and it never gets there."

Grace leaned closer. "How long have you been standing here?"

"Long enough."

He handed her the spoon. "Stir."

She did. Slowly.

Ryan's hand came over hers, guiding the motion. "Keep it moving. Don't stop."

Her face warmed for reasons that had nothing to do with cooking.

"You can't rush this part," he said quietly. "You have to watch it. Wait for it to change."

She glanced up at him. He was watching the roux, not her.

But she felt it anyway.

They stood like that for a long moment. The hum of the still in the next room. The soft scrape of the spoon against cast iron. Willow's quiet breathing.

She stirred in sync with the hum of the still.

Ryan stepped back. "You didn't burn it. That's impressive."

I didn't look behind me once.

She smiled faintly. "Low bar."

He added the vegetables to the pot with a loud sizzle, and the rich smell filled the room.

Grace leaned against the counter and just watched him work.

"I had the worst day," she murmured.

"I know."

"How do you know?"

"You didn't say anything about me fixing the cutting board."

She laughed before she could stop herself.

Ryan set two bowls on the table and gestured for her to sit.

They ate in comfortable silence for a minute.

"This is unfairly good," she said. "How do you do this?"

"I know when it's there, which is what it takes for gumbo and distilling."

Grace set her spoon down and looked at him.

"You make this feel easy."

"It is."

Grace let out a slow breath. *Maybe this is what moving forward feels like.*

She shook her head. "I'm used to carrying everything myself."

Ryan stepped closer. "I know."

The room went very still.

Grace reached for him first this time.

The kiss was slow. Intentional. Warm. Nothing like the uncertain one from that morning.

Ryan's hands settled at her waist like they belonged there.

When they pulled apart, Grace rested her forehead against his chest.

"Okay," she murmured. "That helped."

Ryan smiled into her hair. "Told you. I know you."

Ryan stepped back just enough to stir the pot again before the roux thought about sticking.

Grace stayed where she was for a moment, while he did something she hadn't noticed before.

"Do you do this every night?" she asked.

"Cook?"

"Make everything feel... normal."

Ryan shrugged. "I like normal."

She leaned against the counter while he dished out seconds neither of them needed.

Willow stationed herself strategically between them, hopeful.

Grace slipped her a tiny piece of sausage under the table.

Ryan didn't look up. "I saw that."

"She looked hungry."

"She always looks hungry."

They ate slower this time. Talked about nothing important. The parade route. Whether Willow had always been this spoiled. Whether gumbo counted as soup.

At one point Grace got up to rinse her bowl.

Ryan took it from her. "You cooked. I clean."

"I chopped one onion badly."

"Still counts."

She didn't argue.

He moved around the kitchen, wiping off the stove, lining the towel neatly along the counter, and setting the spoon in the sink.

The quiet hum of the still filled the space between them.

Grace felt it then.

She didn't feel the need to be anywhere else.

Ryan dried his hands and leaned against the counter. "Do you want to watch something? Or sit and pretend we're tired?"

Grace smiled. "Sit and pretend."

They ended up on opposite ends of the sofa that slowly and naturally became not opposite at all.

Willow climbed up and wedged herself between them like a furry chaperone.

Grace laughed softly. "She does not trust us."

Ryan's arm rested along the back of the sofa behind her, not touching; just there. Sliding off the sofa, Willow abandoned them and curled up on her rug.

They talked in low voices about nothing until Grace's eyelids grew heavy. She didn't realize she'd leaned into him until Ryan shifted slightly to make it easier.

After a while, he said quietly, "You should go to bed."

She nodded, but didn't move.

"Grace."

"I know."

She stood reluctantly and then paused.

"Goodnight, Ryan."

He held her gaze. "Goodnight, Grace."

She hesitated a half-second like she might say more.

Then she went to her room and closed the door softly behind her.

For a moment, she stood there listening to the quiet hum of the still and the faint creak of the sofa in the other room.

Ryan was still awake.

She didn't know why that comforted her.

Chapter Seventeen

Grace woke with a small, uncertain twist in her chest.

For a moment, she lay still. Replaying the night before... *Did I let my imagination get away from me?*

The faint smell of coffee drifted down the hallway.

She slipped out of bed and slowly dressed.

Grace's hand hovered over the doorknob, then pulled back.

She turned instead, eyes darting. Jerking clothes out of her suitcase and stuffing them into the tote bag. She smoothed the bedspread flat, pulled out a neatly folded soft cotton shirt, and shook out the shirt and hung it in the closet.

A soft whine sounded at the door. *Willow.*

Grace opened the door, giving Willow a scratch behind the ears before walking more quietly than usual toward the kitchen with Willow softly padding alongside her.

Ryan stood at the counter with his back to her, pouring coffee into two mugs.

He nudged one of them so the handle faced her before she even stepped into the room.

"Morning, Grace."

Just like always.

"Morning," she said.

Lured into the kitchen by the snap of crumbling crisp bacon, the snick-snick of grating cheese, and the rapid whisking of scrambling an egg, Grace sat on her barstool and sipped coffee. When Ryan pulled a tortilla out of the oven, waved his hands, and set a plate in front of Grace, she was tempted to applaud.

"Breakfast taco. Would you like to try homemade salsa?" He set a small bowl of green chile salsa and a spoon next to her plate.

Joining her at the breakfast bar, Ryan nudged Grace's elbow with his. When she side-glanced at him, he smiled, and his nose twitched in that cute, funny way that always exasperated her.

"Quit being annoying; I haven't had enough coffee." Her smile sneaked past her words.

While they were eating, Grace's phone rang. "It's Granny. I'm almost afraid to answer it."

"Have you seen today's paper? They published a special edition for the parade. Don't miss the editorial page, and dress warm today." Nora hung up.

"What did she say?" Ryan asked.

"Dress warm." She took another bite while he chuckled.

"It's going to be like that, is it?"

"Of course," Grace said, "and she asked if we've seen today's special edition from the paper."

Ryan raised an eyebrow and pulled out his phone. “Should I be excited or concerned?”

“Dealer’s choice.”

He glanced at the screen and let out a low whistle. “Oh, this is fancy.”

“What?”

He turned the phone toward her. “Front page is all parade. Photos of floats everywhere.”

Grace leaned closer. “That’s actually nice.”

“Headline says, ‘Briar Glen goes all out for its annual St. Patrick’s Day Parade.’”

She smiled faintly. “I like that.”

Ryan scrolled. “Subhead says record floats, record attendance expected.”

Grace exhaled. “Well. That’s something.”

Ryan tilted his head. “You’re waiting for the part you’re not going to like, aren’t you?”

She nodded. “Keep scrolling.”

Grace scrolled past the front page and stopped. “Granny said to check the editorial page, and she wasn’t kidding.”

Ryan leaned in to see the screen, his shoulder brushing hers. Grace didn’t move away.

He read for a second, then gave a low hum. “Oh... that’s sharp.”

“What?”

Ryan pointed. “‘The parade belongs to the people, not institutions that refuse to stand with them.’”

Grace winced. “Well. That went straight to the till.”

Ryan kept reading. “They never say ‘bank,’ but they absolutely mean ‘bank.’”

Grace shook her head. "I almost feel sorry for Piper."

Ryan glanced at her. "Almost?"

"Very almost. Piper never even bothered to pretend she was concerned about the town, did she?"

Grace set the phone down on the counter and took the last bite of her taco. "What are your plans for today?"

"I'm going to Mack's place this morning to help with the float. What about you?"

"I suspect my morning will be devoted to wrapping the gifts for the volunteers or putting them in gift bags, depending on what Zoey has decided. If I have time, Gordon has some things he found in Bella's notes he wants me to review."

"If we don't finish the float this morning, we'll break for lunch. Want me to bring something to your office?"

Grace topped off their coffee. "You don't have to do that."

"You're right," Ryan said. "I'm going to anyway. Twelve-thirty?"

She studied his face while he talked and unconsciously drifted a step closer.

Willow whined.

"Ready to go out?" Ryan shrugged into his coat and headed for the door with Willow at his side.

Grace drained her cup, picked up her backpack, and slipped her holster into place inside her waistband before following them outside.

Ryan fell into step beside her as she walked toward her car. "Any special requests?"

She shivered as she opened the door. "Something hot."

"I'll see what I can do."

Grace slid into the seat and glanced at him.

Ryan winked.

She glared as she firmly closed the door and sped down the driveway. Stopping before she turned, she unzipped her coat partway to cool herself as her face warmed and her heart pounded.

"Totally caught me off guard," she grumbled as she headed into town.

Shamrocks and dancing leprechauns on storefronts on both sides of the street lit her way as she drove through downtown. The yellow security light in the back parking lot softened the shadows, making easier to see the surroundings.

Hurrying inside, Grace flipped on the office lights and blinked at the abrupt harshness of the fluorescent lights that centered on two folders and a note on her desk. *Gordon.*

She read the note. "I found more than I expected on the abandoned city building. I haven't read through everything, so much of it might be irrelevant. The other folder has the personal papers I told you about."

After starting the pot of coffee in the conference room, Grace sat at her desk, reading the city council minutes and taking notes as she went along.

When Gordon's outside office door opened, Grace hurried to his office as he carried in a large cardboard box.

"The gifts for the volunteers are in this box along with the gift bags we'll have to pack them in. It isn't heavy, it's just awkward." Gordon set it on his desk. "I have two more boxes in my car's trunk."

"Do you want this in the conference room?" Grace asked.

"Yes, if you can manage it."

Grace picked up the box. Gordon was right; it wasn't heavy, but she couldn't see around it. She cautiously searched with her foot before each halting step to be sure it was safe to continue. When she finally reached the conference room and set the box down on the table, she exhaled.

Gordon carried in a second box with a smaller white box precariously balanced on top of it. When Gordon tipped the larger box only slightly, the smaller one slid off, but Grace caught it before it hit the floor.

"Good catch. I ordered cookies yesterday from the bakery and picked them up on my way home yesterday evening. The mechanic from the dealership will be at my house in twenty minutes with the truck. I'll be back after we've installed all the signs."

After Gordon rushed out the back door, Grace put the cookies next to the coffee pot and returned to her desk.

The office was unusually quiet without the parade chatter and phone calls, and the coffee pot's abrupt gurgle amplified the silence. Glancing toward Bella's vacant desk, which only compounded the sense of desertion, Grace shuddered, then began with the thinner file.

She had expected detailed notes, careful lists, and crossed off reminders. What she found read more like thoughts Bella hadn't meant for anyone to see.

After she'd read the first few sheets, she rolled her shoulders then went to the conference room and poured a cup of coffee for strength and grabbed a cookie for comfort.

Grace returned to her desk with the folder spread open in front of her.

She turned to the next page, then leaned back slowly in the chair.

This wasn't a diary. This was Bella trying to convince herself she had done the right thing.

Bella's careful handwriting filled the page.

"Mother always said there is only one correct way to do a thing, and that is the right way. I have tried to remember that this week.

"Sometimes following the rules feels uncomfortable, but rules exist to protect people from confusion and mistakes. If the old records cause confusion now, then removing them is the responsible choice.

"I didn't like changing passwords. It feels secretive. But I was told it is important to be thorough. Thoroughness prevents errors.

"I hope I didn't miss anything. Mother said people who are calm usually know what they're doing."

Grace set her cup down mid-sip.

Bella had always loved rules. After her father died, rules were how she made the world make sense.

Grace looked toward Bella's empty desk, the coffee mug still angled toward the computer as if she might return.

Bella hadn't erased records because she was careless.

She had erased them because someone had spoken to her in the language she trusted most.

“Bella...” Grace whispered.

This wasn’t negligence.

This was manipulation.

Grace’s eyes drifted back to the page.

“Why?” she murmured.

Because if Bella had been talked into this, someone had needed those records gone.

Grace straightened in the chair.

Now, I dig.

She took a distracted bite of her cookie without tasting it and pulled the larger folder toward her.

Grace flipped through the city council minutes until she was three years back. When she found the first page, she started reading, pen already in her hand.

A sudden gust of wind from the front door interrupted her concentration and startled her. When the door closed, she jumped up from her desk, but the front door opened again.

“You and me, door. One of these days,” Leah grumbled.

Nine o’clock already.

Leah rolled in. “What’s the orders for the day, Your Honor?”

“You’re as bad as Ryan.” Grace set down her pen and quietly closed the folder and her notebook.

“I’m flattered. So, what are we doing this morning?”

“Gordon dropped off the gifts and maybe instructions from Zoey. I haven’t checked. I thought we’d just call her. Everything is in the conference room.”

"Let's see what we've got. Maybe we can figure it out on our own, then we'll call Zoey and she'll set us straight. Do I smell coffee?"

"Yes, and Gordon brought cookies, too. Probably because he felt guilty. He's working on the sponsors' float."

"Speaking of which, did you see today's special edition?"

Nodding, Grace said, "It was a shocker, but I'm not complaining."

While Leah poured a cup of coffee, Grace opened the boxes and pulled out a stack of small green sacks, bags of chocolate coins wrapped in gold foil, and rolls of sparkly shamrock stickers.

Nibbling on a cookie, Leah said, "So far, I'm thinking assembly line."

Opening the second box, Grace said, "And you're right. Zoey must have stayed up all night."

She carefully lifted out a white tea towel that had been neatly folded to show off the printed design of a pot of gold with a rainbow and tied like a package with green twine. "What do you think? Prep the sacks first? I'll put on the stickers."

While they sat at the table with stickers and sacks, Leah said, "Bella's not doing well."

"Does she have any family with her?"

"The hospital told the sheriff they expected her niece from Tennessee to arrive this evening."

"According to Bella's notes, the volunteer sacks are handed out by the sheriff's department. Is that what you'll be doing tomorrow?"

"No, a woman in payroll always hands out the volunteer gifts. She likes to do it, and I'm glad it's not me. We'll take them over today so she can organize them. I'm assigned to the mayor's office until after the parade."

After they had packed half the sacks into a large box, Leah said, "Let's take a coffee break. I was afraid to have a cup around our sacks."

"A spilled cup of coffee would have fallen right in line with our luck, wouldn't it? How about a change of scenery?"

"We can use my desk as our breakroom," Leah said.

Sipping her coffee, Grace asked, "Do you know why the city council didn't approve the donation of the city's abandoned building to the volunteers' association?"

"Just the scuttlebutt I've picked up from being stuck at the front desk at the sheriff's department. Mack didn't understand why the volunteers couldn't share the building with other organizations just like it always had been. From what I've heard, Dr. Higgins had charts and data and to back up her case, but Mack wasn't impressed."

"Is that the same Mack who has the St. Patrick's float?"

"Yes. He's a farmer. I understand he and Mr. Pearce Senior have been friends since they were kids. Both of them are highly respected in the community, so Dr. Higgins couldn't find anyone to plead her case for her."

Her charts and data would be in the city council minutes. "That's interesting. How long ago was that?"

"I'm not sure. Just guessing, maybe six months ago."

Gazing into her empty cup, Grace said, “Break time’s over.”

Leah groaned. “Okay, but you need to work on your procrastination skills. They’re the same as they were when we were seven.”

Just as they finished setting the last sack into a box, Gordon rushed in.

“I’m so sorry I was gone longer than I expected. We had four more merchants who brought banners to my house because they wanted to show their support for the parade. The newspaper's support has injected new life into Briar Glen. What do you want me to do?”

“Would you take the boxes to the sheriff’s department?” Grace asked.

“I was planning on it. I had thought I was the only one looking for a job somewhere else, but turns out I was wrong. Instead of swapping job leads in Atlanta, the discussions this morning were centered on what types of businesses could thrive in Briar Glen. Even our dour curmudgeon from the Chamber of Commerce perked up.”

“The boxes are ready whenever you are,” Grace said. “We kept fifteen for us to have here tomorrow for any unofficial volunteers who help the mayor’s office.”

“I’ll take them now, then be back after lunch.” Whistling while he carried the boxes to his car in the back, Gordon paused in the doorway. “I’m glad you’re here, Grace.”

After Gordon left, Grace’s phone buzzed with a text. “Lunch might be later than I thought.”

Grace replied, "I'll take care of my lunch. Don't worry about it."

"Anything wrong?" Leah asked.

"No. Just Ryan letting me know he wouldn't be here for lunch."

"You won't starve. I packed my lunch, and you know I always..."

"Packed an extra sandwich for your imaginary friend, Petey. You still do that?"

"Yep. Sadly, Petey's not around since I got old, but there's always somebody who could use a sandwich. Do you want to eat now or later?"

"Later, unless you're starving. I've got a couple of things to do first."

"Later is better for me too. I have a couple of thoughts I'd like to run past Zoey."

Opening her folder with the city council minutes and picking up her pen for notes, Grace picked up where she'd left off.

Reviewing her notes after reading the first six months of the minutes from three years ago, Grace exhaled. *Walt, Mack, and Henry voted against every idea Mayor Dorsey proposed, while Valerie voted in favor.* He said 'progress'; they said 'risky'.

"Ready for lunch?" Leah asked. "Today's special is a ham and cheese sandwich and chips."

Rising from her desk and hurrying to the conference room, Grace said, "Sounds perfect. Do you want coffee? I can make a fresh pot."

"No more for me."

While they ate, Gordon joined them carrying a case of bottled water. "I thought we'd need this for the weekend."

He surveyed the conference room. "We could use a refrigerator in here. I think I saw one at the thrift store. I'll call them. Anything going on?" He set three bottles of water on the table, then grabbed a cookie before he sat down.

"I've been reading the city council minutes. It looks like the mayor votes only in case of a tie."

"That's true. The voting rules are three pages long, but you got the gist."

While they were eating, Gordon's phone rang, and he stepped out of the conference room to answer.

When he returned, Gordon said, "Ted Conway asked if you would come to the newspaper office for a quick interview this afternoon. I told him I'd call him back."

Grace swallowed hard. "Do you expect this to be a verbal ambush?"

Gordon shook his head. "Oh no. Mr. Conway is not that kind of publisher. This is a great opportunity for a follow up to the parade."

Grace side-glanced at Leah, who nodded.

"Okay. When is he expecting me?"

"At your convenience. I'd suggest this afternoon."

"Take him one of our volunteer appreciation gifts," Leah said.

"Call him back and tell him I'll be there soon."

When Gordon left to call Mr. Conway, Grace moaned. "I'm not ready for this."

Leah snorted. "You were born ready. Just think of it as another one of your projects. Mr. Conway is just another stakeholder. Maybe you can pick his brain."

Grace furrowed her brow, deep in thought. *The Briar Glen Feed and Seed warehouse.*

"Okay, Grace." Gordon interrupted her thoughts. "You can go whenever you're ready."

Pulling on her coat, Grace sighed. "Hopefully, I won't be long."

As Grace drove toward the newspaper office, the growing excitement over the parade was evidenced by the new handmade signs in shop display windows and gold and green balloons on lampposts.

The newspaper's small parking lot was nestled behind the building. After parking, Grace rushed to the front door, then, taking a big breath, pushed the door open. The bell over the newspaper office door gave a tired jingle when she stepped inside.

The place smelled like printers' ink, stale coffee, and lingering cigar smoke. Stacks of back issues leaned against one wall, and a single desk lamp cast a warm circle of light over a cluttered workspace.

"Grace!" Mr. Conway popped up from behind a computer monitor like he'd been waiting for her to arrive. He held a partially smoked, unlit cigar between his teeth. He set his cigar down on the edge of his desk. "Come in, come in. I won't keep you long."

Grace smiled politely. "I appreciate it. I brought you a gift from our team. It's what we're giving to the volunteers who will be helping with the parade tomorrow. We wanted to recognize how much help the special edition was in reviving the excitement for the parade in Briar Glen." She handed the gift bag to him.

"This is a surprise. Thank you. Sit, sit."

He motioned toward the chair across from his desk while he peered into the sack. "Very special. The volunteers will be delighted."

She took the offered chair, easing a pile of papers out of the way.

"I thought it might be nice," he said, settling back into his seat, "for folks to get to know the woman who's wrangled this parade into shape. People like stories. Makes them feel connected."

Grace laughed softly. "Wrangled is generous."

"Modest, too," he said, tapping a few keys on his computer. "All right. Simple questions."

Grace folded her hands in her lap. "That sounds suspicious."

Mr. Conway peered over his screen and chuckled, "You never know, but I like how you think. So, what brought you to Briar Glen?"

She hesitated a fraction too long. "My grandmother lives here, and I lived here for most of my elementary school years. Short answer: family and history. The usual reasons people come home."

He nodded, satisfied. "And how does it feel stepping into such a visible role in the community?"

Grace shrugged lightly. "It feels like a lot of lists and phone calls and hoping I didn't forget something."

He grinned. "People will like that answer."

He asked about the parade, the volunteers, and the town traditions. Nothing difficult. Nothing sharp.

Grace relaxed without meaning to.

Then he said, “One last thing. How do you handle the pressure when things don’t go as planned?”

Grace thought about Daniel. About Bella. About the article. About Piper.

She smiled instead. “You fix what you can and keep moving forward.”

Mr. Conway nodded slowly as he typed. “That’s a good line.”

He tilted his head. “Do you have any questions for me?”

“I remember the old poultry processing plant and how many of my friends’ parents worked there. Now that Fair Valley Manufacturing has bought the plant, do you see more opportunities for employment for our residents?”

He raised his eyebrows. “Have you thought about running for governor? You’re a natural-born politician. Short answer, it depends, but according to their filing with the state, it has possibilities.”

Mr. Conway scurried to a stack of newspapers that was near the front door. “If you have a little time, I have something in the classifieds somewhere.”

While Mr. Conway carefully dug through the stack of papers, Grace wandered to the display case that was next to the front counter to admire Mr. Conway’s typewriter collection.

“The oldest typewriter I have so far is from the 1910s, but I’m always searching for any older ones.”

Returning to his desk a few minutes later, while he waved a newspaper, Mr. Conway said, "Almost wore myself out, but I found it."

Grace joined him at his desk, and he handed her the paper. "When Fair Valley Manufacturing bought the plant, the county required it to run a classified ad in the local paper for a week. Dr. Higgins paid for the ad in cash, but here it is."

Dr. Higgins? Grace ducked her head to hide her surprise as she read the classified ad. "I see what you mean. Is this their Georgia state tax identification number?"

His face was flushed from his effort as he smiled with satisfaction. "Exactly. Depending on how deep you want to dig, this will help you research the company further."

He leaned back in his chair with his hands folded across his stomach. "What else can I help you with?"

She smiled. "What can you tell me about the Briar Glen Feed and Seed warehouse? Why is it abandoned, but in such demand?"

Mr. Conway chortled as he leaned forward, his chair creaking. "Despite everything on your shoulders, you've taken the time to read the city council minutes, haven't you?"

Mumbling, he turned to his computer. "I know I've got it somewhere."

While Mr. Conway moved closer to his screen and taped on the keyboard, Grace glanced at her surroundings, a hoarder's delight and a fire marshal's nightmare with old newspapers stacked on every surface and along the wall.

"Got it." Mr. Conway leaned back. "I wrote a piece a year or so ago but never published it. It's the history of the Barnes family who established the Barnes Feed and Seed Warehouse. The town renamed it when Mr. Barnes left the warehouse to the town of Briar Glen in his will with the stipulation that it would never be sold."

Mr. Conway strolled to the printer across the room and removed a stack of papers. When he returned to his desk, he stapled them together then slipped them into a folder. He handed the folder to Grace. "This should help you understand your hometown."

"But it could be donated."

Mr. Conway furrowed his brow. "You might not want to say that aloud. Very few people have made that connection."

Grace stood when he did. "Is that it?"

"That's it. See? Quick."

She paused at the door. "Thank you for the information about the Briar Glen Feed and Seed warehouse."

He waved a hand dismissively and met her gaze. "Don't mention it. Seriously."

Chapter Eighteen

Stepping into the cold air, Grace pulled her collar together to protect her neck. Feeling oddly exposed, like an unprepared actor stepping into the spotlight on a stage, she put her head down and rushed to the back parking lot, the chill air biting at her cheeks.

Reaching into her coat pocket for her keys, Grace was startled by a bitter voice.

"You proud of yourself?"

Grace instinctively placed her right hand on her hip, lightly rubbing her thumb on her holster.

Standing beside Grace's car, Piper had folded her arms across her coat, holding it tight against the wind with white knuckles. Her face was pale and drawn, and her hands were trembling.

"Piper?" Grace glanced around the empty lot. "What are you doing here?"

"What am I doing here?" Piper's voice was thin and sharp. She let out a brittle laugh. "I should be asking you that."

Grace kept her voice even. "If this is about the parade sponsor..."

"They fired me this morning."

Grace gaped at Piper, then blinked. "What?"

Piper's eyes burned. "Corporate doesn't like bad press. They especially don't like being painted as the villain in a small-town parade story. According to my termination notice, my performance 'doesn't align with the bank's community image.'"

Grace swallowed. "I didn't write that article."

"You didn't have to," Piper snapped. "You stirred it up. You put the spotlight on us, and you made me a problem corporate needed to solve."

She stepped closer, and her coat blew open.

"They started looking at every file I touched. Every loan. Every 'community project' I approved."

The warehouse loan. Grace slightly shifted her weight to avoid reacting.

"I had nothing to do with your job," Grace said.

Piper's jaw flexed. "You should have stopped asking questions when Daniel died."

Grace went very still.

The wind rattled a loose piece of siding on the building.

"What does Daniel have to do with this?" Grace asked quietly.

Piper looked like she wished she could swallow the words back.

"Nothing," she said too quickly as she patted the disc on her necklace. "You just don't know when to leave things alone."

Grace studied her. "What am I not leaving alone, Piper?"

Piper shook her head, anger rising again to cover the slip. "You think this is just about a parade? About sponsorship? You ruined things that were already in motion."

The words hung between them.

What was in motion? The collapse of Briar Glen?

"Maybe I should thank you. Being fired gives me an excuse to disappear. You aren't as lucky. You think you're smart, but you have no idea what you've done," Piper said quietly.

Grace's voice stayed calm. "What have I done, Piper?"

Piper glanced toward the street, then back at Grace. For the first time, the anger faded just enough to reveal something underneath it.

Fear.

Piper stepped back. "You should go home to Atlanta where you belong," she said. "Before you get yourself hurt."

She turned and walked away, leaving Grace standing beside her car with her keys still in her hand.

For a long moment, Grace didn't move.

Her hand shaking, Grace unlocked her car and climbed in.

She furrowed her brow. *It wasn't just about the parade.*

As she drove through town, Piper's words echoed in her head. *No idea what you've done.*

When she walked into her office, Leah said, "You just missed Ryan. I told him you went to the newspaper office, and he said he had an errand and would see you later."

Grace nodded and continued to her office and pulled out Daniel's files.

While she flipped through the files, Leah rolled into her office with a tote bag on her lap. "Nora came by while you were gone and left you this. She said to tell you she added your shamrock shirt for tomorrow. How did the meeting go with Mr. Conway? Was it rough?"

Grace paused and smiled. "It was actually enjoyable. I think he was pleased we pulled together a gift bag for him."

"Are you okay?"

"I'm fine. I'm looking for the documents I saw earlier. I didn't understand why Daniel had them..."

"Let me know if you need any help." Leah put the delivery from Nora on Grace's desk and left.

Grace found what she'd been looking for. An application for a one million dollar loan to improve the Briar Glen Feed and Seed warehouse approved by Piper Franklin with 50% of the funds released, dated six months ago with the borrower listed as Briar Glen Volunteer Association LLC.

Turning to the last page, Grace gasped at the signature. *Valerie Higgins.*

As she stared at the page, highlighter in hand and coffee forgotten beside her, the scent of soap and fermenting grain filled the room before a shadow fell across the desk.

Ryan.

She looked up and flinched at his expression.

“Grace, we need to talk.”

“You’re right,” she said. “We do.”

He nodded toward the back door. “Outside.”

Something in his voice made her grab the loan application and her coat without arguing.

The cold hit them hard as they stepped behind the building.

Ryan scrubbed a hand over the back of his neck. He only did that when he was thinking through something he didn’t like.

“Sully met me behind the grocery store,” he said. “Truck driver from the diner tipped him off. A bunch of rigs were supposed to pick up loads at the Briar Glen Warehouse last night. They got told to stage in the old poultry plant lot instead.”

Grace’s pulse kicked. “There’s nothing at the warehouse.”

“Right. They left this morning,” Ryan continued. “Nobody would tell them when or even where they’d be loaded. Drivers were losing money just sitting there.”

“What were they supposed to be hauling?” she asked.

“He didn’t know. Just said the poultry place reeked. Concentrated cat urine and rotten eggs.”

Grace’s stomach dropped. “That’s not chicken feed.”

Ryan’s mouth twitched despite himself. “No. It’s not.”

She swayed slightly, and his hand came out automatically, steadying her at the elbow.

“I told Sully I’d check it out tonight,” Ryan said.

Grace’s head snapped up. “You what?”

He frowned. “Grace, this isn’t theory anymore.”

“Sully was afraid to get close,” she said.

“So I’ll be careful.”

“You are not going alone.”

“I wasn’t planning on...”

“You just said you were.”

He exhaled slowly. “I know you. You’re going to march into Valerie’s office and demand answers.”

The accuracy of that stung.

“I’m positive she’s at the bottom of this.”

They stood there in the sharp cold, Grace shivering, then stepping closer to Ryan for warmth. Ryan automatically put his arm around her.

Grace shoved the loan application into his free hand. “Then read that.”

Ryan removed his arm as he scanned each page, his jaw tightening as he reached the signature.

“Valerie Higgins,” he said flatly.

“And approved by Piper Franklin.”

Ryan frowned at the line. “Do bankers get commissions?”

“Not like salespeople.” *Only kickbacks.*

He glanced at Grace. “One million dollars for upgrading an old building might be reasonable.” He read through the pages again. “Was there a payout schedule included?”

Grace shook her head. “Fifty percent already released.”

Ryan let out a low breath. “That’s not a coincidence.”

"No, and there's more. Valerie Higgins paid for the required classified ad for Fair Valley Manufacturing in cash."

He met her eyes. "You were going to confront her."

Grace took half a step away as she lifted her chin. "Yes." *Piper saw money. Valerie saw leverage.*

"And you think I'm going to let you do that alone?"

"And you think I'm going to let you sneak around that plant after dark?"

They both stopped.

Ryan's voice dropped, steadier now. "We're past the point where either of us gets to be reckless."

She crossed her arms, but her shoulders weren't as rigid as they had been. "That sounds like something you'd say while doing exactly that."

A small smile slipped across his mouth then disappeared. "Probably."

The tension eased by half an inch.

"So," he said. "What's the plan?"

Grace watched the bats stitching the dusk together with quick, precise turns. Her mind was already doing the same.

"You're right," she said finally. "We don't split up. We don't surprise anyone. We gather proof first."

Ryan studied her. "That's my line."

She looked at him. "I'm allowed to learn."

He stepped closer, lowering his voice. "Talk to me before you confront Valerie."

"Yes."

"Before."

"Yes."

He slid his arm around her shoulders, less protective now, more steadying.

"It's too cold out here to think," she muttered.

"Then let's go inside and think," he said.

They walked back in together.

When they were inside, Gordon asked, "What's our transportation plan for tomorrow?"

Forcing herself to shift into her role as mayor, Grace focused on a reply to Gordon's question.

"Let's meet here then walk together to the high school. I think trying to go anywhere in a vehicle before the parade is over will be too challenging," Grace said. "Everyone should park in the back parking lot."

"Zoey will staff the office with me tomorrow," Leah said. "I'll let her know about parking. I'll be here at seven in the morning."

After Leah and Gordon left, Ryan said, "I'll follow you home."

"I'll meet you there. I have to go by Granny's and pick up extra clothes."

"No, you don't. Nora and Murphy dropped off clothes for you. I was here." Ryan pointed to the bag on Grace's desk.

Grace's mouth curved slightly. "I stand corrected."

After locking up, Grace headed toward the distillery. Smiling at the green glow of downtown from the now-familiar St. Patrick's Day lights and decorations, Grace glanced back at Ryan's truck, which was within inches of her bumper.

Once on the dark highway, Ryan dropped back so that his lights didn't blind her, but close enough so no other car could slip between them.

Slowing for the turn at the driveway, Grace exhaled. After parking, she waited while Ryan nudged his truck close to her car.

She grabbed his hand with both of hers for the warmth when he climbed out of his truck. Chuckling, he put his arm around her while they rushed to the distillery.

Once inside, Grace dropped off her backpack in the living room and carried her clean clothes to her bedroom while Ryan and Willow went outside.

Hanging her shamrock shirt on the closet door handle in readiness for the morning, Grace inhaled the now-familiar distillery aroma of a sweet, malty cloud with hints of fruity and spicy notes from fermentation mixed with her bedroom's unique Gracie-soap fragrance, as Ryan so annoyingly called it.

Putting away the last item from the tote, Grace smiled as Willow nudged the bedroom door open.

"Hello, pretty girl." Grace stroked Willow's back and rubbed her face, and then the two of them headed for the kitchen that beckoned her with the scent of garlic and butter.

Ryan stood at the stove, wooden spoon in hand, steady as ever. The rhythm of it, stir, pause, adjust heat felt almost meditative.

Grace leaned against the counter, sleeves pushed up, watching him without meaning to.

"You're hovering," he said without turning.

"I am not."

"You are."

"So what?" She stepped closer and peered into the skillet. "What is that?"

"Chicken piccata."

Grace inhaled the aroma of seared chicken mingled with garlic. "That sounds complicated."

"It's not. It just sounds impressive."

She smiled faintly. "You like things that sound impressive."

He glanced at her over his shoulder. "We absolutely do."

Willow shifted her weight expectantly near the island.

When Ryan pointed the spoon at the dog, Willow sat immediately.

Grace laughed softly and reached for the lemons on the counter. "What can I do?"

"Zest those."

She picked up the tool that was next to the lemons and frowned at it. "This looks dangerous."

"It's a grater, Grace."

She picked it up daintily between her fingers and wrinkled her nose. "I stand by my statement."

He moved behind her to adjust the cutting board, his arm brushing lightly against her back.

Neither of them commented on it.

She worked carefully, concentrating harder than necessary. "You check the time yet?"

Ryan didn't answer immediately, then said, "Twice."

She nodded once. "Okay."

She exhaled after zesting one lemon and pointed to the small pile. "Is that enough? Say that's enough."

Glancing over his shoulder, he said, "One more."

Glaring at his back while she pushed her hair away from her face with the back of her arm, she zested a second lemon.

The pan sizzled as he added the wine, and steam rose in a quick white bloom, then settled.

Grace inhaled. "That smells like a bona fide restaurant."

"Because it is."

"You know what I mean." *Annoying, as usual.*

His smile gave it away. He did.

They moved around each other easily after that. She set the table without being asked while he poured the water. Willow positioned herself exactly between them, hopeful.

When they finally sat, the house was smaller in the best way, warm and contained.

Ryan bowed his head briefly out of habit. Grace watched him.

When he looked up, she said quietly, "We'll be smart."

"Yes," he said.

Not *I will.* Not *You will.* We.

They ate slowly, discussing the weather and sneaking bits of chicken to Willow, and intentionally pushing aside the tension and apprehension ahead of them. No rush, no strategy session. Just chicken drenched in lemon and butter, interrupted by soft clinks of silverware against plates.

Afterward, Ryan washed and rinsed the pots and pans while Grace dried them.

When he handed her the sauté pan, their fingers lingered a fraction longer than necessary.

"So, is your battery good?" he asked casually.

"Fully charged."

He nodded. "Mine too."

She set the last pot in the cupboard and gazed at him. "What about your holster?"

He met her gaze. "Yes."

Silence again, with no tension, only awareness.

Ryan flipped off the kitchen light. "Ready?"

Grace took a breath and followed him into the living room. "Yes."

He cocked his head as he examined her. "Will you be warm enough?"

Grace glanced at her long-sleeved shirt, then turned on her heel and rushed to her bedroom. Putting on her sweatshirt, she returned to the living room and grabbed her coat. "Yes."

They stepped out into the cool, moonless Georgia night and rode in comfortable silence. When they reached downtown, the barriers were in place for the parade, so Ryan drove around and through a residential area.

When they passed the city park, Ryan said, "Do you remember the time we took on the big kids?"

Grace nodded. "I haven't thought about that in a long time. I got grounded for fighting, but it was worth it."

"You fought pretty good for a scrawny little girl. You were certainly tougher than you looked." Ryan side-glanced at Grace.

"If Leah hadn't come riding in on her bicycle screaming 'Cops,' we could have finished it."

Ryan snorted. "I don't know about that."

As they neared the water treatment building, Grace sat up straighter in her seat, and her breathing quickened. When she glanced at Ryan, they exchanged a look. His hands were tight on the steering wheel.

After the former poultry processing plant came into sight, Ryan put his hand on her shoulder, and she relaxed.

The old poultry plant shouldn't have been lit up at ten-thirty at night, but it was.

A dull industrial glow leaked through grimy windows along the side of the building; not bright, and not obvious, but just enough to say something inside was alive.

The acrid chemical smell hit them as soon as they stepped out of the truck. A sour burn that didn't belong in a farming town.

Grace pressed her sleeve to her nose. "That's not feed."

Ryan's mouth twitched. "No. It's not."

They moved along the fence line, keeping to the shadows.

A forklift whined inside the loading bay. Metal clanged, and a man's voice barked something unintelligible.

Ryan crouched beside a stack of discarded pallets and peered through a gap in the warped siding.

His body went still.

"What?" she whispered.

He didn't look at her. "They're cooking."

Through the crack, stainless steel tables lined one wall. Large industrial burners roared beneath metal vessels that definitely hadn't been used for chicken in years. Clear tubing ran between tanks, and steam curled upward in thin chemical threads.

Men in gloves and industrial respirators moved deliberately, transferring liquid into blue plastic barrels.

Railroad cars sat open along the tracks beyond the loading dock as temporary storage, ready for distribution.

Grace's pulse pounded in her ears.

Ryan lifted his phone and took a quick photo through the gap, and then another.

When he leaned closer, she breathed, "Ryan."

"I need one clean shot."

He slipped along the wall toward a window where the glass had been replaced with cloudy plastic sheeting.

Grace grabbed his sleeve. "That's close enough."

He met her eyes. Calm. Determined.

"I'll be careful."

He moved before she could stop him.

Grace crouched alone in the shadows, her heartbeat loud enough to give her away.

From where she hid, the nearest railroad car, half loaded with barrels, was visible. The forklift operator jumped down and walked toward the building, disappearing inside.

The railcar was unguarded.

Grace's mind raced as she calculated distances.

She hated this feeling, but she understood it. Before she could talk herself out of it, she moved.

The metal ladder was cold and gritty beneath her palm. She lifted herself just high enough to photograph the barrel labels.

Chemical codes. Hazard warnings. *Proof.*

A voice shouted from inside the plant.

She dropped flat against the side of the railcar just as a beam of light sliced across the yard.

Flashlight.

Grace barely had time to slide beneath the railcar before boots crunched on gravel nearby.

Her breath froze in her lungs as the beam paused.

Swept again.

"Thought I heard something," a man muttered.

Grace stayed perfectly still.

After an endless few seconds, the boots retreated.

She counted to ten before moving.

When she slipped back toward the pallets, Ryan was there.

His face was pale and furious.

"What were you thinking?" he hissed.

"You don't get to ask me that."

"You could have been caught."

"So could you."

"Grace..."

Headlights suddenly flared across the lot.

Ryan grabbed her hand and pulled her down behind the pallets as a truck rolled slowly through the yard.

The vehicle paused and then idled.

Ryan's grip tightened around Grace's fingers, and then the truck moved on.

They didn't breathe until the gate clanged shut behind them.

Holding hands, they raced to the truck and rode in silence back to the distillery.

Once inside, the front door shut behind them with a heavy click, and Willow whined.

Grace waited in the kitchen for them to return from the outside break.

Ryan paced into the kitchen, then turned on her.

"I thought I was going to have to drag you out of there."

"I thought you were going to get shot looking through that window."

His anger faltered.

They stared at each other.

"You scared me," he said, quieter now.

Grace's voice softened. "That's how I feel every time you walk toward something I can't stop."

Ryan stepped toward her and rubbed a hand over his face. "I shouldn't have gone that close."

"I shouldn't have climbed the railcar."

The silence hung like a suffocating fog.

"We don't split up like that again," he said.

"We stay together," she added.

He stepped toward her and cupped her face in both hands, firm and steady.

"You matter too much."

The kiss wasn't gentle. It was the kind you give when you realize you don't get unlimited chances.

When they broke apart, their foreheads rested together.

"We're in this," he said.

Grace nodded once. "Then we stay."

Ryan took her hand and led her to the living room. Sitting so closely together on the sofa, even the adoring Willow couldn't wiggle in between them.

Ryan wrapped Grace in his arms, and she leaned against his warmth and listened to the familiar faint drip of condensation from the back of the distillery while she closed her eyes.

"Grace? Grace..."

Waking from a deep sleep, Grace mumbled, "Need fairies."

Ryan chuckled. "You're probably right, but it's two o'clock. We've got a busy day tomorrow."

Grace nodded and padded off to her bedroom.

Chapter Nineteen

Opening her eyes, Grace giggled at Willow's nose that was inches from hers. "I didn't close my door very well when I finally crawled into bed, did I?"

Chuckling from the doorway, Ryan said, "Willow woke me up, so I thought we'd wake you up too. It's parade day, and coffee's ready."

"Get out of here so I can get dressed."

"Come on, Willow. Gracie's not good company until she's had her coffee."

Ryan closed the door, and Grace gathered her clothes and then showered.

After she dressed, Grace strolled to the kitchen and her cup of hot coffee that she knew would be waiting for her.

As she drank her coffee, a knock at the door startled all three of them. Not a polite knock. A firm one.

"This can't be good. It's six in the morning." Ryan strode to the door, with Grace and Willow following him.

Ryan glanced at Grace before opening the door, and she stepped back.

The sheriff stood on the porch, hat in hand. A deputy waited by the cruiser.

"Morning," Ryan said cautiously.

The sheriff's eyes shifted past him. "I need to talk to both of you. Inside." Grace crossed her arms. "What's wrong?"

The sheriff ignored her and stepped in without invitation.

Grace and Willow led the way to the living room, with Ryan bringing up the rear.

"Would you like to sit, sheriff?" Ryan asked.

The sheriff shook his head. "I won't be here long. You two want to tell me why you were at the old poultry plant last night?"

The only sound was the drip of condensation from the still.

Ryan didn't look at Grace, and Grace didn't look at Ryan.

The sheriff nodded once. "That's what I thought."

Grace lifted her chin. "We were concerned."

"You were ten yards from blowing a six-month operation."

Grace blinked. "Six months?"

"Yes, ma'am." His tone stayed calm, but it was as dry as a summer drought. "Six months of surveillance, and six months of coordination with state narcotics, and you two decided to go sightseeing."

Ryan's jaw tightened. "We didn't know..."

"No," the sheriff cut in. "You didn't."

He narrowed his eyes at Grace. "You climbed a railcar."

Her stomach dropped.

"You were seen," he continued, "by one of my deputies who was praying you weren't about to get yourself shot."

Ryan's head snapped toward her. "You were seen?"

Grace swallowed. "Apparently."

The sheriff let that hang for a moment. "Let me be very clear. You are not law enforcement, and you are not undercover. And if you step foot on that property again, I will arrest you for interfering with an active investigation."

The room went very still.

Grace's voice was steady, but softer now. "People are getting hurt."

"I am aware," the sheriff said evenly.

"Then why..."

"Because building a case that sticks takes time. You want this shut down permanently? We do it right."

Ryan nodded once.

Grace exhaled slowly.

The sheriff's gaze softened just slightly. "I know you both mean well. But meaning well and staying alive are not the same thing."

He turned toward the door.

"And Miss Callahan?"

"Yes, sir."

"If you have information, you bring it to me. You don't go collecting it yourself."

He stepped outside, then paused.

"Parade's today. Let's get through it without any drama."

The door shut.

Silence.

Ryan gazed at Grace. "You climbed a railcar."

She met his gaze. "You went inside the building."

He exhaled, and so did she.

For a second they just looked at each other with equal parts guilty and relieved.

"I guess we've been fired," Ryan said softly. "Together."

Grace nodded. "Together."

"So," he said, voice lighter now, "breakfast taco or omelet?"

Grace huffed a breath that was almost a laugh. "Does getting scolded by law enforcement come with breakfast?"

"Only on Saturdays," he said. "No extra charge."

She opened the fridge without asking, handing him the eggs automatically.

He took them like she'd done it a hundred times.

She bumped her shoulder lightly against him. "You're fun."

"Don't tell anyone."

"Breakfast taco," she decided.

While Ryan cooked, he asked, "Didn't you want to be at the office by seven?"

"Yes."

"I'll wrap the tacos in foil, and we can eat there. Are you ready to leave?"

"Give me two minutes."

Grabbing a long-sleeved flannel shirt, Grace returned to the kitchen with her backpack.

"I'm ready."

"Holster?" Ryan asked.

Grace patted her right side.

Ryan picked up a sack. "Would it be okay if Willow stayed at the office? I've felt guilty about leaving her alone so much this week."

"That's wonderful. She can keep Leah company."

"That's what I was thinking."

On their way into town, Grace said, "I'm excited the parade is today, but I've nervous that something will happen, and it will be a colossal flop."

Ryan side-glanced at her. "You always got the jitters right before a big event."

"I did? I don't remember that."

"Because after an event is over, you just move on to the next project. What's your next project?"

Furrowing her brow, Grace said, "I don't know."

"There you are. This one's not over yet."

Grace side-glanced at Ryan. *Why is he smiling?*

Ryan parked in the back parking lot. While Grace unlocked the back door, Willow investigated the parking lot then bounded to Grace to go inside with her.

After turning on the lights and unlocking the front door, Grace made a pot of coffee while Ryan placed Willow's water and her favorite dog mat in Grace's office.

Moving his chair close to Grace, Ryan handed her a taco. While they ate, Gordon joined them in the conference room.

Pouring himself a cup of coffee, Gordon said, "I printed the two float lists from Zoey. One is by float number, and the second one is by the owner's name. Here's your folder. I think we're ready."

"What's my assignment, Grace?" Ryan asked.

"You'll be our pinch hitter. Stay at the office with Leah until Zoey shows up, then join me at the staging area. Leah should be here soon."

Walking to the staging area, Gordon asked, "What are your plans after the parade? Are you going to stay on as mayor? I wish you would."

"Daniel hired me to make the parade successful, and that's all I've thought about since Monday. So, to answer your question, I think after the parade I might take a day off."

Chuckling, Gordon asked, "Are you sure you know how?"

"I might have to research it first."

"Do I check the floats in, or make sure they're in the right spot?"

"Why don't you check them in, and I'll make sure everyone is in the right spot. I need to release some energy, and being bossy sounds fun."

"I forgot to tell you I finally finished the map of the staging area. I put a copy in your folder." Gordon stopped at the entrance to check floats in, and Grace walked to the exit where the floats would leave for the parade, waved to the deputy on traffic duty then returned to the middle of the staging area, ready for the project to take off.

The staging line looked like someone had shaken a snow globe full of pickup trucks and shamrocks.

Grace stood in the middle of it with Zoey's printed lineup in one hand and a pen tucked behind her ear.

At the entrance, Gordon waved vehicles in one at a time, clutching his copy of the list like it was a lifeline.

"Veterans' trailer first float!" he called, voice already hoarse. "Garden club behind them! High school band, you're at the front. Go past the veterans' trailer and take your position!"

A tractor decorated with green garland bypassed Gordon and chugged forward.

Grace stepped into its path and held up both hands.

"Sir. You're number seven."

The driver blinked down at her. "We've always been fifth."

"Today is your lucky day. You're seventh."

He glanced toward the entrance as if Gordon might rescue him.

Gordon avoided eye contact.

Grace pointed. "After the soccer team."

The tractor idled in protest before backing up with a reluctant grind.

Two floats edged too close together, their decorations brushing.

"No touching!" Grace called. "We are not starting a parade with combat shamrocks."

Someone laughed.

Grace waved her thanks.

A group of elementary students in glittering green hats clustered too near a tire.

"Behind the cones, please," Grace said, gentler now. "If you get run over, I have paperwork."

The students' chaperones herded the children back to the cones.

The marching band began warming up off-key.

"Grace!" Tristan waved his clipboard at her. "You're the most talked-about woman in Briar Glen today."

Checking her float list, she said, "Please tell me it's about the parade."

"Mostly." He lowered his voice dramatically. "Also, three different theories about the bank."

Grace kept walking. "I don't want to hear any of them."

As she moved past, Tristan turned to the nearest float owner and announced proudly, "Grace and I go way back. Old friends."

Grace didn't even turn around.

A woman with a clipboard bustled toward her. "We were told we'd be closer to the front."

Grace didn't look down at the list. "You're twelfth."

"But our banner is new."

"That's wonderful. The crowd will appreciate it at twelfth."

The woman hesitated, then retreated.

Grace exhaled.

Generators sputtered to life. Engines rumbled. Someone tested a microphone and produced a shriek that caused three people to wince, a baby to cry, and one dog to bark.

Across the lot, Gordon jogged toward her.

"Kiwanis is asking if they can swap with the Lions." He was out of breath.

"Why?"

"They think they'll get better photos in the sunlight."

Grace closed her eyes briefly. "No swapping."

"Copy that," Gordon said with visible relief.

She scanned the rows.

Band steady in front.

Veterans ready.

Soccer team bouncing in place but contained.

Rescue squad float was centered neatly where it should be.

It wasn't perfect, but it was moving toward order.

For a moment, Grace let herself feel it. The sheer volume of coordination, the phone calls, the lists, the revisions, the second-guessing.

And it was working.

"Five minutes!" Gordon shouted from the entrance.

Grace straightened and walked the line one last time, adjusting spacing with slight gestures and a steady voice.

The parade was ready with a little jealousy, a little good-natured banter, and a lot of noise.

The fire engine blasted its air horn as a signal, and the parade began.

The floats rolled past Grace in a wave of green and noise.

Children darted along the curb, collecting candy. The marching band found its rhythm at last, brass notes bouncing off storefront windows. Applause rose and fell in uneven swells as each float made the turn onto Main.

Grace stood near the edge of the route, scanning for gaps, for stalled vehicles, for anything about to go wrong.

So far, everything was going close to the plan.

Gordon rushed to join her, slightly breathless.

"It's running smoothly." He grinned. "My wife is texting me photos like I'm missing history."

Still tracking each float as it passed, Grace said, "I'll run take a quick peek and check in with the office, then you can watch the parade with your family. There's no reason both of us have to stand in an empty parking lot waiting for floats to appear."

"Really? I'd appreciate it," he replied.

"I won't be long." Grace slipped along the sidewalk, moving against the flow of the crowd. The air smelled like popcorn and kettle corn and diesel fumes.

Hurrying to glimpse the St. Patrick's float, Grace stood with a group of preschoolers as the float appeared. Mr. Pearse Sr. sat high on the float like a man accustomed to being observed, his green cloak draped neatly over broad shoulders rather than worn like a costume.

A silver-threaded stole crossed his chest, and the staff in his hand looked less theatrical than ceremonial, something borrowed from history rather than imagination.

His white hair caught the morning light, and when he lifted a gloved hand to wave, it carried the quiet dignity of someone blessing a crowd rather than entertaining it. The children jumped, waved, and cheered.

The crowds and parade filled the air with laughter, music, and whistles. All normal.

She almost missed her.

Valerie stood half a block down, just beyond the thickest part of the crowd. Not cheering. Not waving. Watching.

Her hands were clasped neatly in front of her coat, posture straight, expression composed. A faint smile touched her mouth, but it didn't reach her eyes.

Those eyes were fixed on Grace.

Grace slowed.

For a heartbeat, the noise of the parade seemed to thin.

Valerie's gaze didn't waver. It wasn't hostile, but it wasn't friendly. It was measuring.

Grace felt it then. Not panic, not yet, but a tightening awareness.

Valerie gave the smallest nod, as if acknowledging something only the two of them understood.

Then the band crashed into a triumphant note, and the spell broke.

A group of teenagers surged between them, laughing and jostling.

When they cleared, Valerie had shifted slightly. She was still there, still watching, but farther back now, partially obscured by green balloons.

Grace forced herself to keep walking; her pulse quickened.

Behind her, the parade rolled on.

When she reached the back door of the office, Grace slipped inside, grateful for the relative quiet. Parade noise drifted through the walls like distant thunder.

Ryan stood near the front window with Willow at his side. Leah was stationed at the curb, waving like she personally owned the parade.

Ryan turned, and his expression softened immediately. "You're back."

"Just for a minute," Grace said, moving beside him. "Gordon wants to watch part of the parade with his family. I told him I'd cover."

Ryan studied her face a second longer than necessary. "You holding up okay?"

She smiled faintly. "Only a few complaints, but no fistfights. I'm calling that a win."

His mouth curved. "Bossy suits you."

She nudged his arm lightly with hers. "Don't say you didn't know that."

Willow shifted eagerly toward the front door, then backed away from a burst of drums.

Ryan glanced down. "She wants to go out, but the noise isn't her favorite thing."

"Smart dog," Grace said.

Their shoulders brushed as they watched the parade pass, close enough that Grace felt the warmth of him through her coat.

"I should get back," she said, though she didn't move.

Ryan nodded slowly. "You always say that before you stay another minute."

She glanced up at him. "Maybe I like this minute."

His eyes held hers a beat too long.

The noise outside swelled, then faded again.

Grace exhaled and stepped back first. "I'll see you after the parade."

"Yes, you will," he said quietly.

She turned toward the door, then paused. "I'm taking the quiet route back. West side streets. Less crowd."

Ryan's expression shifted, just slightly, like he filed the information away.

"Be careful," he said.

"I always am."

He didn't answer, and somehow that felt like an argument they didn't have time for.

Grace slipped back outside and was once again immersed in the music, noise, and excitement of the parade. She walked quickly back to the high school where Gordon waited.

"Only ten more floats to go. Isn't this wonderful? I'm glad you told Zoey to negotiate extending the route for the parade. My wife tells me the streets are packed all along the route." Gordon examined Grace's face. "Are you sure you'll be okay here by yourself?"

"I'll be fine. There's a deputy at the high school exit if I have any problems."

"I'll be back after the sponsors' float. My wife claimed a perfect spot near the beginning of the parade."

After Gordon left, Grace headed back to the entrance to wait for the high school band and the first few floats.

It was quieter here. Not silent because the tunes of the distant marching band carried in waves, but muted enough that her own footsteps sounded loud.

She scanned automatically. The marching band was a block away, which meant the first float was nearly at Main. A deputy at the barrier at the far intersection with his back to her was waving at a car to turn around.

Everything was in motion and where it should be.

"Grace."

She didn't startle. She turned.

Valerie stood in the middle of the road in the crosswalk to student parking, coat neatly buttoned, posture perfectly straight. Too straight.

Grace's eyes went first to the necklace.

Piper's.

"You chose the route away from the parade," Valerie said mildly. "Very efficient."

Grace's pulse steadied instead of spiking. "You made a mistake," she said.

Valerie's smile flickered. "I don't make mistakes."

"The loan for the so-called volunteer association. You signed it."

Valerie's gaze sharpened. "You don't understand what was necessary."

"Bella thought that too." Shifting to face Valerie square on, Grace widened her stance with her feet in line with her shoulders.

A flicker of fear appeared in Valerie's eyes. The crack revealed. It was small, but it was there.

Valerie's hand casually slipped inside her coat.

Grace's hand moved to her hip at the same time.

Valerie's pistol came free.

From behind Grace and to her left, Willow's bark shattered the air.

Ryan.

Willow tore forward, snarling before Ryan could stop her.

Valerie's control snapped, and she swung the gun toward the movement.

Reverberating in the once-quiet space, the shot exploded, and birds fled from the trees.

Concrete burst near Willow's paws.

Grace didn't think. She fired; Ryan fired. Two shots in perfect sync, sounding as one.

Valerie jerked backward, the force spinning her off balance. She hit the pavement hard, her weapon skidding across the asphalt.

Willow lunged forward, snarling, planting herself between Grace and Valerie.

"Sheriff's department!" a voice thundered from down the block.

Grace lowered her pistol and placed it carefully on the ground. Rising, she removed the two objects from her jeans pocket.

Placing his pistol on the ground, Ryan reached Grace in three strides.

The deputy ran toward them, weapon drawn but not firing.

Valerie lay on her side, futilely struggling to reach her pistol, blood darkening her coat at the shoulder and knee.

The calm was gone. Her eyes were wide now, finally human.

Ryan had fear in his voice. "Are you hit?"

"No." Her voice caught in her throat. "What about you?"

"I'm good."

His hand hovered at her waist anyway, checking.

The band rounded the corner a block away, and the applause swelled.

The deputy kicked Valerie's gun away and called for backup and an ambulance.

Grace stood still with Bella's coin pressing into her palm, and Daniel's tie tack cool against her fingers.

Ryan's hand slid into her other hand, and their fingers intertwined.

Valerie lay on her side, breath shallow. When her eyes found Grace's, the calm was gone, replaced by darkness.

Reaching toward her throat slowly, deliberately, Valerie glared at Grace as she yanked the necklace free, and the clasp snapped.

The chain hit the pavement between them with a thin metallic sound. She never looked away from Grace.

Then she closed her eyes as sheriff's department cruisers surrounded them.

Grace's mind snapped into motion.

"We need to divert the parade," she said.

The sheriff looked at her once as he parked, then nodded sharply as if the thought had already crossed his mind.

When he climbed from his cruiser, Ryan met him halfway. Their conversation was quick, low, and efficient, with no wasted words.

Within seconds, orders barked across radios.

Two deputies moved to block the road. The marching band was redirected with confused gestures and frantic waving; the music faltered before picking back up as they turned toward the football field entrance instead of the front of the school.

The parade rolled on, now hidden from the scene by a bend in the road.

Confetti drifted lazily across the empty lot.

The ambulance doors slammed shut around Valerie.

Grace watched the ambulance pull away, sirens silent until it reached the main road away from the parade.

Only then did she let out a breath.

The sheriff strode toward them, expression carved from equal parts relief and frustration.

Ryan moved subtly closer to Grace without touching her.

The deputy who had run in first hovered nearby, still catching his breath.

Somewhere in the distance, the crowd cheered.

The parade continued as if nothing had happened.

Staring in the direction of the sirens, the sheriff said, “She’s talking to nobody right now.”

The sheriff’s words hung in the air. He moved away to confer with his deputies.

Chapter Twenty

For the first time since Valerie's shot rang out, there was nothing for Grace to do.

The parade music drifted faintly toward them, cheerful and oblivious.

Rubbing her palms against her jeans, Grace's hands shook. Not much, but just enough.

Ryan glanced at her hands and stepped closer, his shoulder brushing hers as if anchoring her without making a point of it.

"Cold?" he asked quietly.

She nodded even though she wasn't sure that was quite it.

Across the lot, confetti skittered in the breeze.

Grace's gaze dropped to the shimmering gold speck on the pavement where Valerie had fallen.

She bent down and picked up the small gold disc; its chain snapped cleanly away.

Piper's necklace.

Grace turned it over once in her fingers before slipping it into her pocket beside Bella's coin and Daniel's shamrock tie tack. The coin and the disc rested together, unexpectedly heavy.

She straightened and realized Ryan was close, not crowding, just there.

For once, she didn't step away. Without thinking, she reached for his sleeve. Ryan remained close didn't comment.

Grace stared at the empty patch of pavement, standing very still. She should have felt alone there, but she didn't, and that unsettled her almost as much as the shooting.

"You okay?" Ryan asked.

Grace nodded and crossed her arms, as if trying to hide the tremble in her hands.

"I shot someone," she whispered.

"You stopped her," he said.

She furrowed her brow at the empty patch of pavement, then turned toward the office.

Ryan fell into step beside her, but still giving her space to breathe.

The parking lot already looked almost normal again, and something about that felt wrong.

Too normal.

Grace glanced at Ryan. His jaw was tight, his expression unreadable, but when she touched the pocket where the gold disc rested, he didn't ask.

He just nodded once, like he understood anyway.

She kept walking.

He caught up beside her and brushed her shoulder, the gesture gentle and automatic. A piece of confetti floated to the ground.

"Let's go home," he said quietly.

She nodded.

When he took her hand, she held on.

They walked together toward the office, Willow investigating every bush along the way.

When they reached the truck, Grace exhaled. "I should tell Leah goodbye, so she'll leave and I can lock up."

Ryan nodded. "Project wrap-up."

"Exactly." Grace headed toward the door.

"We'll wait in the truck."

Going inside, Grace sighed with relief. *Only Leah is in the office.*

"I knew you'd stop by," Leah said. "The sheriff is taking full credit and all the heat for the Valerie bust. Well done, anonymous tipster." Leah chuckled.

"How do you know I had anything to do with it?"

Leah snorted. "Show me your pistol."

Grace automatically touched her empty holster then dropped her hand. "I left it at the distillery."

"Isn't that a coincidence? Are you locking up or working?"

"Locking up."

"I've already reminded Gordon my assignment was for the duration of the parade, and I won't be here Monday. The doc says in two weeks I'll be cleared for active duty and back in my cruiser. What about you?"

"The parade was a success, and it's over."

Leah studied her for a moment. "Is that what this is?"

After Leah left, Grace locked up behind her, then turned off the lights one switch at a time.

She stood in the quiet, keys resting cold in her palm.

Temporary. That's what this had always been.

She rolled the keys over in her hand, feeling the grooves press into her skin.

No. She'd give them to Gordon herself.

She sent him a text. "I'd like to drop off the keys."

His reply came almost immediately. "I don't want them, but okay. We're home."

She smiled.

As she closed the door on her way out, the quiet settled behind her.

When she climbed back into the truck, Ryan glanced over. "Good news?"

She lifted an eyebrow. "You noticed."

"You smiled," he said lightly. "I didn't mean to pry."

"Just Gordon. Can we go past his house so I can drop off the keys?"

"Sure."

As Ryan backed out, Grace said, "I hope you know where Gordon lives because I don't."

"If I told you they bought Sara Norton's house, would that help?"

"I would know exactly where Gordon lives."

When Ryan pulled in front of the house, Grace hopped out of the truck, and Gordon met her at the door.

"I didn't want to slow you down, Grace. You've worked hard and deserve some time off before you go on to your next project."

Grace handed him the keys. “Thanks for everything, Gordon. You made a difference. I couldn't have done it without you.”

Gordon's cheeks reddened. “Thank you, Grace. I learned a lot from you.”

They shook hands, then Grace hopped back into the truck.

Grace leaned back and watched the passing scenery on the way to the distillery. Neither one of them spoke, and Willow fell asleep in the back seat.

When they went into the distillery, it was quiet, almost too quiet after the parade and sirens. Grace watched as Ryan strode to the kitchen. She went into her bedroom and pulled out her small suitcase and her tote.

After pulling out all her clothes and laying them on the bed, she folded each item more carefully than necessary.

Ryan was in the kitchen making coffee neither one of them wanted.

“Are you ready for lunch?”

“It's a little early.” Folding shirts one after another, she layered them like tiles into the suitcase.

“Yeah. You should get some rest.”

“So should you.”

“You still haven't found anyone to run that gift shop,” she said absently.

Ryan shrugged. “Didn't seem like the right time.”

Silence settled between them. Not uncomfortable, just careful.

After she had filled the suitcase, Grace rolled a sweater carefully and placed it into the tote.

The zipper rasped softly.

Ryan leaned against the doorframe, arms crossed, watching.

"You don't have to pack today," he said.

"I'm just getting organized."

He nodded like that made sense.

Willow sighed and settled near the bed.

Another shirt disappeared into the bag.

Ryan pushed off the frame, then stopped halfway across the room.

"Grace..."

She glanced up. "Yeah?"

His jaw tightened slightly, like he wasn't sure he wanted to say it anymore.

"I can't keep doing this."

Her hands stilled on the fabric.

"Doing what?" she asked quietly.

He exhaled, eyes steady on hers.

"Waiting for you to leave."

Silence expanded between them.

Grace didn't answer.

Ryan's shoulders lowered a fraction, as if something settled into place.

Grace zipped up her tote.

Ryan glanced at it, then away.

Willow nudged Grace's hand, and Grace stroked Willow's neck.

"You staying at Nora's tonight?"

"Probably. I haven't decided."

"You always decide fast," he said softly.

She waited for him to say more. He didn't.

Later, when she passed him in the hall, his hand brushed hers briefly, then he let it fall away.

Grace stood still after he moved on.

Something felt different, but she wasn't sure what had changed.

She picked up her tote and small suitcase and took them to her car then returned for her backpack and computer, but first, she went to the kitchen.

Sitting at the counter with his back to the door and an empty coffee cup in front of him, Ryan asked, "Ready for lunch before you leave?"

"I'm good, but how did you..." She rolled her eyes. "Gracie soap."

He nodded.

"Thanks... for all of this."

"Yeah." His hand tightened around the mug.

Grace carried her backpack and computer bag to the door and hesitated, waiting for him to say her name.

She trudged to her car, and after glancing in her rearview mirror for one last look, she headed down the driveway.

Before she pulled onto the road, Grace automatically reached for the button to turn on the radio, then lowered her hand as she headed for Nora's house.

She parked in front, like she always did and carried her backpack, computer bag, suitcase, and tote inside.

Nora's house smelled of cinnamon and old wood polish.

Safe.

Grace set her tote by the door and slipped out of her coat.

"You're early," Nora said from the kitchen.

Murphy padded to the door, and Grace rubbed his ear.

Heading to the kitchen with Murphy at her side, Grace said, "Parade's over."

Nora studied her for a moment, then nodded toward the table. "Tea?"

Grace nodded.

They sat in comfortable silence while the kettle hissed.

Outside, distant parade sounds drifted faintly through the windows, laughter, a horn, the last echoes of celebration.

Grace wrapped her hands around the mug when Nora set it down.

The warmth didn't help. Murphy leaned against Grace, and she absently stroked his back.

"You okay?" Nora asked finally.

Grace hesitated. "Yeah."

Nora arched an eyebrow.

Grace sighed. "I thought I'd feel... done."

"And?"

Grace looked down at the steam rising from her tea.

"I don't."

Nora didn't respond right away. She simply took her seat across from her, patient.

Grace glanced toward the living room. The familiar couch, the knitted blanket, and the quiet she'd run to more than once.

Everything was exactly as it had always been, but something felt missing.

Her gaze drifted to the tote by the door, packed and ready.

She felt nothing looking at it.

Then she thought of the distillery and the smell of grain, Willow's sigh, Ryan standing at the counter with his back turned.

The ache hit quietly.

Nora followed her gaze.

"You look like someone forgot something," she said gently.

Grace blinked. *Not forgot. Left.*

She set the mug down.

"I think I'm supposed to be somewhere else," she whispered.

Nora smiled slightly, as if she'd been waiting for that.

"I thought you might figure that out."

Grace stood before she could second-guess it.

"I'm not staying here tonight."

Nora nodded once. "I know."

"I'm going to pack the rest of my clothes into my suitcase."

As Grace went into her room, Nora called out, "Do you need a larger suitcase?"

"No, I'm fine."

After Grace packed her suitcase, she set it in the hall then joined Nora in the kitchen.

She pulled the shamrock tie tack, the coin, and the golden disc out of her pocket and put them on the kitchen table. "These aren't mine."

Nora closed her hand over them. "No, they aren't."

Grace exhaled deeper than she had all day. She picked up her suitcase on the way out. “Thanks, Granny.”

Chapter Twenty-One

Nora opened the door before he knocked a second time. "Ryan," she said softly. "Come in."

He stepped inside, wiping his feet on the doormat out of habit. "I won't stay long," he said. "Just wanted to check in."

Nora studied him for a moment longer than was comfortable. "Grace isn't here."

He nodded as if he had expected that.

"I figured." His smile was polite but thin. "She's probably getting ready to head back."

Nora's eyebrows lifted slightly. "Back?"

"To Atlanta," he said simply. "Once things settled."

Something in Nora's expression softened.

"You care about her," she said.

Ryan glanced toward the window. "Always have, but it doesn't matter much if she's meant to be somewhere else."

Nora didn't answer immediately.

"She talk to you?" he asked.

"About leaving?" Nora shook her head. "No."

Ryan exhaled quietly, as if that didn't change anything.

"She always knew this wasn't permanent," he said. "I just wanted to say goodbye before she took off."

Nora stepped closer. Ryan..."

But he had already stepped back toward the door.

"Tell her I stopped by," he said.

He hesitated only once.

"She made this place better," he added quietly.

Then he tipped his head politely and left.

Ryan sat in his truck for a moment.

As he drove back to the distillery, the clouds darkened.

The driveway was lonelier than usual.

When the distillery was in sight, he swung to park, then he saw the tote bag sitting by the front door. When he peered closer, a figure...

He parked crooked and strode toward the porch with Willow at his side and then slowed, not believing it at first.

Grace sat in the chair beside the door, her small suitcase resting nearby.

She didn't move.

"Grace..."

She looked up, calm and steady.

"I'm here," she said softly.

A breath passed.

"It's where I'm supposed to be."

He drew in a quiet breath through his nose, that familiar habit she'd once teased him about, but this time it trembled.

He reached for her without thinking, hands sliding under her arms.

She moved into him immediately, rising easily as he lifted her to her feet.

For a moment, he simply held her there.

"Okay."

Ryan kept one hand on her as he reached for the key.

The lock turned with a soft click.

He opened the door, and Willow slipped past them into the warmth.

Ryan reached for the suitcase and tote, but Grace took the tote from him without a word.

Together, they crossed the threshold. Ryan pulled the door closed behind them, the soft click of the lock sounding final in the best way.

Warm air carrying wheat and bourbon drifted toward them as Ryan reached for the light.

"The sheriff called while you were with Nora," he said quietly. "Bella's out of surgery. They think she's going to make it."

Grace's shoulders relaxed as she released a breath she hadn't realized she'd been holding.

"And Valerie?" she asked.

"Alive. Under guard." He hesitated. "Sheriff thinks she was running the entire operation. Piper just financed it."

A beat passed.

"Mayor too?" he asked.

Grace shook her head, her hand tightening around his.

"Nope. I'm fulltime at the distillery."

As they sat on the sofa together, Ryan put his arm around Grace, who snuggled close.

Willow circled once and settled at their feet with a deep, contented sigh.

Home.

Did you love Grace and Ryan's story?
Next to read:
The Elusive Embezzler
A Romantic Suspense

Widow and accountant Jenna Ross thought inheriting the Peach Blossom Retreat would be her chance to start over.

But when a decade-old embezzlement scandal resurfaces and one of her guests turns up dead on the inn's property, Jenna's quiet life spirals into chaos. As her intuition pulls her deeper into a web of blackmail and deception, she finds herself relying on the one person she never expected to trust.

And the closer she gets to the truth, the more she realizes the killer's next target is her.

Join Judith's Reader List

Get new releases, bonus content, and exclusive reader offers.

Subscribe Here: judithabarrett.com

More About the Author

Judith A. Barrett, award-winning author, lives on a farm in Georgia with her husband, two dogs, and very sassy chickens. She writes series for her readers: thrillers, mysteries, and romantic suspense novels. Stories with a twist: not your typical characters from not your typical author!

Her motto: You keep reading; I'll keep writing!

When she isn't writing, Judith is meeting readers at arts and crafts fairs, working on farm chores, hiking or camping with her husband and dogs, or rocking on her front porch while planning the next plot twist in the book she is writing.

Website judithabarrett.com

VIP Readers judithabarrett.com/newsletter

Exclusive Discounts and Sales barrettbookshop.com

Not into emails, even though Judith's story-focused newsletters are interesting, Not-Your-Typical newsletters? Follow Judith on Barrett Book Shop, Bookbub, or your favorite bookseller for news of her latest release!

Let's keep in touch!

Find your next book(s) and buy direct from the author at the Barrett Book Shop!

www.ingramcontent.com/pod-product-compliance
Lightning Source LLC
LaVergne TN
LVHW010638110826
845149LV00014B/2876